INTO ᴛʜᴇ DARK
MARKET

Tracey Lander-Garrett

GLASS CAROUSEL PRESS

ISBN 978-1-7334545-3-7 (print) | ISBN 978-1-7334545-2-0 (ebook)

This book is a work of fiction. Names, characters, places, and incidents are either the product of the author's imagination or are used fictitiously, and any resemblance to actual persons, living or dead, business establishments, events, or locales is entirely coincidental.

First printing, 2020

Glass Carousel Press
Pflugerville, TX 78660

Cover Design: Steven Novak, Novak Illustration

For Ric Saterstrom

(1955 – 2016)

who spun dreams for me to grow on

A DARK-HAIRED WOMAN IN SCRUBS FINISHES medicating a young child and tucks him in. The room is dimly lit. Her hand lingers on his forehead and her face takes on a wistful expression. The windows are large and dark behind her as she exits the child's room.

In the hall, she feels eyes on her back: that uncanny feeling of someone watching her.

Because it is the graveyard shift, the hospital corridors are quiet. She turns slowly, and at the end of the hallway, the lights flicker. She sees a figure. The silhouette of a large man. The silhouette looks just like that of her late husband.

She gasps, a shock running through her. Her co-worker, standing at the nursing station nearby, calls to her in concern, startling her. "Hannah? Are you okay?"

When she looks back, the figure is gone.

The next time it happens, she is at the grocery store, a small basket of various items cradled in one arm. She turns a corner and again—this time at the end of an aisle—there stands her husband. She steps backward involuntarily, knocking over an endcap display of canned peaches. After the bewilderment and embarrassment of the tumbling, clanking avalanche, she looks again.

He's gone.

Her therapist suggests it is wishful thinking. That she is seeing men with the same general shape as her husband, but it cannot be him. The therapist puts in a call to Hannah's doctor, who prescribes sedatives.

It is raining steadily outside when Hannah is home the next evening, with occasional rumbles of distant thunder. While making dinner at the stove, Hannah once again has that uncanny feeling that she is being watched. She turns slowly.

"Hank? Hank, is that you? Are you here?" she asks softly, fear and hope intermingling in her voice.

Just then, lightning strikes nearby, illuminating the sky. It silhouettes a figure standing outside the kitchen window, casting light on his face. There can be no doubt this time. It is her husband, his hair drenched, his skin pale, his lips a dark purple.

The color drains from Hannah's face. The figure is repulsive to her. An abomination that looks like—yet is nothing like—the man she loved. She screams, "Just leave me alone!" as the night outside her window goes dark again.

But she cannot look away. Her eyes stay fixed on the window, fearing what she'll see the next time lightning ignites the sky.

When it does, showing nothing but the empty yard, she slides to the floor, sobbing.

A body lies in a mortuary room.

Its dark hair is disheveled in greasy clumps.

Its eyes are gone, as are its ears. All that remain are bloody, blasted pits.

A handsome face, a wide forehead, chiseled chin, with full lips.

The body is shirtless. Long cuts, burns, and missing strips of skin on the pale torso reveal levels of torture that are horrific to contemplate.

It wears leather pants, and its feet are bare. Vulnerable.

The mortuary room is cold, sterile, impersonal. So is the body.

Then it sits up.

And somewhere across the city, an old man plans.

CHAPTER ONE

"ANOTHER ONE?" JULIE ASKED, GAPING AT THE green tentacles of the aloe plant in the kitchen window.

Our new roommate, Sylvie, had a strong liking for green, growing things. She'd begun with a few plants in her bedroom, then a few in the living room, and now, the kitchen. "Are you sure that thing's a plant and not, you know, like an alien or something that's going to rise from its clay pot and kill me in my sleep?" Julie said while fixing herself a cup of coffee.

I was sitting at the table, finishing a bowl of cereal. "It's an aloe," I offered. "She said the juice from the leaves is good for sunburn and rashes and things."

Julie stared at me suspiciously over the rim of her I'M NOT A MORNING PERSON mug. "Has she gotten to you too? Are you a plant person now?"

"She offered to give me a small plant—" I began.

Julie's perfectly-shaped eyebrows rose. "And?"

"And I said I didn't know how to take care of it and she said she would. It's in the living room."

Julie shook her head, looking perturbed. "Well, I guess it's better than having a baby screaming all night. But seriously, she needs to cut down on the plants. It's like living with . . . help me out here. Aren't there some plant villains in comic books?"

"Sure. Swamp Thing, Poison Ivy—"

"Yes. It's like living with Poison Ivy!"

"But better than living with Oscar the Grouchy baby and his under-slept Mommy. Poor Kara. Have you talked to her lately?" The last time I'd spoken with our former roommate, the baby would not stop wailing in the background. She had moved in with her boyfriend in her last month of pregnancy, a relief for me and Julie, but also a stress that necessitated locating a new roommate to help pay the rent.

"Oh, she posted the cutest picture on Instagram yesterday! I commented on it. You want to see?" Julie asked.

"Sure?"

Julie scrolled through photos on her phone until she found the one she was looking for and handed it to me. The screen was dominated by an image of a baby and a pug sleeping next to one another in matching striped shirts.

"Oh my God. That *is* the cutest."

"See what you're missing?"

She was always teasing me about getting a smartphone and connecting to social media, saying I needed to join the 21st century.

I had bought a used silver flip phone at the end of the summer, but it was apparently very 20th

century. It could text and take pictures, but it didn't have the internet.

"Photoshoot today?" I asked, changing the subject. She was dressed in black slacks and a dress shirt instead of pajamas, a pretty good indication that she was working.

"Yes, a catalog job. I'm hoping it will lead to more later. Oh! Speaking of Poison Ivy, she's the redhead wearing green leaves, right? What do you think of that for my Halloween costume?"

"What about the Red Riding Hood outfit you showed me—with the red cloak and basket? You looked really cute in it."

"Yeah, I don't know. The dress was a little big on me." A petite woman who was larger on top than she was on the bottom, Julie sometimes had issues finding clothes that fit her just the way she wanted them to.

She glanced at her watch. "God, look at the time! Gotta run!" She finished her coffee in a gulp, set the mug into the sink, and left.

After I washed up the breakfast dishes and put them in the rack to dry, I left for work too.

Christopher Street Comics, as advertised, sells comics on Christopher Street in Manhattan's Greenwich Village. Those of us who work there call the store Chris Street, which seems to annoy the owner, Mac. When I arrived, Mac was unloading our weekly Marvel shipment from cardboard boxes with the help of Jackson, our newly-hired assistant manager. I greeted them both, receiving a grunt from Mac and a lifted-chin acknowledgment from Jackson.

Mac wore his typical uniform of jeans and a dress shirt rolled to the elbows. He had a slight sheen of perspiration on his ever-growing forehead, which nearly reached his ponytail. He was counting the spines in the stack of comics he held. "You're cashier again today, Madison," he said as I passed him to clock in and put my backpack in the office.

"Thanks for that," I heard Jackson say. Since Jackson was something like six-foot-three, built like a string bean with long arms and legs, he didn't exactly fit in the niche behind the cash register and had to hunch. Maybe he was a little shorter than that, and it was just his hair that was tall, his dreadlocks tightly bundled in a knit cap he always wore.

"How's your first week?" I asked him once I'd taken up my station behind the register.

"Can't complain," he replied. He had just a bit of an accent when he spoke—an almost lilting musicality—that made his voice pleasant to listen to.

"I meant to ask you. Where are you from, Jackson?" I asked.

"Brooklyn, but I was born in Jamaica—not the one in Queens. Where are you from?" he asked, removing a bound stack of comics from a cardboard box.

"Oh, haven't you heard?" Mac said. "She's our own Bucky Barnes." He flipped the box he'd just emptied and scored the tape on the bottom, then flattened it.

"Your arm doesn't look made of metal," Jackson said.

"He means I've got amnesia. I don't *know* where I'm from."

"Oh, come on. You've got to be kidding."

"She's *not-not-not*," sang Nidhi, a film student who manned the bag check area directly across from me. "We think maybe she's a government assassin. Possibly from Canada."

"I doubt I'm from Canada. I don't really know anything about it."

"Except that they say *eh* a lot," Nidhi offered. "And play hockey. And love maple syrup, am I right?"

"Wolverine and Deadpool are Canadian, you know," Mac said. "Not to mention Alpha Flight, or Northstar who was one of the first gay superheroes to come out of the closet. And obviously Captain Canuck."

"Wait, Deadpool is Canadian?" Nidhi said. "How did I miss that? I would think he wasn't polite enough."

"Nice job going all in on those stereotypes, Nidhi. You're sure to offend someone soon." Mac handed her a stack of comics. "Shelve these, please."

"Ten-four," Nidhi said. She held the stack with both hands and got to work putting them away.

"I'm just . . . boring, I guess," I said. "If I could say, 'Oh, I'm from New Jersey,' at least you could imagine something about where I'm from. But yeah, I don't know."

Jackson shook his head. "So you don't know anything? No memories? At all?"

"From last year on October 13th to today, I have memories. That's it though."

"I can't imagine. Everything I am is my family and where I'm from. You see these dreads? I've been growing them my whole life. Not having them as a connection to my past? Let alone no connection at all? I would be lost." He shook his head again and continued unboxing.

"Oh," I said. I wondered if I should feel more lost than I did.

"Didn't mean to offend," he said. "Can you take these?" He extended a stack of comics as a peace offering.

I told him I wasn't offended and went to shelve the stack.

The day passed quickly as the regulars came in to get the newest issues of their favorite titles. At the end of the night, Jackson locked the front door and began sweeping, while Nidhi straightened the comics on the shelves and I worked on replacing the register tape and counting my drawer. Nidhi and I had been chatting off and on all night. Now she was complaining about her parents, who had recently announced that while they agreed that Nidhi should finish college, they also agreed that upon graduation she should marry a nice Indian boy they had in mind.

"Like, why would I do that?" she asked. "I want to meet someone and fall in love! But oh no, if arranged marriage was good enough for them, it should be good enough for me!"

"Their marriage was arranged?" I asked.

"By my grandparents, yep." She stood on her tiptoes to arrange some stacks on the top row.

"And they're still married?" asked Jackson.

"Yeah, they're still together," Nidhi said.

"And they get along?" I asked.

"Pretty much. I mean, my mom's an educator. She teaches psychology, so I always feel like she's five steps ahead of whatever I might say or do, which also goes for my brother and my dad. She kind of manages all of us."

"So if it worked for your parents, what's the problem?" Jackson asked.

"It just isn't, you know, romantic," Nidhi said. "Like, where is my prince? Where's the guy who's going to ride in and save me from the dragon? Who will make my heart beat faster and my breathing stop because he's so handsome?"

"Oh brother," Jackson said, sweeping a small pile of dirt and detritus into a dust pan. "You watched too many Disney movies as a kid."

"I did not! Oh, I know, that's not reality, but what about a meet-cute? What about sharing milkshakes and stealing each other's fries, laughing at inside jokes, running to meet each other at the train station?"

"I take it back." Jackson laughed. "You didn't watch too many Disney movies. You watched too many with Meg Ryan."

"What's a meet-cute?" I asked.

"It's a film trope: A romantic situation in which the main character and his or her love interest *meet* for the first time in a *cute,* memorable way. Cute meeting, meet-cute."

"Well . . . you haven't met this nice Indian boy yet, right? What if he turned out to be your meet-cute? Maybe you bump into each other in the street on your way to meet and you think he's funny and amazing and perfect for you?"

She snorted. "Yeah, right. How likely is it that the perfect guy for me lives in India and is the son of my mother's best friend from when she was a little girl? Plus, I *have* met him. We used to play together as kids when I would visit in the summer. He's kind of . . . I don't know. Boring. Plain." She frowned and straightened a stack of *Movie Fan* magazines with a picture of a handsome man with dark hair on the cover. "Not like Tom here. I could eat him up with a spoon." She made an *Mmm-mm* noise at the cover and grinned. "Did you ever get a chance to listen to those poems he recited on YouTube? So yummy. I could listen to his accent all day."

"Which Tom?" I asked. It seemed like all of the actors she liked were either named Tom or Chris. I had no idea who any of them were.

Nidhi snatched up the magazine she'd been drooling over and showed me the handsome, dark-haired man on the cover. He was wearing a horned crown made of gold. "He played Loki in the *Avengers* and *Thor* movies!" she said.

"Is he the one who always plays bad guys?" I asked. "Vampires, murderers, supervillains?"

"So?" she asked.

"Don't you think that's a bad sign?"

"Oh, come on, bad dudes are super sexy, especially vampires. Now if I could just find one who likes short, dark, and curvy, I'm all set."

Vampires. I know a few things about vampires, and none of it is good. Not that I could actually tell her about it. There was no way she would believe me.

Jackson, who'd seemed ready to chime in about the wisdom of dating "bad dudes" suddenly changed expression and walked off in the opposite direction. Wait, was he crushing on Nidhi?

"So what else is your type besides bad?" I was done wrestling with the register tape and started counting bills.

"Hmm. Tall, handsome. Rich would be nice, of course. And he should cook. And not listen to country music. And love dogs."

Jackson was sweeping over an area he'd already swept, listening in.

"And a dreamy accent you could listen to for hours?" I asked, watching him for a reaction. He noticed me watching and quickly looked away.

"You know it," she said, straightening the *X-Men* and *Zombie Boy* comics on the bottom row of the last shelf. "All done!" she announced, wiping imaginary dust from her hands.

"Me too," I said, dropping the last of the pennies into their slot. The total matched the register tape perfectly, as usual. "Drawer's good."

"Same-same?" Jackson asked.

"Same-same."

He took the cash drawer to the office and put it in the safe, and Nidhi and I left him to lock up. She headed off to meet some friends, and I walked towards the F train.

I liked my co-workers fine, but I missed Billy. Billy and I had worked together at Chris Street for several months. He was always cracking jokes and looking out for me. He had sold me his old laptop cheap and bought me soup sometimes when I was broke. Maybe he'd had a crush on me, maybe he hadn't. I could never quite tell.

Back in late April, Billy had called Mac out of the blue to say his parents had moved upstate and he was moving with them. No two-week notice, no goodbye party, nothing. And here it was, nearly October, and we hadn't heard anything from him. I called his number a few times, but it always went to voicemail. *This is Billy. Say something.* I never did.

I suspected that the upstate move story wasn't true. I wasn't even sure that it was Billy who had called, though Mac said it sounded like him. Then again, it was unlike Billy not to show up on his last payday.

Was he even alive? The question might seem melodramatic, but not if you know what I know. A couple of weeks before Billy disappeared, my life had turned upside down when I'd learned my apartment was haunted. I tried to find out the identity of the ghost and the person who killed her.

I got way more than I bargained for. My investigation led me to Sleepy Hollow and that was where I learned that vampires were real. And so had Billy. Because of me, he'd been attacked by a vampire named Michael Adderly. Adderly had some kind of hold on Billy, a weird interest in me, and a hideout in the sub-basement of the Empire State Building. The last time I had seen Billy, he literally disappeared into thin air after jumping off the 86th floor observation deck. No body, no witnesses, nothing.

I wanted no part of that creepy supernatural world, but I had gone back to the sub-basement in the Empire State Building a couple of times to see if Billy was there. He wasn't.

Neither was Adderly, and that was fine with me.

It was hard enough for me to live a normal life as it was.

When I got home, Julie and her boyfriend Tad were cuddled on the couch in the living room in front of the TV. Two empty wine bottles and glasses with take-out boxes on the coffee table indicated further binge-watching of *Mad Men*, which they'd been watching for weeks. The show was paused and they were laughing and making bets on who would sleep with who by the end of the episode.

"Hey, Maddy. Do you want to watch with us?" Julie asked, slurring her words slightly.

"Did you eat?" Tad asked. "There's plenty of salad and falafel left if you want some."

"Sure, thanks," I said. "To the food. I mean. Not so interested in the show."

"Aww, you're missing out! So much *drama*," Julie said, in a sing-song voice.

"Do you guys want some water?" I asked. I'd learned over time that Tad handled his wine better than Julie did in general, but they both forgot to drink water, which led to awful hangovers.

"Yes, please!" Tad called as I went into the kitchen for a plate and fork.

I opened the fridge to grab the Brita pitcher and noticed a large mason jar of kimchi sitting next to it. "Did you have lunch with your sister again?" I asked Julie as I returned with the pitcher and glasses.

"Ha! Yes. You saw the kimchi?"

"How could she miss it?" Tad asked. Julie's older sister Soo-jin specialized in their mother's recipe, making her own pickled vegetables and distributing it to her siblings and friends. Julie knew better than to offer me any. I'd tried it once and it was far too spicy for me. Sylvie, on the other hand, loved it.

Tad began to pour glasses of water while I went to get my eating apparatus.

"So what about that nurse? His neighbor," Julie was saying when I returned.

Tad said, "I think he overplayed it."

I helped myself to their leftovers and sat with the plate perched on my lap.

"You're right, I guess," said Julie. "What about Dr. Fay?"

"Too early, maybe. But she *has* got her eye on Don," Tad said.

Julie took a sip of water and held onto the glass. "What about you, Maddy? Haven't you got your eye on anyone these days?" she asked.

"I don't know. Not really."

"Well, I think you should. Didn't you ever call back what's his name? Eric?"

"Derek. No. I don't know. We just drifted apart." Derek and I had dated very briefly while I was embroiled in my unfortunate supernatural investigations. Every time I thought of him, I thought of how he hadn't believed me. I didn't need that in my life.

"You know you *are* pretty, right?" said Julie. "Seriously, Maddy. You go around wearing jeans and t-shirts all the time and I know you've been through some stuff with your head injury and all, but you should be dating! Getting out there, meeting cute guys, not just geeks at the comic book store, but guys with jobs, who will take you on actual dates, not just have you over for Netflix and chill."

"There wasn't any Netflix *or* chill," I said primly, deciding not to correct her about the head injury. Derek was a movie buff with a wall of DVDs. He didn't go out much. We'd hung out at his apartment and kissed once, but that was it. "And I don't know, I just haven't really met anyone. There are a couple of regulars who seem nice, but none of them have really caught my interest."

"Hey, it's late, sugar blossom," Tad said, kissing the top of Julie's head. "What say we call it a night, huh?"

"Aw, come on, let's finish the episode?"

Tad pointed the remote at the TV and the red line at the bottom of the screen indicated sixteen minutes remaining. "You can watch by yourself if you want," he said, stifling a yawn. "I'm beat."

"But that's no fun," Julie said and pouted as she stood, wobbled, and sat back down on the couch hard. "Whoa. I think the wine is kicking in. I'm dizzy."

"You. Are. A. Terrible. Lightweight," Tad said, punctuating the sentence with kisses on Julie's head. "Come on." With one hand behind her back and the other scooped beneath her knees, he picked her up easily, grinned at me, and said goodnight, whisking Julie down the hall into her room. The door closed and giggles came from behind it moments later.

They were so cute I thought I might barf.

The next evening at Chris Street, I had bag check duty and the other assistant manager Erica was on register. Mac left early to pick up his twin boys from pre-school, leaving me, Erica, and Trendon on duty. Trendon mostly kept to himself during store hours, but he knew a lot about comics and gaming. He also knew quite a bit about baseball, and baseball cards, which was why he spent most of his time in the back of the store, either reading or obsessively going over our inventory.

With Trendon in the back, there weren't any guys in sight at the front of the store. Maybe that was why Brently Kaczor—a regular customer whose last name I was unsure how to pronounce—decided to chat me up on his usual Thursday night visit. Clutching the comics he'd claimed from the customer reserve box in the back, he smiled at me before putting his purchases on the counter for Erica.

While Erica was ringing him up, he kept turning around and chatting at me. "God, I love this store," he said.

"Me too," I said.

"I could spend hours here," he said.

"Trust me, it's not that exciting," Erica said.

"But you're here when the new issues arrive, every week!"

"Oh, yes," Erica said. "We are. Every week. Eventually, the novelty wears off." She finished ringing up his purchases and told him his total.

He handed her a credit card and turned back to me. "Nice night, huh?" He wore a checked dress shirt and khakis with a light jacket over the shirt. "I'm glad it hasn't gotten too cold yet."

I nodded. "Yeah, it's nice out."

"Though the temperatures are supposed to drop later on tonight," he said.

"That's what they say," I agreed.

He handed me his bag check ticket: half of the six of clubs. I unclipped the other half of the card from his rucksack and umbrella and handed it back to him. "Here you go."

"They said it might rain. That's why I have the umbrella. I mean, I don't carry it every day," Brently said. Over his shoulder, Erica, caught my eye and raised one double-pierced eyebrow.

"Well, better to be prepared, right?" I said.

"Right! Yes, exactly." He seemed relieved that I wasn't judging his umbrella.

Erica ripped the receipt out of the credit card machine and cleared her throat. "I need you to sign," she said.

He looked a little different than he had the week or two before. I was trying to place it when he turned away from me to sign the receipt. Then I saw it. He'd had his hair cut. The back was trimmed meticulously.

"So, uh . . . hey, have you ever seen *Rocky Horror Picture Show*?" he asked.

"That's playing at the IFC, isn't it?" Erica asked.

"No . . . I've never seen it," I said. "Not really my thing."

"Oh," he said, seeming deflated. "I was going to ask if you'd like to go with me."

"That's . . . really nice of you," I said. "But I, uh, have a boyfriend."

"Oh, right," he said. "Of course you do." He picked up his rucksack and slung it over one shoulder, tucked his umbrella and the bag of comics under the same arm, and left, telling us to have a good night with a sad smile before the door jingled closed.

Erica seemed to be holding her breath and then burst out laughing after he'd gotten out of earshot. "Oh Madison, you're such a heartbreaker," she said. "Why didn't you say yes?"

"Sure, with you rolling your eyes at me in the background?"

"I was rolling them at him, not you!"

"So you think I should date the kind of guy who you roll your eyes at?"

She shrugged. "I dunno. Should you? I mean, he seemed pretty harmless. Nice. Safe, you know?"

I thought of Nidhi's description of her dream guy versus the guy her parents wanted her to marry. "He was plain."

"Yeah, kind of. His face was kind, though. A kind face. Don't see those very often in this city."

"Oh yeah? Why don't you date him then? Oh right. You've sworn off men."

"I got tired of nerdy dudes trying to outnerd me. Always checking my nerd card. My lesbian lover and I are very happy, thank you very much," she said and smiled sweetly.

A customer came up asking for help getting a Wonder Woman t-shirt in the right size and then someone needed help finding *Arkham Asylum* in the Batman graphic novel section and then it was questions and answers for the rest of the night until closing time.

"You know what bugs me?" Erica said, pulling the register tape as I straightened the stacks.

"What?"

"When guys ask women out at the places they work. Like, sorry, Romeo, but I'm not part of the goods for sale, you know? It just makes everything awkward."

"Yeah?"

"Absolutely. You watch, the next time Brent Cocksore comes in, he'll be even more awkward than he was tonight."

"His last name is *not* Cocksore."

"I know. But I don't know how the hell to say his name, so he's Cocksore now."

"You're terrible! Now that's all I'll be able to think every time I see him!"

Trendon paused in his sweeping, looked at the two of us, and shook his bald head in disgust. "Y'all're mean," he said, and walked towards the back of the store. Trendon had grown up in Kentucky and his accent was noticeable even without the *y'all*s. Erica teased him about it when he first started until she realized it kind of hurt his feelings.

"Okay, okay, it was mean," Erica called after Trendon. "I didn't mean it!"

"Yes, you did," I whispered.

"Shush!" she whispered back.

He returned to the front of the store, brandishing a dustpan and brush. "How the hell is a guy supposed to meet a girl, then? Y'all don't want to be catcalled, you don't want to be talked to on the subway, or at school, or at work, or anywhere else as far as I can tell. So where is a good place to ask a girl out?"

"Well, I don't want guys to ask me out at all," Erica said. "I'm in a relationship with a woman."

"But Erica, you did date guys before you and Saraya got together, didn't you?" I said.

"Yeah, I'm bi. And it isn't like dating women is all *that* different. But . . . what women *don't* do is hit on other women while they're just going about their lives. Who wants to be asked for her number on the way to the dentist? Or be told to smile when she just heard her grandfather is in the hospital? Yes, that happened to me."

"Okay, I get it," said Trendon. "Men are trash."

"It's not that. It's just, you know, women aren't here *for* men. We're just . . . here. Living. Doing regular stuff. If we dress sexy, it's because we want to, not because we're walking want ads for dates," she said, pulling at the hem of her blue plaid dress.

"So how did you meet your last boyfriend then?" I asked.

She pulled her lip piercing into her mouth for a moment then released it and said, "We were in the same Star Wars RPG."

"D20 or D6?" Trendon asked.

"D6," she said with a smirk. "Oh, sorry, Madison. We're talking about dice. D stands for dice, the number for the number of sides of the die."

"Yeah, I knew that, somehow."

"You're a gamer? You never said!"

"I'm not?"

"Oh, right. It's ironic that I forget that you wouldn't remember, isn't it? So, Trendon, you play Star Wars?"

"Nah, I never played, but I heard the D6 one was better."

Erica rolled her eyes and gave me a look. *See? Dudes. Checking my nerd card.*

I wanted to find out more about how she and the former boyfriend had gotten together, but Erica was now counting silently to herself as she went through the stack of ones in the drawer. When she got to the end of it and wrote the total down, I asked, "So you played the same game together and started dating?"

"We were friends, and then it turned into more than friends."

"No meet-cute?"

"Why are you and Nidhi obsessed with that term?"

"I don't know! I guess I like it."

"Ugh, it's so contrived."

"Where'd you meet your boyfriend?" Trendon asked. It took a few seconds to realize he was talking to me.

"Oh. I don't have a boyfriend."

"Then why did you tell that guy you did?" He held the dustpan and brush at his sides like a shield and sword, ready to do battle if a dust dragon appeared.

I thought a moment. "I guess I didn't want to tell him I wasn't interested in him?"

"So you were just letting him down easy?"

"I guess?"

Trendon made a disgusted noise, kneeling to sweep up the dust pile. "Women. So when you *did* have a boyfriend, how did you meet?"

"Um . . . well, he wasn't my boyfriend, but the last guy I dated I met at his work."

"Ah ha!" Trendon pointed at me with the brush. "Hypocrite."

"Wait a second! *I* never said anything about being asked out at work . . ."

"Not listening," Trendon said. "Not listening!" He finished sweeping up the dirt pile, continuing to mutter the same phrase every time I tried to explain myself.

Ten minutes later, as Erica pulled down the security gate over the Chris Street storefront, Trendon remained standoffish as if he truly disapproved of everything Erica and I stood for, whatever that was.

"Are you still mad at us, Trendon?" I asked. It was starting to bother me. I didn't like feeling as though I'd done something wrong.

He crossed his arms and scowled at me. Then he winked, turned on his heel, and stalked off.

"Man, he's a weird one, huh?" Erica said as we both walked away.

"Oh, he's not so bad," I said.

We reached the corner, where Erica turned off towards the PATH train, and I continued on to the F train at West 4th. Approaching the station, I was surprised to find a flood of humans pouring from every exit and entrance in the vicinity. The streets were crowded with commuters and there was a distinct smell of smoke and burnt plastic in the air. Two MTA workers in orange vests with reflective patches were arriving to direct people away from the station, but they did little to quell the chaos.

And then chaos knocked me sideways, grabbed me by my elbows, and took my breath away.

Chapter Two

I'D NEARLY BEEN THROWN TO THE GROUND, BUT his hands steadied me. The first thing I noticed was that he was several inches taller than me. The next thing was his startlingly vivid green eyes. His hair was dark and wavy, longer in the front and on top, shorter on the sides in kind of a messy punk rock pompadour. He had one pierced ear with a silver hoop and the fullest, most sensual lips I had ever seen on a guy.

"God, I'm so sorry," he said.

I opened my mouth to say something but nothing came out. He was stunningly handsome, with high cheekbones and a strong jaw, and he was still holding onto my elbows and forearms.

I finally found my voice when he steadied me once more and released my arms. "Sorry?" I said. It came out with a bit of a squeak at the end so I cleared my throat. "Oh, for bumping into me? No problem."

He was still looking at me, a strange mixture of relief and surprise apparent on his face. I continued to stare at him because he was just that pretty. The throng of frustrated commuters continued to rush around us as if we were rocks in a stream. A woman bumped into me and muttered, "The fuck outta my way."

"Ah, let's see . . ." Green Eyes looked around the area for a moment and seemed to make a decision. "Come this way," he said, taking me by the hand and leading me through the crowd expertly.

He wore a fitted black suit jacket over a white V-neck t-shirt and dark jeans. He was tall, maybe as tall as Jackson, but more filled out—he was thin at the waist, but his shoulders weren't as narrow as Jackson's.

The crowd thinned out within half a block and he released my hand. "There, that's better. I could barely think back there." His voice had a bit of a lilt, again making me think of Jackson, but his consonants were more clipped. Maybe English? Or Irish?

"Ugh. Do you know what was going on?" I asked, my fingers tingling slightly from his touch.

"Track fire. Whole station's closed for now."

"Oh, that's great. I need the F train to get home to Brooklyn," I said. "Maybe I can go to . . . what's the next station down? Broadway-Lafayette?"

"Those stations are going to be madhouses until they figure out how to reroute everything. I also need to go to Brooklyn. Share a taxi?"

"Can't afford it."

"Coffee?" he asked.

"Huh?"

"Would you like to get some coffee? With me. To kill time until the trains are running right again."

I didn't answer right away because a million thoughts were crashing into each other in my head.

Coffee at this hour? How much does a cup of coffee cost? Why is he asking me to coffee?

"Or maybe a movie? There's the theater right there . . ."

Wait. Is he asking me on a date? To a movie? Oh, brother . . . yet another movie date guy! What will Julie say?

"Ha!" I laughed.

"Well, I can't say I've gotten that reaction before," he said, looking bemused and puzzled.

"I'm sorry. It's just, a movie? Not very original."

"So coffee then."

"I don't drink coffee. More of a tea person."

He looked back toward the station entrance where additional MTA workers were now tying pink and orange tape across the doorways. "So what do you plan to do? You've got some time to kill now if you can't take a taxi home and so do I."

"I have no idea."

"So come, take a walk with me. Tell me about yourself."

"Why are you doing this? I don't even know you."

"My apologies." He bowed at the waist and tipped an imaginary hat. "Kipling Jack Donovan at your service. Call me Kip for short."

"I'm Madison. Uh, Madison Roberts."

"Well then, Miss Uh-Madison Roberts. We're introduced now. How about that walk?"

He was winsome, endearingly eccentric, and incredibly attractive. "Sure," I said.

We turned a corner and crossed with the light, headed east on Bleeker Street. "So, tell me about yourself," he said. "Are you in school? Coming from work?"

"From work. At Christopher Street Comics."

"And you live in Brooklyn, you said—"

"Not so fast! Your turn. Do you go to school or work?"

"Aye, I work. I drive a carriage at Central Park."

"Ooh, that's a cool job. You like it?"

"Yeah, yeah. It's fine. Good work. I like the horses. Tourists? Not much, but some are decent folk."

"You have an accent," I said.

"I do at that. Care to guess where from?"

"Nope," I said, practically before he'd finished speaking. He laughed.

"Ireland. I grew up in Ireland," he said.

"Wow. What brought you here?"

"My uncle. Moved here to help him out. And what about you—"

"Hey, doesn't this place look interesting?" I interrupted. I knew where his question was headed and I didn't want to answer it.

There were velvet ropes outside what appeared to be an art gallery. I could see neon-colored art glowing under black lights through the front window. Thumping dance music came from inside. A bored looking girl in a short and tight black dress stood behind a podium with a clipboard.

"Yeah? Let's go in then," Kip said.

I looked down at my ripped jeans, open flannel, and faded t-shirt. "I don't think they'll let me in like this," I said.

"Leave that to me," he said. He approached the podium girl and leaned in close to speak to her. She asked him a question, he answered, and she laughed. I couldn't hear the words they were saying, but understood the body language and tone. He asked her a question, and she ran her fingers through her long hair and smiled at him coquettishly. After a moment she shrugged and unclipped the velvet rope from the stanchion.

"Come on," Kip said, gesturing toward the door with a toss of his head.

I didn't know what he had said, but whatever it was, it had obviously worked. We walked through a small vestibule into a wide dark space lit only by black light. The room was warmer than it was outside, so I peeled off my flannel and tied it around my waist. My light blue t-shirt was glowing and so was the white stitching on my Converse sneakers. Kip's white t-shirt also glowed. The walls were covered with huge, glowing neon-painted canvases. A man and a woman stood close together in the corner, each holding glowing beverages, seemingly talking about one of the paintings.

We stood and marveled, pointing out different images to one another: hot pink roses in a lime-green bush; an orange fish-headed man in old-fashioned lemon-yellow clothes; an electric purple mouse swimming in a neon blue puddle; a glowing green caterpillar sitting on a magenta mushroom, smoking from a sky-blue hookah.

"Curiouser and curiouser," Kip said, observing a painting of a glowing white rabbit wearing a purple vest and green bowtie. "I'm sensing a theme."

The thumping music seemed to be coming from an archway across the room, over which a glowing sign read

WE('LL) COME TO
WONDERLAND

"Shall we?" Kip asked.

"We've come this far," I said cheerfully.

The second room was much larger than the first, maybe twice the size of a basketball court. It was also lit with black lights. Several cages, one suspended from the ceiling, featured gyrating androgynous figures in neon body paints. A dance floor dominated the space, and ten or so people in dress clothes were dancing, while other small groups at the edges stood and talked. A DJ wearing a red dress and a crown stood on risers at the back behind turntables. On our immediate left, a small bar was set up against the wall, and a man in rabbit ears was pouring glowing drinks into stemware.

I suddenly felt awkward with my flannel around my hips and folded it over one arm. Kip turned to me. His eyes looked crazy in the black lights. The pupils almost disappeared into the glowing iris and whites of his eyes. "How old are you, if you don't mind me asking?"

"Your eyes look crazy!" I said, both because his eyes really did look bizarre beneath the black light, but also to stall for time before answering his question. I wondered how old he was. He seemed young. Maybe nineteen? As old as twenty-two?

"Yours do too. It's the black lights," he said, shouting over the music. "So how old are you?"

I didn't want to tell him an age that would make him think I was too young, so I split the difference. "I'm eighteen," I said, like I meant it. I mean, I could be eighteen. Or seventeen. Even as old as twenty. The doctors hadn't been sure. "How old are you?"

"Twenty," he said. "Soon to be twenty-one."

"Looking forward to that legal drinking age?" I asked.

"No. Not at all. I can't stand the stuff. But I'll buy you one if you'd like," he said, gesturing towards the bar.

"No, that's okay, I don't drink either."

He seemed pleasantly surprised. "A couple of sodas then?"

"Sure," I said. We walked over to the small bar. The two men ahead of us took their drinks and left. When we moved up to the bar, the handsome bartender smiled and offered a handshake to Kip. "Hey, Jack!" he said. He wore a white shirt and white pants, with green suspenders and a green bow tie. The rabbit ears on his head looked incredibly realistic. Very thin and almost translucent but with downy fur on the backs. They'd been blended seamlessly into his own ears.

"Hey, Jonas!" Kip took the hand and leaned forward, embracing the man in a half hug.

"What can I get you?" Jonas asked.

"How about a couple of Shirley Temples?" Kip said.

"Coming right up." Jonas put some ice into two glasses and opened up a bottle of ginger ale.

"I thought you said your name was Kip?" I asked.

"It is. Kip, short for Kipling. Kipling Jack Donovan. Some of my friends call me Jack," he said.

Right. He'd said his full name when he introduced himself. Which was kind of weird? But I guessed that was just how he introduced himself.

Jonas poured grenadine into the ginger ales and stirred them, dropped a maraschino cherry into each, and slid them forward.

"How much do I owe you?" Kip asked.

"These are on me," Jonas said. For a second, I thought one bunny ear twitched.

"God, your ears are so realistic!" I said.

"You think so?" Jonas asked with a broad smile.

"Yeah, really incredible effect. Did you do them yourself?"

"Oh, no, I was cursed by a blue fairy for . . . stealing a pie?" He paused partway through and made an odd face at Kip, then laughed as he finished.

Kip was completely expressionless. I chuckled. "Well, thanks for the drink."

"You're quite welcome, my dear."

"That was nice," I said to Kip as we moved away with our beverages. "He's funny."

"Oh, yes. A laugh-a-minute that guy."

We came to stand next to a tall round table with a couple of empty glasses on it. I placed my folded flannel on it and my knapsack beneath. "That's kind of crazy that you'd run into someone you know here. How do you know him?"

Kip took a drink of his Shirley Temple. "Oh, he used to bartend at a pub near Central Park I used to go to."

"I thought you said you didn't drink?"

"I don't. But my friends do."

The music changed from the instrumental heavy thumping music to a song with two male vocalists and guitar over synthesizer and drum machine. It was still dance music, but I liked this one. Kip must have noticed me nodding my head in time with the beat.

"You want to dance?"

"No. I don't dance."

"Oh, come on, everyone says that but everyone can dance a little."

"Not me."

"I could show you how . . ." Kip trailed off.

"No, thanks."

"You mind if I do?" he asked dubiously.

"Not at all. Be my guest," I said, and waved him toward the dance floor.

He went right to the center, which was vacant. Most of the other dancers—of which there were now seven—seemed to prefer the perimeter. Kip began moving his head in time with the music. The movement continued down his body, animating his shoulders, arms, torso, hips, legs, and feet. Then he was moving across the floor, his legs pumping, shoulders swinging. He turned and I could see that his eyes were closed while he danced, seeming to lose himself in the song. A few of the other dancers were turning to watch him. The music paused a moment and then the guitar segued into a solo that sent Kip sliding across the floor near two girls. He mimicked their dance style for a few beats, then shimmied his shoulders, and approached a couple who were dancing several feet away. He did the same with them. A few more people got onto the dancefloor and then a few more, and Kip borrowed each of their moves in turn.

The song faded out as another began and more people began dancing. I wasn't even sure where they'd all come from. One minute the dance floor seemed nearly empty, the next it was teeming with bodies.

Kip appeared next to me, shrugging off his suit jacket. "You sure you don't want to join me?" He smiled and folded the jacket in half, placing it on the table.

"Are you kidding? There's no way I could keep up!"

He held out a hand, and said, "Last chance."

When I shook my head, he nodded and disappeared into the swarm of waving arms and moving feet.

The cage dancers were still undulating and I wondered how long they had to stay in them, especially the suspended one. I sipped absent-mindedly at my drink, but it was just a cherry and ice cubes.

"Need another?" Jonas asked, seeming to

materialize at my elbow.

"Oh! Jeez, you scared me," I said.

"My deepest apologies," Jonas said, taking a step back and bowing his head. He'd already placed my new drink on the table.

"How much are they?" I asked. I had about four dollars on me and wanted to be sure I could give him a tip.

"On the house," he said with a smile, scooping my old glass up. "It's the least I could do to make up for giving you a scare. Plus, any friend of Jack's." He waved a hand through the air dismissively and made his way back to the bar.

A few songs later, the music changed genres again, this time to a melodic ambient instrumental. This seemed to be a cue, as the cage dancers left their stations, the majority of dancers drifted away, and the suspended cage began to descend to the floor. Kip emerged from the crowd, glistening a bit from his exertions and brimming with happy energy.

"Man, that Red Queen really knows how to read the crowd," he said, taking the cocktail napkin from beneath his glass and wiping his brow with it. He then drained his glass in a single gulp, leaving only mostly melted ice cubes and a bright red cherry with a long stem.

"So . . ." he said.

"So?" I inquired.

He speared the cherry with the stirrer and looked at me. "I know this will seem like the cheesiest thing ever, but . . ."

"But?"

He smiled mischievously. "Do you know anyone who can do this?" Before I could ask what, he tossed the cherry into the air and caught it in his teeth. I applauded politely. The cherry disappeared inside his mouth and he held up a single finger as he began making grotesque expressions while his tongue poked around inside his cheek. Seconds later, he opened his mouth and plucked out the stem, which had been neatly tied into a knot.

"Neat trick," I said, and suddenly yawned. "God, what time is it? How long have we been here?"

"About an hour, maybe?" Kip guessed.

"You think the trains are running again?"

"Probably. You want to get going?"

"Yeah. I'm tired," I said, stifling another yawn. He picked up his jacket and began putting it on. "Don't you want to stay?" I asked.

"Nah, they'll be closing up here soon and the best set is over, I think." Jacket on, he focused his attention on me and saw me putting on my flannel. "Stop!" he exclaimed with an alarmed look on his face.

I stopped, wide-eyed. Was there a spider on it? Had a drink been spilled on or near it? "What's wrong?" I asked.

He seemed to recover his composure. "Well, first of all," he began, taking the flannel from me, "it's inside out. Can't have you going out like that." He pulled the sleeves out and shook it into shape. "Second of all, please, allow me." He stepped behind me and held it out by the shoulders so I could slip my arms into it easily. "Much better," he said.

Outside, the velvet ropes were gone, as was the podium. The temperature had dropped further and thinking to put on my jacket, realized I had left my knapsack beneath the table in the dance room. "Gah, I left my bag inside. Sorry, I'll just be a sec—"

Kip handed it to me. "No need. I picked it up as we were walking out."

"Wow, thanks! Very observant of you," I said, getting my jacket out of the bag.

"It is important to always remain vigilant," he said in a resonant voice, as if he were quoting something.

"What's that from?" I asked, pulling the jacket on.

"Huh? Oh, just something an old friend of mine used to say."

"Weird friend."

"You have no idea."

We walked west along Bleeker Street. The streets weren't exactly deserted, but they were much emptier than I was used to. I unzipped a pocket in my knapsack and surreptitiously pulled out the silver flip phone that everyone made fun of but made me feel like I was on Captain Kirk's crew.

"When can I see you again?" Kip asked.

"What? I . . . you . . . want to see me again?"

"Why wouldn't I?"

"Why would you?"

I took a glance at the little screen on my phone. The time read 3:02AM. "That can't be right!" I exclaimed, forgetting that I was trying to hide my outdated technology.

"What can't be right?"

"The time!"

"What time is it?"

I told him. "According to this thing, anyway," I said. I held it out and he let out a surprised laugh. "I know, I know," I said. "I need to 'join the 21st century'."

"No, no. You don't understand," Kip said, still chuckling. He reached inside his jacket, and his hand emerged with a black version of the exact same phone.

I laughed. "You have got to be kidding. You haven't joined the 21st century either?"

"Nope." He grinned at me. I grinned back. "Do you text?" he asked.

"Yes. Slowly, with one finger, but yes. It's very 20th century."

"What's your number?"

I gave it to him and he typed it into his phone, using his thumbs. Then my phone beeped. I opened it and a new text had appeared. It read: **Kip.**

Chapter Three

THE NEXT MORNING, I WOKE WITH A HEADACHE. I heard the sound of a whistling kettle and knew that Sylvie was in the kitchen, making her habitual cup of tea.

Kip and I had taken the same train, caught up in conversation about comic books, which he knew very little about. He almost missed the stop for his transfer so we didn't really get a chance to have an awkward hug or handshake. He yelled "Fuck!" and dashed out as the doors were closing. We waved at each other as the train pulled away.

Now it was morning, my head hurt, and I needed to pee. I opened my bedroom door and crossed the hall to the bathroom.

"Goooood morrrrrning!" Sylvie cheerily sang from the kitchen.

"Morning," I replied, closing the bathroom door. When I'd finished my business, I splashed my face with water and brushed my teeth before coming out again.

"Cup of tea?" Sylvie called out.

"That would be great," I said. "I don't suppose you have anything that's good for a headache?"

"Let me see," she said. I heard cabinet doors opening and closing as she rummaged around.

I stole into the living room and curled up on the couch, massaging my pounding temples.

Sylvie emerged from the kitchen some several minutes later and presented me with a steaming mug. "Chamomile and willow bark. I already strained the leaves out of it, but it's still hot, so you might want to blow on it before drinking."

As I could any time that Sylvie stood near me, I caught a scent that was a mixture of tilled earth, freshly cut grass, and carnations. Julie had said it was Sylvie's patchouli perfume, but I'd smelled patchouli before and it didn't smell like Sylvie.

I wondered how old she was. Her thirties, maybe? I wasn't sure, but she certainly acted older and wiser than me and Julie. It seemed rude to ask, and after all, it didn't really matter. I didn't even know how old *I* was. Why should I care about how old my roommate was?

Tall and slender, she wore her dark hair in thick braids wrapped around her head and scoop neck t-shirts or tank tops with capri pants. I'd only seen Sylvie with her hair down once in the two months she'd lived with us. It was waist length.

She also loved plants. I mean, *loved* plants. She spent a good amount of time every morning misting them with a spray bottle, checking over their leaves, and talking to them. And they thrived. I'd remarked on this to Julie the week before and she shrugged, saying, "Well, she *is* Canadian," as if that explained anything.

"You got in late last night, didn't you?" she commented.

"Oh, I'm sorry, did I wake you? The trains were all messed up from a track fire."

"No, you didn't wake me. It's just that you don't usually sleep so late."

"And you aren't usually home during the day on Friday," I said.

"I'm taking my road test in Queens today," she said.

Sylvie worked for the NYC Parks Department, climbing and pruning trees. One of the requirements of the job was a commercial driver's license, and she'd been working on getting hers.

My phone chirped from my room, announcing a text message. My immediate hope was that it was a message from Kip, which quickly turned to dismay as the phone dinged four more times in fast succession. I approached it warily, and saw that I had five unread messages. I flipped it open and was surprised to see they were all from Zoe.

Zoe was a ghost hunter, or if not exactly a hunter, a medium who could contact ghosts and help them move on. She'd helped with the one in my apartment, and I was more than grateful.

The texts read:

> Having trouble with a haunting
> I dont see spirit but hauntee does
> not just @ home - other places 2
> shes really scared
> could really use ur help

Crud cakes. I sighed heavily. My stomach turned as if it were tying itself in a knot. "Nooo . . ." I moaned, scrunching my eyes shut as though I could make the messages disappear by not looking at them.

"Everything okay?" Sylvie asked from the living room.

No, everything was not okay. I wanted nothing to do with hauntings. No hauntings, no spirits, no ghosts, no vampires, no anything weird and mysterious. "Yeah, I'm fine," I said.

I was not fine.

What the hell did Zoe expect me to do? I had done my best to forget about the events of the spring, to avoid getting caught up in the creepy supernatural world, but now here I was, being dragged back into it.

"Okay, I'm heading out," Sylvie called. "Feel better!"

"Thanks," I said. "And thanks for the tea!" The front door banged closed and I heard our two deadbolt locks clank into place.

I read over the messages again and stared at one in particular.

could really use ur help

What could I do? Zoe was convinced that I could see ghosts. Or that I had some kind of magical energy. Possibly both.

Sure, it sounds cool, but then a ghost almost makes your pregnant roommate have a miscarriage, a possessed girl tries to kill you, and a vampire maybe kills the only friend you have and then begins to stalk you and it's not cool at all.

I skipped back to the previous message.

shes really scared

Hell.

Actually, *hell* was not a strong enough word.

"Fuck," I said aloud.

CHAPTER FOUR

HANNAH FRANKEL LIVED ON STATEN ISLAND IN A beautiful two-story home with a manicured front lawn. Zoe's battered 1970's station wagon with its wood paneling sat in the driveway in front of a small garage. I wished that I'd taken her up on her offer of a ride instead of taking the ferry and two buses to get there, but there I was, and only about twenty minutes after I'd hoped to arrive.

I walked up the steps and rang the bell. Zoe answered the door and waved me in. She wore a gray dress over black leggings and her hair was longer than when I'd last seen her. She looked like she hadn't been getting enough sleep. But if Zoe looked bad, Hannah looked worse. A woman in her thirties with a lank brown ponytail, her clothes hung on her and she had dark circles the color of bruises beneath her eyes. What a contrast to the framed photo on the side table at her elbow, a glowing bride and handsome groom with huge smiles.

"Hi, I'm Madison," I said, extending my hand to her.

"Hannah. Thank you for coming," she said, placing her hand in mine. It was smooth and cold and limp.

I let go and resisted the urge to wipe my hand on my jeans. Instead, I stood awkwardly in her living room, looking around. The room was cozy, with a blue couch and chairs arranged facing a fireplace with a big screen TV mounted over it. Color-coordinated blankets and pillows were arranged artfully, complementing the tan walls and multi-colored rug. Two more framed portraits of Hannah and her husband on their wedding day adorned the walls.

A plate on the coffee table held a cheese Danish with one bite taken out of it, and a cup of coffee had a dark ring around the inside from sitting too long between sips. A glass of water and an orange prescription bottle sat next to a plant on the side table.

"I'm sorry. Please . . . have a seat," Hannah said, gesturing toward one of the upholstered chairs.

I sat, and looked at her, waiting. When she didn't say anything, I looked at Zoe, who shrugged helplessly. I guessed I'd have to start.

"So, um, Zoe said that you were having a problem . . . ?" I prompted.

Hannah nodded several times, closing her eyes and breathing out of her nose. She pressed her lips together, swallowed, and then spoke. "Yes. My— my husband. He—he—passed. But I've—" Her voice broke and tears welled then overflowed as she continued. "I've . . . seen him. Here."

Zoe passed Hannah a tissue and I noticed a few others crumpled in her lap. She dabbed at her eyes and took a drink of water.

"I'm sorry for your loss," I said sincerely.

She nodded. "Thank you. I appreciate that."

"When did it happen?" I asked.

"When he . . . passed? Or when I saw him?"

"Both, please, if you can."

She dabbed at her eyes once more and crumpled the tissue. "We'd been married just over a year," she said. "He was a highway patrolman for the New Jersey State Police. It was a—a stupid accident. Not his fault. A drunk driver. That happened . . . a little over a year ago. I stayed with my parents for a while, and then came home. I went back to work. I tried to get into a routine. And then, about two weeks ago, I thought I saw him at the hospital."

"Why were you at the hospital?" I asked.

"I'm a nurse."

"You said you *thought* you saw him?"

"Yes. And then he was gone. I thought . . . well, my therapist said that it was probably just wishful thinking, that I'd seen someone who resembled him and imagined it was him. But then I saw him again, at Pathmark."

"At the grocery store? Out in public?" I asked, looking from Hannah to Zoe. Zoe nodded, as if to say, *See? This is why we need your help.*

"And he disappeared just like the first time?"

She nodded. "No one else saw him either."

"How long was that after the first time?"

"About four days."

"Were those the only times?"

"No," she said. "I saw him twice more. Here. Once across the street when I was getting the mail. I was so startled I ran into the house. When I looked again, he was gone. That was Monday, and I contacted Zoe Tuesday. Then last night, I saw him looking in the kitchen window." She wound the crumpled tissue tightly around two fingers. "I didn't know what to do so I screamed at him. 'Just leave me alone!' or something like that. And then, just like the other times, he vanished.

"My therapist said I was hallucinating and wanted me to see a psychiatrist. But I know what I saw. I know it was Hank." She burst into tears after saying the name and mopped her face with the tissue she was still holding. "Excuse me," she said, and left the room. The sound of footsteps ascending a staircase came from down the hall.

"Yikes," I said to Zoe.

"Yeah," Zoe said. "I don't even know where to begin with this one."

"I'm guessing you've ruled out a long-lost twin brother?"

"I can't rule anything out at this point. The thing that gets me is the diversity of the locations. Most of the time, ghosts are stuck where they died or where their bodies are lain to rest. That's why places are haunted, not people. But when a person is haunted and they aren't a medium like me? Well, that's poltergeist territory. Or possibly demonic."

"Demonic? Tell me you did not just say 'demonic.' "

"Wish I could."

"Zoe, what the hell do you think I can do about a freaking demon? I can't even see ghosts! You should call a priest! Get an exorcism!"

"Shhhh! Keep your voice down. I haven't mentioned any of this to Hannah."

"Why not?"

"Don't you think she's been through enough?"

I looked at the framed pictures of the happily wedded couple. "Yeah. Yeah, I guess she has."

We sat in silence for a while. Upstairs, we heard a shower start. I wondered how close the nearest church was. I wondered how hard it would be to get a priest to believe us. I wondered if Hannah was hallucinating, and whether her husband had a clone.

"Does she have any idea why he'd be haunting her, if he is?" I asked.

"No, none. I asked her if she kept anything of his on her at all times, wondering if it was some item his spirit was attached to. She doesn't."

"Even her wedding ring?"

"She took it off after the funeral. Said it was too painful."

"So, you think that a poltergeist or demon has just . . . what? Taken on his shape or something?"

"Maybe? Or animated his body?"

"Oh my God, like a zombie?"

"I don't know. Like I said, I can't rule anything out at this point."

"Wait. Do you know which window she saw him looking through?"

"Yeah, in the kitchen, through here." I followed her into the kitchen and she pointed. "That one."

Outside the window there were bushes and a small expanse of grass up to a fence. The neighbor's house was on the other side. "I know how we can rule one thing out, maybe," I said. "Did it rain here, yesterday or the day before? Do you know?"

"I think it did," Zoe said. "What did you have in mind?"

"Let's go outside."

We made our way around the side of the house and waded into the bushes. There were footprints in the dirt between the bushes and the house. Large footprints.

"Well," I said. "Looks like it's not a ghost. Unless ghosts wear shoes."

"I wish that was comforting," Zoe said.

"Well, how do we know this isn't some stalker weirdo lost brother person? That would take us out of the equation and we could let the cops handle it."

"True," Zoe said.

"I wonder if she still has any of his shoes around. We could see if they're the same size. Also, we need to test your other theory about how something might have inhabited his body. Well, if he was cremated, we could rule out demonic possession. And if he was buried, we should visit his grave. We might be able to tell if it's been disturbed."

"Good idea," Zoe said. "But we probably don't want Hannah to know that."

"Probably not," I said.

"I know she saved the newspaper article about the accident. She showed it to me," Zoe said. "She probably has the obituary too."

"Do you know where it is?" I asked.

"Yeah, in a scrapbook under the coffee table."

"Let's take a look."

CHAPTER FIVE

WASHINGTON CEMETERY WAS MILES AWAY IN Brooklyn between the Bensonhurst and Midwood neighborhoods. The elevated train tracks for the F line run right alongside a long portion of it.

Zoe had decided to stay behind to keep Hannah company in case the stalker decided to show up. She had written down directions from her smart phone and handed me her keys. I blinked at her twice and then took them without comment. Whether she'd forgotten that I didn't have a license or just didn't care, I wasn't going to argue.

As I parked, an F train rumbled and screeched overhead, pulling into and then out of the station. The day had turned gloomy and overcast and I wondered if it might rain as I left the station wagon parked on McDonald Avenue. Tall iron railings guarded the cemetery's borders, and I turned on Bay Parkway to find the entrance. The first thing I noticed was the office building, a dilapidated brownstone with a sign that read WASHINGTON CEMETERY in foot-tall letters over the front door. Another at the entrance advertised its hours for visitation: 8AM – 3:30PM. I checked my phone. It was 3PM. I had just enough time to make it.

As I stepped onto the porch, a bearded man in a black fedora and black suit with white tassels hanging from the sides opened the door and nearly hit me with it. He seemed flustered a moment and then wobbled back and forth indecisively as he tried to figure out how best to get past me. I took a step back and moved aside, and the man grunted and brushed past.

Inside the dimly-lit office, a gray-haired woman in a long-sleeve shirt didn't bother to look up from the ledger she was writing in as I entered. She sat behind a desk with a computer on it and a typewriter on a table behind her. The windows needed a cleaning and it made the sunlight even fainter. I stood there quietly until she put down her pen and expectantly said, "Yes?"

"Hi. I'm looking to pay my respects to a friend of my dad's. He was buried here." I had practiced this speech on the way over.

"Go ahead. No one's stopping you," she said.

"I don't know where to look," I said.

"Recent burial?" she asked.

"No, not that recent. About a year ago, I guess?"

"A year ... 'not that recent'," she repeated. "Oh, to be so young again. Name?"

"Madison ... oh, do you mean his name?" The woman nodded wearily. "Henry. Henry Frankel." That was what the obituary had said. Hank must have been his nickname.

She typed quickly and consulted the computer screen, then jotted down the details on scrap paper and handed it to me. "Go out this door, take a right, walk along for five rows, take a right, then another right, and start looking over there." She told me the plot number and gestured at the clock on the wall. "Better hurry. We close soon."

The gravestones were crowded close to one another, and there were no trees, or bushes, or curving pathways. What little grass there was was yellow-green in color, perhaps from too much rain or not enough sun. It was just a miniature city of stone monuments, jumbled together in grids and sharp angles, as crowded as the Manhattan skyline. Several tombstones were crooked or chipped. Many were eroded, the edges and lettering worn down, maybe by rain. A few others were broken or knocked over. For whatever reason—maybe the cemetery was short of money or manpower? —they seemed to have been that way a while.

The stone was black and shiny, rectangular in shape, with a foot-tall etching of Hank's smiling face to the left of his epitaph. A star of David appeared at the top of the text, followed by what I guessed was Hebrew lettering. Beneath that it read:

IN LOVING MEMORY OF

HENRY VICTOR FRANKEL

1981 – 2016

NEW JERSEY STATE POLICEMAN

BELOVED HUSBAND, SON, AND NEPHEW

MAY HIS SOUL REST IN PEACE

Looking at the etching gave me the creeps. It had been modeled on his official police photo, the one I'd seen in the scrapbook. His cap and the collar of his uniform were easily visible. It wasn't that they'd done a bad job capturing his likeness—I recognized it at once. They'd even gotten his cleft chin and dimple right. There was just something about it. Maybe it was just the tragedy of it all. That smiling face here in the middle of all this decrepit death. He'd been, what, thirty-five when he died? It didn't seem fair.

Everything seemed to be in order, until I took a second look at the grass in front of the stone. One square of sod was more yellow-brown than yellow-green, and its edges were still clearly defined. I sunk down onto my haunches and contemplated. Was that just normal in the first year after a burial? Should I find another recent grave to compare it to? I stuck a finger under the sod and found it went under quite easily. Too easily. I lifted it and the square rose at the corner. Beneath it, powdery dirt. I thought I could see something glinting in the dirt and dusted it away. The loose soil shifted, revealing the very solid corner of the wooden coffin. I dropped the sod and it seemed I felt a giant centipede walking up my spine. That coffin should have been under several feet of earth. Which meant it had been disturbed.

Which was pretty disturbing.

I had to call Zoe for directions because I got lost in a construction detour coming off the Verrazano

Bridge, but luckily made it back to Hannah's house before rush hour started. I parallel parked across the street from the house and was thinking about Zoe's admonishment about all that smartphones have to offer when I spotted movement out of the corner of my eye.

A guy in a hoodie was walking down the sidewalk toward me. I caught a glimpse of very pale skin, a cleft chin, and a dimple. I knew that chin and dimple. I'd just been staring at an etching of them in a cemetery in Brooklyn.

I got out of the car, intent on speaking to him. "Are you—"

His eyes widened as I spoke. He turned and ran.

"Hey!" I yelled. "Hey!" I took off running after him.

He glanced back after half a block. When he saw I was still behind him, he picked up speed. Low-hanging branches of neighborhood trees pulled my hair and one gouged my cheek, but I kept running. He cut right and hopped over a waist-height picket fence of a little one-story house then ran into its backyard. I tripped over the picket fence, picked myself back up, and ignoring the pain in my ankle, rushed to the backyard, only to see him vault over a tall privacy fence into the neighbor's backyard.

How fast was this guy anyway?

I rushed to that fence as his head disappeared beneath the next one and knew I'd never keep up.

A little kid with one hand in his mouth and the other clutching a teddy bear stared at me from a large picture window in the picket fence house. I waved, and the kid flopped his teddy bear at me. Then I slowly limped back to Hannah's.

"What happened? Why are you bleeding?" Zoe demanded as she ushered me inside.

I touched my face where it stung. My fingertip came away bloody. "I saw him," I said.

"Saw who?"

"Hank."

"You saw Hank?" Hannah's voice came from around the corner. She sounded . . . hopeful.

"Yeah. I tried to talk to him and he ran from me. I chased him, but he was too fast."

Hannah seemed a bit more together than she had when I'd left. She'd changed clothes, her hair was clean and styled and she was even wearing a little makeup. The uneaten Danish had been taken away, as had the old coffee cup, but she seemed calm and alert. "You're sure it was him," she said. It wasn't a statement or a question, exactly. More that she was prompting me to say what she was hoping I would say.

"I saw a guy in his mid-thirties, wearing a hoodie and track pants. He had very pale skin, a cleft chin, and a dimple right here," I pointed at my cheek. "I couldn't swear it was him, but if it wasn't, it was someone who looked an awful lot like him."

Hannah let out a long, shaky breath. Tears followed instantly. "Then I'm not crazy? I'm not crazy!" She stood up, crossed the room and hugged me. "Thank you, thank you, thank you! You have no idea what you've done for me!"

After she let me go, Zoe retrieved the box of tissues and handed one to her.

"No one else believed me," Hannah said, drying her eyes. "No one except you two. I'm so grateful."

"Do you mind if Madison and I talk for a few minutes in the kitchen?" asked Zoe. "Oh, and also, do you have a band-aid or something? This cut on her cheek is still bleeding a little I think."

"Of course, absolutely. There's a first aid kit upstairs. I'll be back in just a few," Hannah said, already bustling out of the room.

I followed Zoe into the kitchen. "Are you limping?" she asked.

"Just a little. I kind of twisted my ankle."

She *tsked* at me and opened Hannah's freezer. "Well, she doesn't have an ice pack in here, but there is a bag of frozen mixed vegetables you could use . . ."

"I'll be alright. I'm just babying it."

She closed the freezer and sat down opposite me at the table, speaking low. "So, when you say he was too fast, how fast are we talking? Vampire fast?"

Zoe had been present when Michael Adderly took off with Billy, but all she'd seen was a blur.

"No, not that fast. But faster than a human, for sure. Like . . . maybe as fast as someone on a bike, except he was on foot."

"So we can rule out vampire?"

"I don't know. I mean, he didn't try to drink my blood. I didn't see any fangs. And you know, the sun is still out."

"Oh, right. It wouldn't make sense anyway," she said. "He died in a car accident after all."

"True," I said.

The sound of footsteps descending the stairs hushed us. We nodded at one another, silently agreeing not to talk about vampires in front of Hannah.

She appeared in the kitchen doorway holding a white box with a red cross on the front. "Let's get you patched up," she said.

"You don't have an Ace bandage, do you?" Zoe asked. "She hurt her ankle too."

Hannah made a scandalized sound and looked at me accusingly. "You should have said!"

"I didn't want to be a bother."

"An injury isn't a bother to a nurse. Now take off that sneaker and your sock so I can see what you've done to yourself," she demanded.

I obeyed her instructions and she examined my ankle, moving it this way and that.

"It's just a strain. I don't think you sprained it. If you did, it's a very light one. You're lucky you were wearing these high tops."

Her demeanor seemed very different. It seemed like having a problem to solve was good for her. This was familiar territory. Safe. Normal.

"Rice!" she said loudly, confusing me.

"Rice?"

"R-I-C-E. Rest. Ice. Compression. Elevation. Best treatment for an injured ankle. And don't take any anti-inflammatories for at least twenty-four hours. Pain relievers are okay, but nothing that reduces inflammation. Let your body's natural response do its work for a little while. And stay off it as much as possible, especially tonight."

"That will be a little difficult seeing as how I need to get back to Brooklyn," I said.

"I'll drive you," Zoe said. "Least I can do."

Chapter Six

I LIMPED INTO MY APARTMENT TO THE SMELL OF peppers and onions cooking. "Hey," I called.

"Hey," came Julie's voice from the kitchen. "You hungry?"

"Always," I replied. I set down my backpack and went to see what was happening in the kitchen.

Julie had her back to me, using a wooden spoon to stir a sizzling pile of vegetables in a large sauté pan.

"Smells good," I said, sitting down at our small kitchen table. "What is it?"

"When it's done, it'll be vegetarian fajitas. Still interested?"

"Sure."

"Ack, what happened to your face?" she asked. I'd been thinking about answers to this question while Zoe drove me back to Brooklyn. "Oh, you know. I was chasing a zombie in Staten Island," I said.

She laughed. "Like you do, right? Tell me another one, Buffy!"

"My friend's puppy got loose. Who's Buffy again?"

"You're hopeless," Julie said.

"Not true. I have much hope."

"So is he okay?" Julie asked.

"Who?" I asked back.

"The puppy!" she said impatiently.

"Oh! The puppy. Uh, yeah. *She* is fine. For a second I thought you meant the zombie."

I didn't know if the zombie was fine, or if the zombie was even a zombie. Hannah had gone to stay with her parents in New Jersey for a while until we could figure out what was going on.

"So what are you up to this weekend?" Julie asked.

"Oh, I don't know. Working mornings this weekend, no plans at night."

"Tad and I are going to a burlesque show in Coney Island on Sunday if you'd like to come."

"What's a burlesque show?"

"You know, old-timey striptease type stuff? They're fun."

My phone dinged from my backpack in the other room. I got up to grab it and Julie barred my way with a wooden spoon that had half a green pepper slice hanging from it. "No, no. No saved by the bell. Answer!" she threatened.

"What the hell? Answer what?"

"Do you want to come with us? Maybe meet some people?"

"Oh. No, thank you."

Julie raised the spoon like a tollgate.

"Alright, but don't blame me for leaving you home with the plant whisperer."

I grabbed my phone and returned to the kitchen. I had one unread text.

Do you like horses. - Kip

I wasn't really sure how I felt about horses. They were okay, I supposed. I typed:

They're okay.

The phone beeped again moments later.

Meet at the park tomorrow? 5pm?

"What are you smiling about, hmm?" asked Julie, carving an avocado.

Which park?

Central Park. At Columbus and 59th. Look for the horses.

"Looks like I have date tomorrow night," I said.
She put down the avocado. "Oh my God. Finally! Tell me *everything!*"

Central Park in autumn is a landscape painting come to life. Leaves, so many leaves, scarlet, orange, burnt umber, gold, yellow, some still green, some almost violet, others brown and tough as leather, the rest as fragile as papyrus. A rainbow of falling, dying leaves laid out like a tapestry, tree to tree.

The air was crisp and cold as I came up out of the subway. Several cars, mostly taxis, were in the roundabout, circling the monument at Columbus and 59th. A small flock of pigeons cooed and fluttered, pecking at pieces of stale bread.

I inhaled the odors of NYC in autumn: decaying leaves, exhaust, burnt pretzels from a vendor cart half a block away, and here, a whiff of horse dung.

A line of carriages stood along Central Park South. A restless horse tossed its head. Another stamped its feet. A few of the drivers smoked cigarettes while waiting for their next fares. One wore a top hat.

It was Kip. He wore his black suit jacket as he perched in the driver's seat of a blue carriage. A white and gray horse was tethered in front of it.

"You're early," he said. I was. I'd gotten off work and headed straight there.

"So are you," I said.

"I work here!" he said.

"Do you want me to come back later?" I asked.

He tilted his head and looked down the line of carriages ahead of him. "Nah, let's go. Climb aboard." He offered me a hand and pulled me up into the driver's seat with him. Once I was seated, he whistled a short piping whistle three times, which was returned by the other carriage drivers. Then he clicked his tongue at the horse, shaking out the reins once and steering us toward the street. The jingling of the horse's harness accompanied the clip-clopping of its hooves. A few more of the same whistles came from his fellow drivers as we pulled past six more horse-drawn carriages. They weren't wolf whistles; just short, loud ones.

"Why are they whistling?" I asked.

"Eh, it's a thing we started recently. When you pull out ahead of the carriage at the front of the line, you whistle. When you're going off shift, you whistle. That kind of thing. A signal."

"Saves the time of yelling back and forth?"

"It does. You look nice tonight, by the way."

Julie had refused to allow me to get myself ready that morning and supervised my "look." First, she had insisted on blowing out my hair. "It's a pretty color," she'd said, referring to my strawberry blonde, "but it needs style." The way she used the brush and the blow dryer left my hair smooth and bouncy on my shoulders.

Next, she focused on makeup application. A dab of light concealer hid the small scratch on my face. Then "Just a little brown eye shadow," she'd said, dragging a thin brush beneath and above my lashes. She then proceeded to darken my blond eyebrows and wiggle a mascara wand on my lashes to make them fuller. "See? It makes those blue eyes pop!"

I'd been concerned I was going to look weirdly artificial, but instead my eyes were just more noticeable. My reflection in the mirror had big blue eyes with long dark lashes.

Deeming my freckles "cute," needing no foundation or blush, she had pronounced me done, advising me to wear lip balm of some sort. Beneath a navy peacoat, I was wearing dark jeans, a royal blue V-neck sweater that Julie said was too large for her, and a pair of knee-high brown boots that Kara had handed down to me when her feet grew a size in her last trimester.

Luckily, my ankle was feeling better, but the boots—with their chunky two-inch heels—were uncomfortable to stand in, which was what I'd just been doing at work. Everyone at Chris Street had remarked on my appearance too, which made me wonder what I looked like the rest of the time.

I thanked Kip for the compliment. He handled the reins with ease, keeping an eye on traffic while maneuvering the carriage and horse alongside taxis and commuter cars. "Where are we going?" I asked.

"Don't like surprises?"

"Not really," I said. None of the surprises I'd had in the last almost-year had been particularly pleasant.

"Do you trust me?" he asked, flashing me a winning smile.

"Hell no, I don't trust you!" I laughed. "I don't know you!"

"Fair. A fair observation. A palpable hit!"

"I don't follow. We're not playing Battleship, are we?"

"What's Battleship?"

"Oh, right, I forgot you didn't grow up here." It was kind of nice being around someone who knew even less about pop culture than I did.

The carriage turned into the park and Kip began lecturing about the different buildings we could see in the distance, pointing out landmarks, explaining the history of Central Park. After several factoids regarding a green expanse called the Sheep's Meadow, he pulled over to the side and tied off the reins. He removed his top hat and placed it beneath the seat. Then he ran his hand through his hair, ruffling it. "That's better," he said. "That hat gets warm! I don't have hat head, do I?"

"No, you don't have hat head," I said. It wasn't really fair. How could his hair go from under a hat to just-tousled and still look so good?

"Come on," he said, alighting from the carriage and holding a hand out to me.

Ahead of us was a squat, octagonal building with several open-to-the-air arches. It was constructed of alternating red and cream bricks with a sort of cupola on its roof. Strains of music came from within—a marching dirge, played on an organ or accordion of some kind.

"Have you been on the carousel before?" Kip asked, his accent coming out on the last syllable.

"I have not," I replied.

We went to the ticket window where a young guy in a tan uniform greeted Kip like an old friend. Kip complimented him on his earring and the guy passed him two tickets.

"How much do I owe you?" I asked Kip, reaching for my wallet.

"Owe me? Are you trying to insult me now? You owe me nothing. I owe Rodney nothing. Rodney owes me nothing."

"Who's Rodney?"

"The young fellow who just gave us the tickets."

"Is he a friend of yours or something?"

"No, I just read his name on his badge."

I gave him a look. "But *why* did he give you the tickets?"

"Maybe because I complimented him? He had a really interesting earring. It was an articulated skeleton that—"

"Ooh!" I said, cutting him off. We'd moved through the turnstile into the main room. In the center was the carousel, lit with a thousand white light bulbs and stable of (I found out later) fifty-seven painted race horses. The carousel was in action, turning and turning, the horses rising and falling with the movement of its marvelous mechanism, making them appear as if they were dashing across a track. The riders were mostly women and children, though a young couple spun by as well, the two of them seated closely in a stationary carriage seat.

The carousel slowed and came to a stop and the various riders climbed off their horses. Handlers in uniforms checked the ride for stowaways and then the music, that same sad dirge, started up again, apparently signaling the next batch of new riders that their time had arrived.

"See one you like?" Kip asked.

I scanned the platform. There were plenty of white horses, arrayed in rainbow colors of barding and saddles, some in red, blue, and yellow, others in gold and silver. A brown horse with a golden mane and a white stripe on its forehead intrigued me a moment, but it wasn't quite right.

Then I saw two black horses standing side by side. The closer one had a white mane and white around its hooves and a painted-on lionskin for a saddle. "That one."

Kip took the black horse next to it. Its nose and head were raised, its mouth open, as though neighing or bucking or both. Several metallic clangs sounded and we were off.

The world spins by when you're on a carousel. The up-and-down movement of the horses combined with the rotation of the platform creates a dizzying combination of sensations. Between hanging on to make sure I didn't fall off and the loudness of the music, I didn't bother trying to make conversation with Kip. He hadn't brought me here for that.

I watched him bob up and down on his horse. He smiled at me and I found myself smiling back. Eventually, the ride stopped and we climbed off, though Kip said they'd let us ride again if we wanted. I didn't think it would be fair to all the people in line, though I was tempted.

"Did you have fun?" he asked, taking my hand as we strolled across the lawn back towards the horse-drawn carriage.

"I did. Did you?"

"Oh, yes. But I think I might enjoy this more."

"This?"

"This," he said, giving my hand a squeeze.

I might have blushed, but it's hard to tell because one of my chunky heels skidded in a pile of leaves and I slipped, falling backwards. My hand slid from his grasp as I collapsed on my back in the grass and leaves. Then I *definitely* blushed. Though this time with embarrassment.

He stood over me, staring down with his lips pressed together, utterly failing to contain his amusement.

"Go ahead, laugh," I said.

He chuckled a bit, but then with sincere concern said, "That was not the most graceful landing I've ever seen. But are you alright?"

"Yeah, I'm fine. A little help?" I asked, holding out my hand.

"Of course!" He grasped my hand and pulled me up so fast that I practically bounced off him. I hadn't realized it, but the heels on my boots made us closer in height, so that he was just a couple of inches taller than me. Our faces were inches from each other. He kept a firm grip on my one hand, while using his other to pick a leaf out of my hair.

Then he kissed me.

Those full lips were as soft as they looked, and I instinctively inhaled through my nose when they touched mine. He smelled of cinnamon, cloves, smoke, and some undefinable delicious sharp-sweet yum. The kiss went on, slowly, tentative, small gentle brushes of his mouth against mine. First, fully on both lips. Then my top lip. Then the side of my mouth, both lips, the other side. He caught my lower lip in his and tugged on it slightly with his teeth, and then pulled it into his mouth.

Now I don't have much experience with kissing—or if I do, I can't remember it. There was that one time that Derek and I had kissed, which was nice, but this? This was erotic. Hypnotizing. Dizzying. The difference between instant hot cocoa and one that's been brewed at home with whole milk and rich Dutch cocoa, topped with fresh marshmallows. A gourmet kiss. Everything a kiss ought to be.

A horsey snort and the jingling of a harness caught my attention as he broke off the kiss.

"Alright, lass, alright," he said to the horse. "We should get going. She's bored. Or maybe jealous?" As we ascended into the driver's seat, she let out a soft nicker.

"What's her name?"

"Oh, that's Rosie, that is. She's a Percheron. Do you know what that is?"

I shook my head.

"She's a working horse. That's what they're bred for. They like to work." He picked up the reins and Rosie set off at a clip-clopping pace.

"Do you really think she likes it?"

"Eh, she gets a bit bored sometimes. If she gets angry, she'll try to take a bite out of you, just like any other mare."

"Is she the only one you drive or do you just drive any of them?"

"Only her. I can only handle one lass at a time," he said, smirking at me and rolling his eyes at himself.

Okay, I admit it. I was smitten.

After we dropped the carriage off, Rosie needed her gear removed and a thorough rub-down, which Kip conducted himself. While he was checking and cleaning her hooves, she kept nosing one side of his jacket. "Here," he said, handing me a small apple he pulled from his pocket. "You give it with the flat of your hand. Just let it sit on your palm. Yes, like that. Exactly."

I held out the apple and Rosie blew air out of her nose and then nudged the apple with it. I stayed perfectly still while Kip watched. She nudged the apple once more and then took it gingerly with her lips, then pulled it into her mouth and began crunching. As soon as she was done, she nudged the side of my jacket. Kip laughed.

"Sorry, Rosie. I don't have any more. Do I?" I looked at Kip.

"No, and that's the third one she's had today. Don't let her fool you."

Rosie blew air from her nostrils again and rubbed herself against the wooden slat wall where Kip was cleaning her. "Alright, alright. Yer done, girl," he said. He led her down the row of stalls to an empty one, then came back to me.

"I'll just wash my hands and we can go to dinner, yeah?"

"Yeah."

We walked east from 11th Avenue to 9th and then headed south into Hell's Kitchen. Our destination was a tiny Thai restaurant with seating for maybe twenty people. All of the tables were full. The hostess, a young Asian woman, grimaced at us and asked, "How many?"

"Two," we said at the same time. Our eyes met and returned to the hostess.

"Twenty minutes. You want leave phone number?" she asked.

That sounded fine, so I gave her mine. "So what now?" I asked Kip.

"Take a walk?"

"Sure."

Kip linked his arm in mine and we walked south along 9th, taking in the snippets of music blaring from each of the several bars we passed.

"So tell me more about yourself," Kip said. "Where'd you grow up, here in New York or somewhere else?"

I took a deep breath and let it out. "You know, that's a story I'd rather tell over dinner, if it's all the same to you."

"As you like. What would you prefer to talk about then?"

There's nothing quite like someone asking you what you'd like to talk about to make anything you might want to talk about flee screaming from your brain so that all you can think is that you have nothing to talk about and that you are probably the least interesting person in the entire world. I glanced wildly around, hoping my eyes would light on a suitable topic, when I heard my phone ringing.

"Saved by the bell!" I said, and picked up.

It was hard to hear the person on the other end over traffic and the rock music blasting from the bar we'd just passed, but I was pretty sure it was the hostess from the restaurant. "Yes, we'll be right there," I said. I would have said goodbye, but she hung up before I could.

"So, out with it. Where did you grow up?" Kip prodded. We had just placed our orders. There was no escape now.

I met his gaze and said, "I don't actually know." The vivid green of his eyes seemed darker in the dim lighting.

He raised his eyebrows a moment and his mouth quirked up in a half smile. "That's one of the things I like about you, Madison. I can never predict what you'll say next."

I spent the next few minutes explaining about dissociative fugue—my formal diagnosis—to the best of my ability. Then, while we ate, told him the story of my awakening and my time at Bellevue. He made concerned faces and asked questions in all the right places. He didn't seem put off by any of it. If anything, he seemed to take it all in stride.

"So you're like one of your superheroes maybe, yeah? Next you'll tell me you have superpowers."

"I don't feel very super, honestly," I said, poking my fork at the last few noodles on my plate. Kip was nearly finished with his dinner as well.

"Oh, I meant to ask you," he said. "What did you do to your cheek?"

I reflexively raised my hand to the spot where I'd scratched it chasing Hank. Apparently the makeup that Julie had applied had worn off.

I'd already told him about my amnesia, so why not tell him the rest? A voice in my head put the kibosh on that right quick. *Are you nuts? Not only do you have no memories but you also chase zombies? Sure! Tell him you lived in a haunted apartment, too! Do you want him to think you're insane?!* I could go with the puppy lie, but it just didn't feel right. I didn't want to lie to him.

After a too-long pause, I met Kip's eyes, and said, "And that's a story for another time. Is that okay?"

"Ooh, another mystery. I love a good mystery," he said.

"Then you—" I started but was cut off by the drunk guy who—having just got up from his table—staggered into the server walking by with a tray of drinks, causing her to lose hold of the tray and dump several glasses of Thai iced tea onto our table.

Kip and I reacted quickly enough to avoid any major stains, though I hoped that the small one on my jeans would come out. I'd just gotten them at the thrift store two weeks before.

Our server and a manager came over and began apologizing as they mopped up the orange liquid. The hostess yelled at the drunk guy and practically chased him out. Our server offered to replace our dinners, but since we were almost finished with our meals, we declined.

"We'll just take the check, thanks," I said.

"You aren't paying," Kip said.

"Watch me," I said.

The manager came back to our table. He told us how sorry he was that the server had spilled the drinks and he wanted to let us know that our dinner was at no charge.

"It wasn't the server's fault," I said.

The man nodded. "Yes, but we want all our customers to have a nice time here. We hope you come see us again."

We both thanked him, and he shook our hands like we'd done him a favor.

Outside, I asked Kip, "Is it just me, or do you never pay for anything?"

We were standing outside the 57th Street F station and could not seem to stop kissing. I'd pull back and say, "I really should get going," and he would say, "Okay," and then I'd go to give him a last peck and next thing I knew, we were at it again.

"Okay, you should go," he'd stop and say, and I'd nod and sigh and he'd kiss my cheek, or my forehead, but then I'd kiss his lips again and off we went.

He smelled like spices and smoke and his lips tasted of cinnamon. His mouth on mine was like a magnet drawing energy from the middle of my brain and the center of my body.

"You should—"

"I should—"

More kissing.

My phone rang.

"I should—" I began, but was interrupted by further kissing.

"—get that—" he supplied, but then, more kissing.

"Or I could just let. It go. To voicemail," I said, between kisses.

The phone stopped ringing, but it started again several seconds later.

"Okay," I said, extracting myself. "Whoever it is, it must be important."

Kip inhaled as if steeling himself against further temptation. "Yeah, yeah. You should check that. Answer."

I dug the phone out of my bag and found that it hadn't rung at all. In fact, the battery appeared to have died. I held it up. "Must be yours. Mine isn't even on."

Kip's eyes opened wide and he reached into his pocket.

"Hello?"

He listened a moment and his face lost a little bit of its color. He turned away from me and spoke into the phone.

"Oh, I . . . I'm out . . . uh . . . 57th. Yeah. Um . . . yeah, no." He glanced at me a moment and then turned away again. "Yeah, I'll be right there. Yeah. Me too. Okay, bye."

"Everything okay?" I asked as he put the phone back in his pocket.

"Yeah. Just a . . . uh . . . friend," he said.

"You need to go?"

"Yeah." He opened his mouth to say something else, closed it, and said, "Yeah," again. He came in for a goodbye kiss, but it suddenly became awkward and he kissed my cheek instead. "I'll . . . uh . . . call you," he said, and quickly walked away.

Chapter Seven

At home, Julie was standing outside her bedroom door in a red corset, matching underwear, garters with stockings, and a pair of red six-inch stilettos.

"Ahhhhh!" she yelled—not in embarrassment or surprise, but excitement. "Tell me all about your date!"

Julie didn't habitually wear fancy lingerie while lounging about at home, but she was quite open about Tad's enthusiasm for it—as well as her Instagram feed's. She often modeled her outfits for me when she first brought them home. I hadn't understood what a garter was or how it worked until she demonstrated for me. So finding her wearing such wasn't the most unusual thing either.

She raised a red plastic hairband with devil horns and placed it on her head.

She was still trying to pick out her costume for the Halloween ball she and Tad would be attending at the end of the month. So far, all the options didn't seem that different from her usual bedroom attire.

While I recounted my date, Julie put on a flashy fashion show of several lingerie-themed costumes. "Did you like devil better?" she asked, emerging from her room in a lacy white one-piece with feathery wings. "Or do you like angel? Or . . . ooh! How about Wonder Woman? Or did you really like Little Red Riding Hood better?"

"Why are you having so much trouble deciding?" I asked, trying on a red mask she'd left lying around.

She adjusted the cap of her current costume, a "sexy policewoman" which involved a skin-tight black mini dress with a plunging neckline and a badge. She'd accessorized with thigh-high stiletto boots, a police cap, and a belt with a nightstick and handcuffs. She stood in her doorway, looking at herself in a full-length mirror, while I watched the show from the hallway.

"Because Tad's old friends from the burlesque scene will be there! It's a big deal."

"Haven't you met these friends before?"

"Like two of them," she said, tucking her long dark hair into a messy bun beneath the cap. "Plus, you know, any occasion for dressing up is an opportunity to get more followers."

"Followers?" I said, and then realized what she meant. "Oh, for your Instagram."

"Do you think I should just leave the handcuffs on, or make Tad wear them?" she said, cocking her hips to get a better view of the metallic cuffs where they hung.

"Are they real?" I asked.

"Only kind of," she said, taking them off her belt. "See?"

They were lighter than they looked and made a ratcheting noise as I opened and closed them.

"Weird," I said.

"What's weird?"

"I don't know. I thought they'd be heavier. Did they come with a key?"

"No. They have an emergency release button right there," she said. "So, you put them on the person," she said, snapping one of the cuffs onto my wrist, "and then—"

At that moment, the front door opened and Sylvie came in, carrying a sack of groceries. I could just imagine what we looked like, Julie in her sexy cop costume, me wearing a mask, her putting the handcuffs on me.

It was an odd moment to walk in on, but she closed the door behind her and walked to the kitchen, not even pausing as she walked past us.

"Hello to you both," she said without changing expression. Julie and I looked at each other for a second and then started giggling.

The next day at Chris Street, Nidhi also demanded I tell her about my date. The day before, I'd told her about running into Kip on the sidewalk, which she'd declared a "real-life meet-cute!"

Nidhi was on register duty, Trendon was on bag check and not particularly happy about it, and I was in the back, taking inventory of the vintage action figures that hung behind the back counter. Whenever the store was empty, Nidhi would steal to the back to ask me about how things had gone with Kip. When I got to the part about the phone call at the end, she frowned.

"Oh, I do not like that," she said.

"I wasn't too crazy about it either," I said, pulling down a package marked *Teenage Mutant Ninja Turtles*. Inside was a bipedal turtle-man wearing an orange mask. It was marked at $200. "What is this guy from?"

"Seriously?"

"Seriously."

"His name's Michaelangelo. It says it right there. Look, see? He has little nunchucks . . . No? Raphael, Donatello, Leonardo?"

I shook my head and shrugged. "They're Italian?" I said.

"You are an enigma, inside a riddle, wrapped in a big cliché," she said. Pretty much all of my co-workers knew about my amnesia at this point. If I hadn't told them about it myself, they'd heard from one of the others.

"Right. I'm . . . what now? An assassin from the future?"

"All I'm saying is that I'm not ruling out the possibility," she said. "But anyway, back to that phone call. I don't like it. I don't think he's single."

"That's what my roommate Julie said. His behavior when he was taking the call was strange. He seemed tense. And evasive. But I don't know. At one point he said he could only handle 'one lass' at a time."

"Ha! Classic womanizing Casanova move. Tell every one of the *mares* in his *stable* that she's the one and only." She nodded conspiratorially, giving me a wink. "You see what I did there?"

Trendon yelled across the store to ask us if we

wanted to order lunch. With more important matters on the table, the topic was dropped.

Monday morning began with a text from Zoe. She'd heard from Hannah, who wanted to know when she could go back home. Apparently, commuting to the hospital in Staten Island from New Jersey several hours per day wasn't to her taste. I suggested we meet at the Brooklyn Library to do some research.

I love the library. The tall ceilings, the relative quiet, the books, the classes, the resources. I'd learned how to research at the library, how to use the databases to hunt through old newspapers for answers. My caseworker had suggested I go there and take computer classes because she thought it was a skill I ought to have. She wasn't wrong.

When I spotted her, Zoe was at the information desk, speaking to a bespectacled librarian who gave her directions to the non-fiction section.

"Roland should be up there somewhere," the woman said.

Zoe thanked her and turned to me. "There you are. Hi!" She gave me a quick hug.

I never knew how to receive hugs. It was nice being hugged but I was never sure how long I ought to hug back for, if I should offer hugs, or just go in for the hug or what.

"We're going upstairs," she said, and so we went.

The non-fiction section was in a part of the library that hadn't been renovated very recently. The stacks had an older, well-used appearance. It wasn't dusty, but the air was full of that old-book smell that was somewhere between dried roses and stale vanilla wafers.

When we found Roland, he was standing on a stepladder, placing a book where it presumably belonged. Zoe nudged me and whispered, "Hipster Santa."

"Hipster what?"

"Shhh!"

Roland was a trim man with white hair and a white beard. He wore a red and blue plaid jacket over a white shirt and red bow tie, with dark pants. Once the book was among its fellows, he took a step down then hopped to the floor. It wasn't very far but he moved much more agilely than I'd have expected for a senior citizen.

He picked up the stepladder with one hand and snapped it shut, then whirled on his heel and spotted us. "Ah!" he said, his eyes shifting from me to Zoe then me again.

"Have we met?" he asked.

"Uh . . . I don't think so?" I said. "Though I come here all the time. I mean, not this area of the library, but at least once a week?"

"My mistake. Okay then. You must need help finding something, correct?"

"Yes. But we don't really know where to look," Zoe said. "The woman at the information desk said you might be able to help us."

"Yeah, we want to research folklore and mythology about . . . well, zombies."

His eyebrows raised. "Is this for a school project? An essay?"

I said, "Yes," and at the same moment, Zoe said, "No."

Roland blinked.

"I'm the one with the essay. She's just helping," I said.

"And you're not interested in fiction or cinematic . . . zombies, correct? No classic literature, film history, or anything of that nature?"

"No, nothing fictional. We're looking for what real people believe happens when a dead person is brought back to life, you know, wrong."

"Not like Jesus," Zoe supplied.

"No, I certainly should suspect not," Roland said. "Follow me this way."

He led us down long aisles of shelves, taking a few turns.

"This is the mythology and folklore section. I'd suggest looking at . . ." He seemed to be thinking it over, then tapped a few books, saying, "Haitian and African voodoo culture, this book on Eastern European belief in vampires, and Egyptian burial rites, perhaps." As he tapped each book, he nudged it forward an inch so that we could pick it out easily. "If you were interested in classic literature, I might direct you to Mary Shelley's *Frankenstein*, or hmm . . . I wonder if the works of Albertus Magnus or Paracelsus . . . Alas, we don't have editions of the latter two, but scanned copies are available through interlibrary services should you wish to peruse them."

I almost didn't know what to say after all of that, so I just said, "Thank you."

"Not at all, not at all," he said, and backed out of the aisle.

"I've got nothing," Zoe said. "Haitian zombies weren't risen dead people so much as drugged people who maybe kinda-sorta thought they were dead? But not really. And Hank definitely died. So he's not that kind of zombie."

I picked up the book on Eastern European burial rituals and gestured with it. "Well, people in the fifteenth or sixteenth century seemed to think that if a black cat jumped over your corpse, or you had red hair, or committed suicide, or maybe were born with a caul—then you would turn into a vampire. Or maybe a werewolf. But not a zombie." I let the book fall to the table.

"Any luck with the Egyptian stuff?" Zoe asked.

"It's interesting, kind of. Things about different parts of the soul being separated from the body after death, *ka, ba, ha,* and others. The *ka* is the personality and the *ba* is the 'intrinsic spark that gives us life, vitality.' The *ha* is the body. Apparently after the *ba* and *ka* separate from the *ha* they become something else that's judged in the afterlife against the weight of a feather. Which is pretty weird. They believed a good soul would weigh *less* or the *same* as a feather, whereas an evil soul would weigh *more* than a feather."

Zoe made her voice gruff and intoned, "Guilt. It's soooo heavy."

"And tasty. If the soul was evil, it would be eaten by a weird monster crocodile-hippo-thing called Ammit."

"Damnit, Ammit . . ."

"Then there's an entire chapter about mummification: Taking out the body's organs and putting them in jars, taking out the brain, washing the body with wine and wrapping it with herbs and amulets and stuff so that the person can live in the afterworld."

"How long did it take before it rose from the coffin and began to kill?" Zoe asked.

"Sarcophagus," I corrected. "Seventy days from embalming, covered in this dehydrating stuff called natron. After a while, they stuffed it with sand or whatever, and then when the seventy days was over, they would wrap it in linen and then it officially became a mummy."

"Do you think Hank is a mummy?"

"No. He seemed too lively. He's not a dehydrated bandaged corpse. He's, like, built?"

Zoe paged through a book about Jewish funerary practices, since Hank had, after all, been Jewish. "It says here that 'the soul of a person is confused after they die and they stick around the body.' Well, that's true, in my experience."

"Do you see a lot of ghosts?"

"Not a lot. Just, I mean, do you see any people with mustaches in here?"

I looked around and saw the librarian with his white mustache and beard. "One."

"But it depends on what neighborhood you're in, right? Ghosts are like that. So in some areas, like cemeteries, I see a lot. In others, maybe one, maybe none."

"Here?"

"There's one I saw earlier. I'm not sure where she went."

I shook my head wonderingly. "So weird."

"This is interesting," Zoe said, scanning the page. "As soon as a Jewish person dies, his or her body is *never* alone until it is buried. It says the soul stays with the body for seven days, mourning for it. But I remember my Gram said that some souls are confused for years and years. The ones that stay in cemeteries get upset about being eaten. Not by a hippo monster. By worms and things."

"OKAY," I said, shuddering as I thought about being eaten by worms. "That is enough research for me."

"Yeah, me too," Zoe said, throwing down the book. "I don't want to get stuck on the BQE. I'm heading back before rush hour starts."

Chapter Eight

WHEN I GOT HOME FROM WORK THE NEXT NIGHT, Julie was home, clothed in a set of baby-blue pajamas with monkeys on them. Her eyes were red and she was sitting on the couch with the remote in her hand and half a bottle of wine on the table. A bag of chips sat on the couch. She appeared to be watching a period drama of some sort.

"Hey, Jules, what's going on?" I asked.

"Oh, this stupid movie," she said, pausing the action. "They are all so mean, except for this one character. She is the sweetest. And this . . . this *moron* is obviously in love with her, but nooo his pride. God, I hate him."

"Stupid men," I said.

"Stupid men," she agreed.

"Trouble in paradise?" I asked.

She made a sound of disgust. "Tomorrow, Tad will be having lunch with his ex-girlfriend to help her with her headshots. And it's just lunch and I'm not supposed to be jealous but I am and *ugh*."

"Why aren't you supposed to be jealous?" I asked.

She glared at me. "Don't even."

I wasn't sure what I wasn't supposed to even, so I didn't say anything.

She sighed. "I'm sorry, Maddy. Do you want to order pizza? Bacon and pineapple? My treat."

"Um, yes, please."

"Dessert?" she asked.

"I don't think so."

"I'm getting a chocolate can-no-li . . ." She sing-sang the last word.

"Fine," I said. "But you may have to finish it for me."

"The horror!" she faux-exclaimed and picked up her phone.

I checked mine while she was ordering. Still no text or call from Kip.

When Julie put her phone down, she looked at me sympathetically. "Still haven't heard from him?" she asked.

"No," I said glumly. I was beginning to think that Nidhi was right about him being a womanizer. Some insipid damsel in my brain asked, *But what if he's hurt?*

I told her to shut up.

"Don't worry. It's only been . . . what? Three days? That's nothing," Julie said.

I counted. "It's been four."

"Four? Still. Not so bad. I think it has to be at least a week before you can consider yourself ghosted."

"Ghosted?"

"Yeah, you know, guy pulls a disappearing act, disappears like a ghost?"

"Oh." I said.

Ghosts. I hadn't even mentioned the ghost, but I had told him about my amnesia. "Do you think he was put off by my past? Or lack thereof?"

"You told him?" Julie seemed surprised.

"Yeah. You think I shouldn't have? He seemed fascinated, not weirded out."

"Hmm. Hard to say. I would have waited a little longer than the first date to tell him."

"I think I should text him."

"And say what? 'Did my amnesia bother you?' or 'Why haven't you called?' That is the clingiest. Don't do it."

"What should I do instead?"

"Hang out with me and eat pizza, of course," she said. "But first, ugh. I've sprung a leak. I'll be right back." She left muttering about her light blue pajamas and closed the door to the bathroom.

My mind dwelt on thoughts of Kip. If he already had a girlfriend, then he was just messing around with me. Or maybe when he'd said he could only handle one girl at a time, I misunderstood and he was being sarcastic, letting me know he had a bunch of girlfriends. Maybe his phone kept dying, like mine did. Maybe he was in the hospital. Or the morgue. Or maybe he hadn't taken my diagnosis in stride and had just pretended like it didn't matter. Or had second thoughts about it afterward. There were fifteen million other possibilities. It was infuriating having my thoughts stuck on him, but it was all I could think about.

The next day was new comics day and it was busy enough that I couldn't spend the entire time pining over Kip and wondering further why he hadn't called. I only started obsessing about that during closing and texted Nidhi, who was off that night.

> Can I text him now?

> NO.

> But.

> NO.

The following night, Nidhi and I had a shift together, and though I managed not to say anything for most of the evening, I eventually broke. "I just don't see the harm in one little text," I said.

"You need to forget about that fuckboy. He probably has a girlfriend and you were going to be his side piece but then he got caught by the girlfriend and had to go," Nidhi lectured. The store was pretty quiet and I was Mylar-bagging a collection of comics Mac had bought earlier in the day.

Nidhi had register duty, but she had come back to talk to me while the store was empty. Jackson was up front, changing the window display.

The store bell jingled and a customer walked in.

It was Kip. His hair was tousled and he wore a leather jacket over a white shirt and skinny black tie.

"Well, hello," Nidhi purred, clearly referring to him.

"Oh my God," I said. "It's Kip!"

"I take back everything I said," Nidhi said.

Kip's eyes lighted on me and he walked in my direction.

"Go," I whispered to Nidhi from the corner of my mouth.

"No."

"Yes!"

"Not yet!"

". . . Hi, Kip," I said, smiling awkwardly and wishing I could kick Nidhi.

"Hello."

"Hi, I'm Nidhi," she said, offering him her hand.

"Hello. I'm Kipling Jack Donovan," he said, shaking it. He winked at me, then turned her hand and kissed the back of it.

Nidhi fanned herself with the hand after releasing his grip. "Okay, you can keep him," she said, and walked to the front, giving us relative privacy.

"First, I want to apologize," Kip said, "For leaving so quick when I last saw you and also for not calling you for so long. I had to get a new phone and a new number and some other things happened too . . . I'll tell you about it later. At any rate, to apologize, I have brought you Rosie."

"You've brought me . . . Rosie?"

From his jacket pocket he pulled a small figurine of a white and gray horse and placed it on the counter.

I looked at him.

He grinned at me, spread his hands wide and posed like a game show model, using his hands to frame the miniature horse.

"So does this work with a lot of girls?" I asked.

"I beg your pardon, madam?"

"Okay, beg away," I said, enjoying torturing him.

"Please, oh, please, won't you forgive me for not calling for five days?" he wheedled.

"Six days. Not that I was counting," I said.

He got down onto his knees and looked up at me with those big green eyes of his. "Please forgive me. You have my word as a gentleman that I am sincere," he said. God, he was cute. And weird.

I sighed heavily. "Okay, *fine*. But," I said, pointing at him with one finger. I waited.

"But?" he asked, still on his knees.

"No more horses," I said.

"For a while?" he asked.

"For a while."

"Fair. Pick you up when you get off?"

"Sure," I said. "6PM."

He turned and left and Nidhi came bounding toward me like a gazelle across the plain in a nature documentary. "Oh my God," she said. "Wait, what is that?"

"That would be Rosie, his horse."

"I take everything back," she said. "He's not a womanizer. He's a manic pixie dream boy."

"Is that a good thing?" I asked.

"All I'll say is this: Enjoy it while it lasts?"

The High Line is an urban renewal project, a park constructed over the remains of an old elevated railway on Manhattan's west side. Kip and I entered in the Meatpacking District and meandered uptown, observing views of the Hudson River, lookouts over various streets, and landscaping with native rushes, ferns, and other greenery mixed with wilting wildflowers, daisies, and black-eyed Susans that were the last remnants of the summer season. Most of the young trees had begun to change color. In some areas of the park, the old steel rails show through the concrete, a reminder of a different time.

After walking for several minutes and remarking on various statues and pieces of art, we came across a group of closed vendor stalls and continued on, finding a bench where we could sit together and watch the last bright orange rays of the sunset peeking between tall buildings on the New Jersey side of the river.

"So you never said why you had to leave so abruptly that night," I said, after we'd been shading our eyes against the brightness for a few minutes.

"A friend of mine was attacked—by her shithead boyfriend," Kip said. "A mutual friend of ours called and told me. They needed help moving her things out before he came back."

I expressed my dismay and concern and he grimly acknowledged his own. This conversation segued to talking about my relative non-experience with dating—as far as I knew. Kip admitted he'd dated "a lot" but hadn't had any serious relationships and was not—I'd asked—seeing anyone else.

"Most American girls I meet—they're beautiful, right? And empty-headed. Only interested in television shows and taking—what do they call them? Selfies? And posting on their Facebooks and Instantgrams."

"It's called Instagram," I said. "But I know what you mean. It seems like most of the people I meet are constantly looking at their phones. Smartphones, I mean. I think that's one of the many reasons— aside from holy cow, expensive—that I haven't gotten one. They seem . . . I don't know. Addictive? Everyone's a phone zombie. Except for a few random people I've met."

"I'm a random person now, am I?" Kip asked, teasing.

"No, you're not. You're just . . . you."

And then there was kissing.

Over the next two days, we spent every free moment together. When that wasn't enough, Erica told me she was pretty sure she could get the new girl Mac had just hired to cover one of my weekend day shifts.

One day, we wandered through the Met, had lunch in a café there, and walked over the Brooklyn Bridge in the evening. The next day, we went to Coney Island, where we rode the Wonder Wheel and had our pictures taken in a photo booth.

Nidhi proclaimed that the crash and burn was nigh because Kip and I were spending too much time together. And didn't I find it weird how much time he wanted to spend with me? "Like, clingy much?" she asked.

We were working at the front of the store, her on bag check, me on register.

"It's not like that," I said. "We're just . . . I don't know. Similar. He's the only person I've met who doesn't have a smartphone besides me."

"Oh, God, you were made for each other. Do you know that even my grandmother in India knows how to Facetime now? You are seriously behind the times. And so is your boyfriend."

Boyfriend? Was he my boyfriend? I wasn't sure.

"Um . . . how do I know if he's my boyfriend or not?"

"Oh my God, Madison. You're killing me here." Then her eyes opened wide and she covered her mouth with her hand while staring at me.

"What? Is there a cockroach tap dancing on my head?" We sometimes got those really big water bugs in the store and we always made whichever guy was working kill it. I ran my hand over my hair, just to make sure. It was roach free.

She shook her head.

"Whaaaat?" I asked.

"Are you a virgin? Like, do you even know?" she whispered.

I sighed. "Yes, I know. And no, I'm not." Part of my intake interview at Bellevue had included an extremely thorough physical exam. They wanted to be sure that I hadn't been raped.

I hadn't.

"But . . ." she said expectantly.

"But?"

"But you don't remember, right? Who it was? Or if it was just one or if you had the dreaded 'multiple partners'—God, I hate filling out paperwork in doctor's offices."

"No, I don't remember. I have no idea."

"So you're *like* a virgin . . . kissed for the verrry first tiiiime! Like a viiiirrrrgiiin . . .'" she sang quietly, bobbing her head in time to the music she could hear in her head.

"I kissed someone before, thank you very much," I said.

"I know. Just . . . don't tell me you don't know 'Like a Virgin.' It's a classic!"

"Sure I do. And isn't it 'touched for the very first time'?"

"Oh, yeah. I guess it is," she said. "Memory is a weird thing, isn't it?"

"You have no idea."

A customer came into the store, interrupting our conversation and leaving me to my thoughts while Nidhi helped him find the *Spectacular Spider-Man* issue he was looking for.

Memory *is* a weird thing. Divided into multiple aspects: explicit memory, implicit memory, and sensory, and then those divided again into long-term, and short-term or given other qualifiers like declarative, un-declarative, iconic, echoic, etc., it's hard to keep track of. The doctors explained it all to me, but ironically, I don't really remember what they said. I was so overwhelmed at the time that it all mashed together.

Kara—my old roommate who recently had a baby—looked up "Memory" on Wikipedia one time and we figured out that I maintain my *implicit* memory—knowing *how* to do things like walk and drive and read and play piano—but no *explicit* memory. It's not surprising that early memories, like learning how to walk and talk, disappear. But I have no explicit memories of piano lessons, or French classes, or how to drive. Yet I can still do those things.

I do have the ability to make long-term and short-term memories, just only from the day I "woke up," October 13, 2016.

My memory also includes details about history and pop culture, but I have no memory of learning them or being exposed to them.

And that's the other weird thing.

It's not just that my knowledge started last year, but that there's a gap. I don't know anything that happened between the winter of 1987 and the fall of 2016 unless someone tells me about it.

But I do remember things that happened before that, like that Ronald Reagan was president for two terms, or that a little girl named Jessica got stuck in a well in Texas, or that there was a movie called *The Best Little Whorehouse in Texas* with Dolly Parton and Burt Reynolds . . . it wasn't the weirdest trivia out there, but also things that an eighteen- to twenty-year-old girl in the year 2017 probably wouldn't know off the top of her head.

But what's really bizarre is that the only clue I have to my identity is a flyer and newspaper article about a girl named Christina Taylor who went missing in . . . you guessed it: 1987. A girl who was eighteen years old in 1987, who looked just like me.

It made no sense at all.

How could it be me in 1987 at age eighteen when even now I looked like I was about that age? Not *fifty* like she would be.

I had tried to get myself to look her name up online, or in the library newspaper databases, but it made me feel queasy every time I even considered it. Besides, wouldn't she have shown up in the Missing Persons files that the police went through when I was first "found"? Granted, they hadn't been looking as far back as 1987, but you'd think that someone would have recognized me. The resemblance was uncanny, and the clothes I was found in? They were exactly the ones she'd disappeared in.

The flyer and article had been anonymously delivered to my apartment after the spooky happenings in Sleepy Hollow. I thought—but wasn't sure—that the vampire Michael Adderly was the one who'd sent them, along with a record player and an old record of a song he'd recorded when he was a popular crooner in the 1930s or '40s.

Adderly had even called me "Chris" twice—short for Christina? So, if I *am* Christina, what kind of girl was I that a vampire knew me well enough to call me by a nickname? Did my lack of apparent aging have something to do with vampirism? I didn't think I was a vampire. I didn't thirst for blood and got along with the sun just fine. I got freckles, not set on fire.

Curiouser and curiouser. None of it made any sense.

"Hey," said Kip.

I jumped. I'd been so lost in thought I hadn't realized he had entered the store. He seemed jittery somehow, as though he was hyped up on too much coffee. He even seemed a little sweaty and disheveled.

"Are you okay?" I asked.

"Sorry," he said. "Yeah. Just . . . whew." He ran his hand through his hair. "Was crossing the street, almost got hit by a bus." He was talking fast and his accent seemed stronger. He looked back toward the store entrance and sighed. "You want burgers tonight?" he asked.

"You came here to ask me if I want burgers?"

He sniffed and coughed a second. "It's important for me to know your every desire so I can plan accordingly," he said. "Also, you hadn't answered the text I sent ye."

"I didn't get it," I said. "And sure, burgers sound great."

"You get off at 6PM, yeah?"

"Yeah. That's, like, twenty minutes from now."

"I'll just hang around while you finish, shall I?"

"Um, that should be okay. Don't do it when Mac is here, though. He'll have you arrested."

While Kip went to the graphic novel section, I checked my phone and saw the text I'd missed, plus a new one from Nidhi:

Is he on drugs or what?

I glared at her and she put her palms in the air, gestured toward Kip and made an expectant face.

I typed:

He almost got hit by a bus.

Nidhi's phone vibrated. She looked at the screen and looked at me and then started typing furiously.

That sounds like what someone on drugs would say.

I shook my head at her and put my phone away. She stuck her tongue out at me.

Sitting at a picnic bench in the oasis that is Madison Park, Kip and I were eating burgers and fries from Shake Shack when I got a text from Zoe.

will u take stakeout 2morrow?

She knew I had the day off and I knew she needed one.

Sure.

"What's that all about?" Kip asked. His accent seemed to have reverted to its less exaggerated version.
"I need to go and um, housesit for a friend of a friend tomorrow," I said.
"Can I join you?"
"Well, hmm. You may not want to."
"Why not?"

"Let me tell you about my friend Zoe and how I met her." I told him about the crazy events of the previous spring when I'd discovered my apartment was haunted and how I'd gone to Sleepy Hollow to investigate and that was where I'd met Zoe, the girl who could talk to ghosts. I left out the vampire part because I figured ghosts were bad enough.

While I recounted all of this, Kip's face went through several expressions, but none of them seemed particularly incredulous. He seemed more interested in how it had affected me, rather than trying to explain any of it away. He was so different than Derek, whose only interest in the paranormal was about trying to prove it didn't exist.

I then explained that Zoe and I were working on a new case and that was where the "housesitting" came in.

"Would you like company?"

"What? Don't you think I can defend myself against a zombie ghost?"

"Maybe I should protect it from you, hmm?"

I made a scandalized sound and he threw a French fry at me.

The stakeout was just as uneventful as the last one had been. Either Hank knew that Hannah wasn't around and hadn't bothered to come by, or he was successfully avoiding detection. Either way, we were no closer to resolution. Hannah was still terrified and we had no answers for her.

Kip and I took the Staten Island Ferry both ways, getting a closer look at the Statue of Liberty in the sunshine in the morning and seeing it all lit up in the evening on our way back.

The windy deck of a ship is a pretty romantic place, and we'd been kissing off and on during the return voyage. We'd found a secluded area on the side of the main cabin. We stood against the railing with our bodies pressed together, exploring one another's mouths. The chill wind was making our shared body heat all the more welcome, and what he was doing with his mouth, tongue, and hands was making me even warmer. He unbuttoned my navy peacoat and put his hands inside, tracing my neckline and letting his fingers trail down between my breasts.

"Come home with me," he murmured, kissing my neck.

I felt like I was melting, as though a direct link from the spot where he'd kissed my neck went straight to my knees and a couple of other notable places as well.

"Okay," I said, and kissed him back.

While we rode the subway, Kip explained that he lived in the Crown Heights neighborhood of Brooklyn. "It's a traditionally an African-American area, but now all these wealthy developers are coming in, and people fleeing the cost of housing in Manhattan. The residents hate it. Not that I can blame them. They're the worst kind of people—the gentrifiers, I mean, not the people who've lived there for generations. As bad as the English, they are."

"Aren't you a gentrifier?" I asked, teasing him. "Nah, I'm Irish."

Kip's apartment was a fourth-floor walk-up in a brownstone with a couple of apartments on every floor. He checked his mail in the entryway and then we went through the interior door. The stairwell was dimly illuminated by a flickering bulb somewhere above.

"And you live by yourself?" I asked as we trudged upwards.

"It's tiny. You'll see."

It was one large room, maybe twelve feet across and twenty in length, with very high tin ceilings, perhaps twelve to fifteen feet high. Linoleum led from the front door into the kitchen, which took up the entire right wall: fridge, stove, sink. Directly across, a tall window. Cabinets painted robin's egg blue above the sink and stove. A small table with two chairs sat across from the stove, leaving a three-foot walkway.

I put my knapsack on the table and hung my navy peacoat on a chair. Kip shrugged out of his leather jacket and hung it on the other chair.

"It's cozy," I said.

"Yeah, it's home," he said. "You want anything to drink?"

"A glass of water would be fine," I said, looking around the room.

Behind the table, a couch divided the room into kitchen and living areas. A bed sat in the corner, parallel to the other window. It was a full-size with one pillow and a patchwork quilt.

Looked like he usually slept alone.

Kip took a pitcher out of the refrigerator and got a glass down from one of the cabinets. "Here you go," he said.

I took a sip. The water was cold and almost sweet. "I see you like to read," I said. Against the wall next to a bureau was a small bookcase with a modest collection of hardcovers. They looked old, like first-edition antiques. Cloth covers, some with lettering that had faded completely.

And then there was the television. It was antique as well, but I found its appearance strangely comforting. It was an old-style CRT television, built into an ornate wooden frame. On top were rabbit ears—V-shaped antennae that needed to be manipulated to get reception to come in.

"Where did you get that TV?" I asked. "It's older than we are!"

"The guy who lived here before me sold me his furniture and threw the TV in for free. He said he couldn't move it anyway."

"Do you get any shows on that thing?"

"Oh, God no. It doesn't actually work."

"And you say you never know what *I'm* going to say."

I walked to the kitchen window and saw ivy curling around it on the exterior. It overlooked a small overgrown courtyard completely covered in plant life.

Somewhere in the distance, I heard a strange undulating howl. "What the heck?" I asked.

"Just a werewolf," Kip said off-handedly.

"Don't even joke about that!" I said, perhaps a little more strongly than necessary. The *last* thing I needed was a werewolf.

Kip laughed. "Sorry. It's the mosque around the corner," he said. "It's a call to prayer. I think there's something wrong with their . . . what's it called? The PA system. That's why it sounds so strange. You get used to it. I even like it now."

He sat down on the couch and patted the seat next to him. I joined him and put my water glass on the table. I took in the room from there. There wasn't anything hanging on the walls. I wondered how long he'd lived there.

"Now, where were we?" he asked.

"Hmm, here, I think," I said, leaning towards him and kissing his neck.

"Mmm," he said, pulling me into his lap so I could reach his neck a little better. "And here too, right?" he asked, kissing my neck.

Again I felt that current go straight through me.

"And here," I said, tracing the collar of my t-shirt.

He shifted and kissed across my collarbone.

"And here?" he asked, his fingers trailing between my breasts once more.

I sighed without meaning to sigh. "Yes."

His mouth came back up to my mouth while his fingers danced across the top of my breast, then beneath it and around it.

While kissing, I sat forward and began pulling my shirt off. Kip helped me and pulled off his own shirt.

I caught a glimpse of muscled torso and smooth skin before we were kissing once more. One of his hands cupped my waist while the fingers of the other traced around my bra and across the nipple over the lace.

Julie had supervised my first sexy bra purchase, taking me to her favorite reasonably-priced lingerie store where she suggested a pale blue front-closure bra. The bra cost more than twice the matching underwear. I didn't have enough money to get both, so I got the bra, since Julie said it was okay to not be wearing a matching set the first time you slept with a guy. "That way he won't think you planned it," she said.

"Planning is bad?" I asked.

"I don't know. To some guys, maybe. Not when you've been together awhile. But a lot of guys . . . the first time? They like to think it was their idea, which is pretty stupid. There's nothing wrong with a girl initiating sex. But I don't know. I'm pretty sure most guys don't care *what* you're wearing the first time."

The striped cotton briefs I'd bought months ago at Target would work fine.

Somehow Kip and I had slithered down the sofa so that we were now lying on it together, our mouths and bodies intertwined.

He felt around the back of my bra for a time before realizing what he was looking for wasn't back there. His hands moved to the front and nimbly undid the clasp. He kissed along my chin and then my collarbone and then along my breast, before finally reaching my nipple. I shivered in ecstasy and dimly registered the sound of my phone dinging—signaling an incoming text, then another, then another. Kip's mouth opened and he tasted my nipple as the phone dinged three more times.

He sighed. I sighed. Silence.

"I should—" I began to say, but then Kip's tongue flicked out and across my nipple hard and I forgot how to use my words.

His fingers were at work on my other breast, circling, gently squeezing. The two sensations paired was exquisite.

There was a noise. A sound. Aside from the noises that were coming from me unbidden, there was another sound. It was my phone. Ringing. Ringing and ringing from my backpack.

"Do you have voicemail?" Kip asked, his mouth hovering above mine.

"I do," I said.

"Do you want to take off your jeans?" he asked.

"I do," I said.

He got through the two buttons and the zipper, then shimmied them down my hips and pulled them off each leg.

With a hand at the edge of my striped underwear, he began kissing from one hip all the way across to the other. His other hand had returned to my breast but now joined its mate at the sides of my underwear, sliding just inside the waistband.

"May I?" he asked, giving the slightest tug.

I met his gaze, which was some combination of desire and anticipation that was incredibly sexy. His lips looked dark and full.

"Yes," I said, my voice much more whispery than I'd meant it to be.

His long fingers gently pulled the cotton down over my hips, then my thighs, then past my knees and further down one calf before his mouth and tongue met at the most sensitive part of my anatomy.

I'd barely kicked my panties the rest of the way off when I was hit with a wave of pure blissful ecstasy that rose and fell and rose again as his mouth did whatever it was doing.

He paused a moment as my phone rang again, but a moan from me seemed to be all the encouragement he needed to continue. It stopped ringing and my thoughts fled with a flick of his tongue. I was all sensation.

When the phone rang yet again, Kip hung his forehead on my belly.

"It must be important," I said.

He nodded and licked my belly button playfully.

"Hey!" I said, pulling on my underwear and leaning over the back of the couch to grab my bag.

I dug my phone out just in time for it to stop ringing again. Not only were there three missed calls, but *nine* unread messages.

CHAPTER NINE

I FLIPPED THE PHONE OPEN, THINKING IT WAS Zoe—maybe something was wrong, maybe she'd found Hank or Hannah had seen Hank again—only to be greeted by the following messages from Julie:

4:39pm	Tad is a dick!!!!
5:47pm	Having wine after work
7:04pm	You should come to Hoboken!
8:13pm	Ther R probably hobos in Hobbkn
8:14pm	I can't drive. Can u drive????//
8:14pm	Ima hobo wino
8:15pm	R Ualiv e maddy
8:15pm	Mady
8:15pm	Imm callingu

"What the hell?" I said.

"What is it?" Kip asked.

"Julie. She's been drinking. A lot, apparently."

"Your roommate, right? Well, you can just silence it . . ."

"No, she's not at home. She's in Hoboken. Look."

"Oh. Ohhhhhh," he said. "Can't she take a cab home or something?"

The phone beeped. I had a voicemail.

Our eyes met. "I better listen to it."

"Maaaaddy," Julie's voice came tinny and slurred from the small speaker. "I drank too mush. I can't find my wallet . . . I def can't drive. But you! You can drive! Pleeeease come to Hobroken. I will buy you things. And owe you errything a million times. And a new shirt. I need a new shirt. Bring a shirt. Maddy! Please callll meeee baaack." Some of it was garbled but I understood most of it.

"She needs me to drive her back from Hoboken," I said.

"But you don't have a license, do you?" asked Kip. "Have you even driven before?"

"Yeah. I've driven. I don't think the license is the most important thing right now," I said, clipping my bra closed and grabbing my shirt. "I should go."

"Of course. And I'm coming with you," Kip said. "Sounds like you could use a hand with her maybe."

"Bathroom?" I asked pointing at a door.

An archway and five-foot-square "hall" led to a door, with another door against the same wall.

"Closet," Kip said, then pointed at the other door. "Bathroom."

We took the subway into Manhattan, bought an I ♥ NY t-shirt from a street vendor, and transferred to the PATH train to Hoboken. Julie had given me the address of a pizza place and said she was outside it. I consulted the map inside the station, found the street, and figured out which way to go. Kip was duly impressed by my navigating skills.

When we got to the pizza place, it was closed. It had been . . . how long had it been? Subway ride plus t-shirt plus PATH transfers . . . probably an hour and a half? If I had really been smart, I would have copied Julie's number into Kip's new phone before mine died.

Where could she be?

"JUUUUULLLLLIIIIIEEEE!" I yelled, cupping both hands around my mouth.

I heard a moan.

Across the street, catty-corner to the pizza joint, was a bank. It had three marble steps going up to its front doors, and curled up at the bottom of that front door with her head on the wall, was Julie.

We crossed the street quickly and were overcome by a particularly vile smell. "Oh, God, what is that?" I asked, trying to breathe only through my mouth.

Julie was covered in vomit. The bank stairs were covered in vomit. It was purple.

"Hiiiii," she said. "I'm disgusting."

"We're gonna need some paper towels," I said to Kip. "Just towels in general."

"Always gotta have a towel," Julie slurred. "Pete always said. Good ole Pete."

"Who's Pete?" Kip asked out of the side of his mouth.

"Her old boyfriend," I muttered. "God, what a mess. What did you do to yourself, you poor thing?"

"I wassssh drinking. Withh Allen and Todddd from my old job. And then Franz and Arruun showed up. And then I said, 'I should eat something' and so Franz brought me here and I got pizza but then . . . I got sick."

"So Franz just left you here?"

"He did! Before I wasssh sick. I said I was fine. But I wassshn't really fine."

"Poor Julie. Where's your car?"

"Ah! That is the bessst part. I can't lose my car, because I put it in my phone. See?" she said, offering the phone to me. I knew this drill from the summer. The phone was miraculously not covered in vomit, though the screen and sides were slightly sticky. I wiped it on my jeans.

"Keys?" I heard a jingle as she handed them over. The keys had not been so lucky in the vomit department and I wiped them on my jeans too.

"You are the best, Maddy. The absoluuute best." Her eyes then focused on Kip for a moment. "You know I didn't like her when I met her? Wait, who are you?"

Kip opened his mouth to say his name, but I jumped in, "It's Kip. I told you about him, remember?"

"WAIT IS HE THE GUY WHO CAN TIE A CHERRY STEM WITH HIS TONGUE?" Julie said in a very not-inside voice.

Remembering what Kip had been doing just before her calls had interrupted us, I felt my cheeks go red and was glad it was dark.

"So you *did* notice," Kip said, sounding pleased.

"Anyway," I said. "I'm going to go get the car. Will you stay here with her?"

"No, we should just bring her to the car together, yeah?"

"I think it will be faster if just I go."

"But who will protect you from the werewolves of Hoboken?" he asked.

"Cut. That. Out," I said, wagging a finger at him. He really needed to lay off the supernatural jokes. It was starting to make me feel like he was making fun of me for telling him about my experiences.

"Sorry. Okay. You need me to stay with her, I'll stay with her. But hurry, yeah?"

"There isha towel. In the trunk. A biiiiig towel," Julie slurred.

"Ten-four," I said. "Be right back."

I found Julie's dark blue Mini Cooper parked where her map app said it would be and clicked the remote to unlock it. I got in, pushed back the seat about six inches, adjusted the rearview mirror, started the engine, turned on the lights, stepped on the clutch, put her into gear, and drove.

It was much faster getting back to the bank in the car than it had been fast-walking, and I saw Julie sitting much as she had when we'd first arrived. But where was Kip?

I did a K-turn in the street and backed up to the corner so that the car was only ten feet from the stairs.

I killed the engine and popped the trunk, where I found the beach towel that Julie had mentioned, as well as two others. When I closed the trunk, the sound echoed off the surrounding buildings. The streets were eerily quiet. I could hear the buzzing of a street light and there didn't seem to be many cars on the road in the immediate vicinity.

Kip emerged from the shadows inside the bank door's overhang like an apparition and scared me half to death. "Gah! Don't do that!" I said.

I opened the back door and spread one of the towels across the backseat, leaving the other folded over to use as a pillow.

I put another towel around Julie's shoulders as Kip and I walked her over to the car.

"I've got her," he said.

I opened the door and he swept her up and placed her inside. I got into the front and put on my seatbelt. Then I heard Kip make a very strange noise. It was half a whimper and half strangulation.

"You okay?" I asked.

"My, oh, my," Julie said. "I shee you aren't jusssht good with your tongue to make up for other defish—definch—def—shhhort-comingsh," Julie said.

"A little help?" Kip grunted. I couldn't quite see what was going on, but I was starting to get an idea.

"Yep, he's a SHOW-er!" she said. "Jusssht needed to check for you Maddy—"

"Jesus, Mary, and Joseph," Kip said. I thought he was praying for protection from the drunk girl who was groping him, but something about the frightened, whispered tone of his voice made the hair on the back of my neck stand up.

I could see what he was looking at through the windshield. Up the block, in the middle of the road, silhouetted in a streetlight, was a large man. A man wearing a hoodie and track pants. I couldn't see his face from here but I thought—I knew—it was Hank. In one hand, he carried something metallic. A section of pipe, maybe.

He was standing stock still, staring at us. Then he moved. His walk was single-minded and full of purpose, and there was no doubt what that purpose was. He was headed straight for us.

I started the car.

Kip shouted, "Go, go, go!" He threw himself into the backseat atop Julie, who squeaked in dismay.

I stepped on the clutch and slammed her into reverse. With Hank barreling down on us, I floored the gas pedal.

Chapter Ten

I found the high-pitched whine of the transmission (clearly protesting the unaccustomed speed at which I was in driving in reverse) disconcerting, but I kept my foot on the floor.

I knew from firsthand experience how fast Hank could move. And he was moving. I'd seen wild cheetahs stalking wildebeests on a nature documentary over the summer and marveled at their explosive bursts of speed, the way they gained on, then mauled and broke the necks of their prey. I had no doubt what would happen if Hank caught up with us. Whatever had happened since the last time I'd seen him, he wasn't running away anymore.

Facing backward in my seat, I kept one hand on the wheel, a foot on the gas, the other on the clutch, and my other hand on the gear shift. A side street swung into view. I backed into it, then stomped on the brakes, hit the clutch and threw the stick into first.

And Hank was still coming, lumbering, stalking.

I hit the gas and tore down the side street, shifting from first gear to fourth in several seconds, then slamming on the brakes as I realized there was a STOP sign immediately ahead. Julie was moaning in the backseat and Kip was trying to hang on but kept getting tossed about. Finally he extricated himself and climbed into the front with me.

"Seatbelt," I demanded, and he fumbled with the buckle.

I peered anxiously in the sideview mirror to see if I could spot Hank, but all was quiet. I heard a click as Kip mastered the buckle.

"I think we lost him," I said.

SMASH. The driver's side window rained chips of glass all over me as Kip hollered in fear.

Large, pale hands reached into the car and tried to pull me out, but the seatbelt did its job and locked me into place. I had a choice between going forward or going backward and since there was a truck heading into the forward intersection, I threw the car into reverse once more.

The big hands tore away from me as the car jerked and backed up.

I was watching out the back window while going in reverse while Kip was watching Hank through the windshield.

"He's still coming!" Kip cried.

The street widened, with no cars parked at all on one side of the street. Seeing how much room I had, I suddenly knew what to do. The car screeched to a halt as I stamped on the brake to make the front tires lock. At the same time, I yanked hard on the steering wheel, then thrust the stick into first. The car did a 180-degree turn and I stomped on the gas again, continuing forward in the same direction I'd been reversing in, performing a nearly-perfect J-turn.

Our speed picked up fast and soon Hank was a tiny figure in the distance. Then I couldn't see him at all.

"Good God, woman," Kip said. "How did you learn to drive like that?"

I had no idea. I told him so.

"I'm cold," Julie mumbled from the backseat. The cold night air was streaming through the broken window, and a good thing too, because Julie still smelled terrible.

I handed Kip my key and told him which apartment was ours. "Go ahead and bring her inside. I'll be there as soon as I can find parking," I said.

We had driven aimlessly in the back streets of Hoboken for several minutes before I remembered how Julie got around places she didn't know. Soon, Siri had us on the road to Brooklyn. We chose not to talk about what had happened, not while I was driving unfamiliar roads without a license.

We'd stopped briefly at a 24-hour drug store to buy a box of clear trash bags and packing tape, which I used to cover the driver's side window the best I could. It flapped and rippled as we drove, but held.

Now I had the very onerous task of finding somewhere to park in Brooklyn when it was nearly midnight. It wasn't difficult to find parking on a weekday in the late morning and early afternoon, but as of about 5:30PM most days, when most of the commuters began to arrive home, parking spots became sparse. Small cars fit in small spaces, of course, and very small cars fit in even more, but Julie's was one of many in our neighborhood and even the very small spots were taken.

I circled our block and then the next and the next, then came back to our block and checked to see if a car happened to move while I was circling the other blocks. But one hadn't. After circling for nearly thirty minutes, I ended up parking several blocks away and was not pleased. I checked the car for any valuables and grabbed Julie's phone charging cable and her sunglasses. Once I got out of the car, I was even less happy. The temperature had dropped even further and I wished I'd thought to put my ear muffs and gloves into my knapsack and made a mental note to do so tomorrow. Because it was so chilly, there were a lot less people out in the neighborhood than usual. The night had a crisp feeling to it, but also a tangible silence, almost the way the air feels after a church bell has just stopped ringing.

I had just come around the corner onto my own block when the lumbering figure appeared directly in front of me.

Then he locked his hands around my throat, and began squeezing.

Chapter Eleven

THE PRESSURE AROUND MY THROAT WAS MAKING me gag and cough. I couldn't get enough air. I couldn't scream because I couldn't draw enough breath *to* scream.

I would have, had I been able to. I had much to scream about. My assailant was much bigger than I was; I hadn't noticed because I hadn't gotten close enough to him. He was at least six-foot-two and built like a refrigerator. But despite his strength and agility, Hank didn't look so good. Aside from his pallid complexion and purple lips, his eyes were so fogged over, they looked completely white. The look of intense hatred and revulsion on his face wasn't doing him any favors either. The dimple didn't so charming from this angle either.

I have this theory about all the little things you notice when you're dying. I think all of your senses become extra tuned-in, hungry for every last scrap of sensory information before the curtain drops. Because my curtain was certainly about to drop. I could barely inhale through my nose and could smell mildew and cedar chips and incense on Hank, maybe on his clothes, maybe just from him.

My fingers scrabbled at his but they were no use, like a child's plastic sandbox rake versus tree roots made of stone. I tried to kick at him but his arms were long enough that I couldn't reach. I tried to throw myself to the ground but his huge hands just held me in place.

I could hear my heartbeat pounding in panic as my oxygen flow was restricted. I tried and failed to think of some other self-defense technique. This was it. My eyes were closing. He was lifting me off the ground. Or was it my soul flying away? No, he was lifting me. I could feel my feet dangling. From beneath heavy lids, I watched as his hood fell away from his forehead, revealing a weird eye symbol drawn or tattooed on it.

I didn't know what it was. Spots were in my vision and at the same time I was feebly fighting for my life, I also wondered whether I'd imagined it and chastised myself for wondering such a thing while I was dying.

My other theory about things that happen when you're dying is that time dilates. Changes. Slows down. But I digress again.

I knew this was it. I was done for. And I would never find out about who I had been before the amnesia. I'd never know if I was Christina or someone else. And what about Michael Adderly? What was I to him?

Whoever I was, this was the end of her story.

No! I thought. And that was the moment that my fingers caught fire.

Chapter Twelve

THE FEELING OF HEAT, HOT AND WHITE, SO HOT IT almost felt cold, began in my solar plexus and exploded through my chest into my arms and out of my hands at the fingertips, shooting orange-red flames around Hank's fingers.

My fingers had produced flames only once before, when I'd faced Michael Adderly at the Empire State Building. I had pretty much convinced myself that it was something I'd imagined. But here it was, happening again, and I couldn't have been more grateful.

Hank's fingers sizzled like sausages. With an inarticulate cry of pain, he dropped me.

The roaring wall of sound in my ears suddenly broke and I landed on my feet, but my knees were like noodles. I dropped into a kneeling crouch. The sound of my retching and coughing was all I could hear as I struggled to drink in air while putting my burning hands between me and the monster that had just been trying to kill me. Hank—or the thing that had once been Hank—was beating his hands frantically on his track pants, trying to put them out. I could see the symbol on his forehead more clearly now. It reminded me of an Egyptian Eye of Horus, which I'd seen during my research, but this was different somehow, with a cross at the inside corner of the eye and a swoop below it.

As I gasped for air, orange and blue flames licked along my fingers. I held them aloft, trembling. The monster turned and ran—so fast—and disappeared around the corner.

I let out a shaky breath, wheezing with the effort of drawing air through my bruised throat, then clenched my hands into fists. The flames went out. My hands had a pins and needles feeling that abruptly ceased when the fire disappeared.

I stood on shaky legs, still coughing, when a sardonic male voice said, "I see you don't need any help . . . Madison."

I knew that voice. The last time I'd heard it, its owner was jumping off the Empire State Building.

I turned around. There, not ten feet away, he stood: Michael Adderly, in his flawed, all-too-attractive and undead glory. The light blue eyes, the slightly-off center aquiline nose. The full head of not-quite shoulder-length dark hair. The fangs in a lopsided smile.

"It is Madison, isn't it?" he asked. "That's what you're calling yourself these days?"

He wore jeans with a fitted dress shirt that showed off the triangular shape of his torso. The sleeves were folded back and pushed to mid-forearm. It was a chilly night, but he clearly didn't feel it. He looked like he'd been working out. *Do vampires work out?* Shut up, stupid brain.

"How's Billy?" I rasped through my aching windpipe.

"*Billy?*" he said. "That's who you want to talk about?"

We both stood there, me breathing too much and him not breathing at all.

"Billy is fine," he said.

"Alive?"

"I said he was *fine*," he repeated, which did not answer the question. I watched his chest while he spoke and he did seem to take a breath before speaking, which was oddly comforting.

It suddenly occurred to me to wonder what he was doing there. In my neighborhood. Around midnight.

"Are you . . . stalking me?" I asked, my voice still scratchy. It hurt to talk.

"Would you like me to?" He moved and was now somehow only three feet away. I resisted the urge to take a step back.

"No," I said, and swallowed painfully.

His eyes searched my face. He seemed concerned, possibly puzzled. He took a step closer to me. Now he was just a foot away. Kissing distance.

The thought didn't disgust me the way I wished it did.

"Are you sure?" he murmured.

"Yes," I said, with as much indignance as I could muster, given the circumstance.

The sensations flooding my body were very unsure, however. His proximity was intoxicating in every way I could imagine.

"You're just so very . . . different," he said. His expression was still somewhere between concerned and confused. He seemed sincere—a complete shift from the mocking tone he'd used earlier.

"Different . . . how?"

"Just different. You remind me of . . . someone I once knew."

"Christina?" I asked.

"No. Someone I knew long ago. Before." He leaned toward me and stared into my eyes.

It was incredibly intimate.

"Before what?" I asked. My voice was husky, both from the injury and the effect he was having on me.

"You're shaking," he said softly.

"Of course I'm shaking. I was just strangled by a monster."

But it wasn't just that. I was still breathing too hard but now it was for a different reason. Some part of me—not quite my solar plexus, but above it . . . my heart, perhaps?—*yearned* for him. Yearned for his eyes to look upon me with tenderness, for his mouth to turn up in a delighted grin as he laughed, for his hand to reach out and tuck the hair in my face behind my ear. I swallowed painfully.

"What are you doing to me?" I asked.

"Nothing. Nothing at all," he said. He came just a few inches closer.

I closed my eyes, thinking that perhaps he had somehow hypnotized me. "Yes. Yes, you are. Is this some kind of vampire trick?" I asked.

"No trick. I swear it," he whispered.

It was worse with my eyes closed. My lips were terrible, traitorous entities with their own ideas, longing for his kiss. I opened my eyes again and that was worse too, because he was so close and his face was somehow the same as my heart and I had no idea why I felt that way or even what that meant.

I shut them again but my erratic breathing was making me dizzy.

"Shall I stop?" he asked. I could feel the breath leave his mouth as he spoke, an erotic wisp of air across my bottom lip. "One word. Just 'stop.'"

It took every ounce of willpower I ever might have had not to close that inch or two of distance and claim his mouth as my own.

"Stop," I said. I immediately wished I hadn't.

A whoosh of movement and then nothing. I opened my eyes.

He was gone.

Fuck.

Fuck!

A high-pitched noise behind me, farther away. Hinges?

Down the block, standing in the open front door of my building, stood Kip. What had he seen?

"Hey," he said, waving.

I waved back as I walked toward him.

"I was getting worried. Thought I ought to come check on you."

I nodded.

"Why's your face all red?" he asked as I climbed the stoop in front of my building.

"Let's get inside," I rasped.

Based on his reaction, Kip hadn't seen anything. He was wearing the I ♥ NY t-shirt we'd bought for Julie because she'd smeared vomit on his shirt and jacket while she was molesting him. He'd managed to get it off the jacket, but the shirt needed laundering badly.

He said that Julie had been alert enough to see to herself to bed, but I knocked softly on her door and peeked in to make sure she hadn't passed out in her own sick. She hadn't. Snoring away in a pink tank top and matching pajama pants, she was adorable.

When I told Kip that the scary guy from Hoboken had just attacked me, he said, "WHAT? How'd he get from Hoboken so fast? Can he fly?"

"God, I hope not."

We sat in my room, him on my desk chair and me on my bed, holding a frozen bag of peas on one side of my neck and frozen mixed vegetables on the other. So this was what my life was like now. Attacked in the dark by a supernaturally strong tracking zombie. Stalked by a vampire. Flaming fingers. Frozen veggies on my neck.

"I need to tell you something," I said hoarsely.

"Okay," Kip nodded, listening.

"You know that housesitting we did? With the dead husband stalking his wife? Well, that was the guy. I don't know what he is, if he's a ghost or zombie or what. I don't know how he found me. Did he follow us to Hoboken? Then here? I mean . . . how long did it take us to get there from here?"

"An hour? More?"

I tried to think of the timeline, but between the adrenaline and other various hormones running amok in my brain nothing made sense.

"I'm not sure how long. I can't think," I said, coughing as the irritation in my throat got to be too much.

"Take a few minutes. It's okay."

I took a few drinks of water before I continued. "I know you took the ghost stories I told you with a shaker of salt, but you saw him, right?"

"Yeah, I saw him," Kip said, shaking his beautiful head. "He was fast. Scary strong."

All I could think was what if Hank had gotten Kip instead of me?

I felt cold. Cold and scared.

Not only was I being hunted by some creepy zombie but there was a vampire to consider, too.

Would Michael see Kip as competition? Would he hurt Kip? Nothing else seemed important.

"Kip . . . I think . . . we should break up. It's not safe for you to be around me."

Kip's face went through several expressions that were hard to interpret. Shock, astonishment, concern, suspicion, hurt, and uncertainty.

"And I haven't told you everything either. I mean, I might as well, right?" I said, my voice ending on a squeak that nearly became a hysterical laugh, which caused another coughing fit. I drank more water, but it didn't help.

Kip got onto the bed next to me and stroked my back while I coughed. The sensation was comforting. "Maybe you shouldn't make any hasty decisions until you can breathe and talk like a regular person, yeah?" he said.

I looked at the hardwood floor. My feet in their striped socks.

Everything looked normal. Boring.

Lies.

"But that's the problem. I'm not a regular person. Look for yourself," I said, pulling my hospital release forms from the top drawer of my desk. "You know that I have a dissociative fugue. Amnesia, right? Well, *cough* it seems that somehow, I used to *cough cough drink* know a vampire. And he appears to be stalking me. Not to mention that I think all of this *cough* makes me sounds like a crazy person!" I finished my little speech with a coughing fit so bad that I finished the water.

Kip went to the kitchen and refilled my glass. I took a sip.

"So—" I said. I was going to tell him the part about my fiery fingers, but Kip cut me off.

"Shh," he said, sitting next to me on the bed once more. "You've said a lot. And your poor throat, which has been through hell, has had enough. Just sit a moment. Breathe. Drink." He ran his hand up and down my back again. "Now you're going to listen, alright?"

I nodded.

"Let's say, putting all of this into perspective, that I believe you. What kind of person would I be if I left you to deal with all of this on your own? A right piece of shite. No. I'm going nowhere. What ye need right now," he said, his accent getting thicker, "is a good night's sleep. What ye don't need is to be alone."

I felt tears welling up. I nodded again.

"Come here," he said, drawing me toward him for a hug.

Kip spent all night in my bed. We slept spooned with his arms around me, and it felt like the best rest I'd had in who knows how long.

My voice came out in a croak when I tried to say good morning, coming out more like "Guhhhh mor . . ." Then it disappeared entirely.

Kip propped himself up with one elbow. "You know what you need? A nice cup of tea with honey."

I nodded fervently. "Syl—" I began to say, only cut off again by the voice-eating frog in my throat. I tried clearing it, but just ended up saying, *Ahem hem hem cough cough* six or seven times.

Kip handed me the water glass with a directive: "Drink."

I sat up and finished the glass. I handed it back to him and said, "My roommate. Sylvie. She has herbal teas." I swung my legs off the bed and stood up. I opened the green curtains I'd inherited from Kara when she moved out and saw that the sun was shining.

"Oh, your poor neck," Kip said.

I put my hand to my neck self-consciously. The area around my throat was tender and painful to the touch. I sat next to him again and Kip lifted my hair. "That animal! You can see the finger marks," he said.

"You think I could cover it with makeup?" I asked, clearing my throat again.

"Maybe a scarf," he said. "Or do you own a turtleneck?"

"I do," I said, making the annoying *ahem ahem* noise again.

"Let's see about that tea, yeah?"

"I'll ask Sylvie."

"This is Kip," I said.

Sylvie gave a curt nod. She seemed to disapprove of my having him sleep over. She moved stiffly around him, shooting skeptical glances out of the corner of her eye. I had never seen her behave that way around Julie's boyfriend, Tad, and I wondered what was different about me and Kip. Maybe she assumed we'd had sex and thought I was too young for that?

"I was hoping I could ask you for a cup of tea," I said, my voice still sounding rough.

"Are you sick?" she asked, then looked at Kip accusingly as if it were all his fault.

I had my cover story ready. "I was attacked last night by a homeless guy. See?" I lifted my hair and turned toward the light.

"Did you call the police?" she asked, her face not changing expression.

"No," I said. "He ran away and I felt terrible and it was late so we just came inside and went to sleep. Do you think I should have?"

Her eyes narrowed as she regarded the two of us and shook her head. "I'll make you some tea," she said, heading toward the kitchen.

There in my sunlit living room, the events of the previous night seemed a million miles away. But wasn't I forgetting something?

"Oh God! Zoe!" I said. I should have called or texted her about the attack. I picked up my phone and began pecking out a message.

"Oh, Madison. You are a brave, danger-prone warrior princess," said Zoe. She almost looked as if she might cry. "I know you don't really like it, but . . . can I hug you?"

How could I say no to that?

The hug didn't feel awkward at all. To me, anyway. The people shuffling around us in the lobby of the Brooklyn Public Library might have disagreed.

Kip had taken the subway to Manhattan so he could pick up Rosie and his carriage. Zoe had suggested we meet at the library. I didn't have to be at Chris Street until 2PM, so we had a few hours to research.

"Are you okay?" she asked after releasing me.

I nodded. My throat was feeling much better after Sylvie's tea, which she had made a huge thermos of, with directions to drink a cup every two hours. It was somehow both bitter and flowery at the same time, which was an odd combination, but it worked.

"My neck still hurts a bit," I said, pulling down my black turtleneck sweater enough for her to see a bruise or two.

Zoe looked stricken. "You fucking *valkyrie*, you could have died," she said.

Then she hugged me again.

Upstairs in the non-fiction room, we found the shelves and books that Roland had showed us before. We searched the catalog for books about symbols. I drew the symbol on Hank's forehead to the best of my ability.

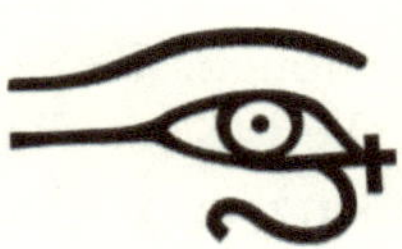

We found an Eye of Horus symbol to compare it to, and Zoe agreed that the symbol from Hank looked similar, but wrong.

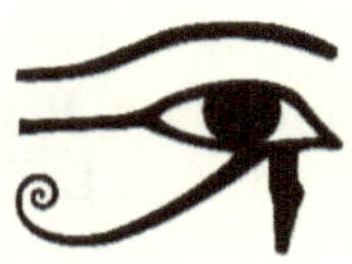

In the reference section, we were scanning the shelves when I thought I saw movement out of the corner of my eye. I turned to look, but nothing was there. I figured it had just been my imagination.

Then Zoe sighed heavily and said, "No."

"No, what?"

"Not you," she said. To the empty air, she added, "No, she can't see you."

"Are you talking to a ghost?" I asked.

She nodded unenthusiastically. "The one I saw before."

A book on a nearby shelf flung itself it to the floor a few feet away. I jumped.

Zoe said, "Huh." She squinted at me.

"*I* didn't do it," I said.

"I know." She addressed the empty air with an accusatory finger and said, "Don't you threaten me."

Two more books fell, closer to us, one missing my right foot by about six inches. "Um . . . Zoe?" I said, uncertain about what to do.

"Okay, that's enough. We're done," Zoe said lightly. It was like she was scolding a child. She got up and started walking away. Halfway to the door, she stopped abruptly.

"Oh, so *now* you'll try being polite?" she asked the air in front of her.

"What's it want?" I asked.

She spoke over her shoulder to me. "Her son. She wants me to tell her son where to find her jewelry. I don't do messages. People don't listen to the crazy ghost lady anyway. Believe me."

Then she was silent for several seconds as the ghost pled its case. Finally, she crossed her arms and said, "*Fine*, Harriet. What will you do for me?"

I kept staring at the empty air between the stacks over Zoe's shoulder, but I didn't see anything there. When I turned my head, I could almost see a shadow in my peripheral vision. As soon as I tried to look *at* that shadow, though, it was gone.

Zoe was right. I could almost-sort-of see ghosts.

"Magical signs and symbols," Zoe said. "And you better not be lying to me or I'll find your jewelry myself and pawn it."

Zoe turned around and faced me, her eyes focused on something above my head.

"Is she . . . floating?" I asked, hunching my shoulders and tucking my chin into my chest.

"No, she's . . . helping. Under duress, I might add. But that's ghosts for you."

I looked where Zoe was looking and two books slid forward on their shelves without jumping to the floor, and I felt the hair on my arms stand up. A third book bumped my left elbow and I squeaked and pulled it away quickly.

"That is incredibly disconcerting!" I said.

"Sorry," Zoe shrugged. She seemed like she was used to this sort of thing.

A few more books slid forward, and then a few more.

"Okay, okay. Enough. What's the address?" Zoe asked. She took out her phone and typed it in. "Yes, I'll remember. You're welcome. Now, if you don't mind, we have research to do."

She turned to me. "You okay? You look a little pale."

"How do you get used to that?" I asked, watching Zoe pull two of the indicated books off the shelf.

"When you've had to deal with it your whole life like I have . . . you just do." She picked up another book.

"Let me help," I said.

"Thanks," she said, handing me stack of books. "It's nice not having to pretend there's no one there, or that I don't see anything, like I usually do in front of everyone else." She smiled. "It's a relief."

"Even your family?" I asked.

"Oh, my family. Especially them." She grimaced. "Can you get that last one? It's too high for me." I got on my tiptoes and pulled the last book down.

With all the ghost's recommendations acquired, she left the aisle and I followed. There were a few tables in the reference section, and we sat down at one of them as far away from everyone else as we could get.

"Why especially your family?" I asked, putting the sketch I'd made of the symbol on the table between us. "I mean, if you're willing to talk about it. I don't want to pry."

"My mom has never actually believed me." Zoe opened one of the reference books and I followed her lead and cracked one too.

"What? With things like that happening around you constantly?"

"Things like that *don't* happen around me constantly." She looked at the symbol I'd drawn and ran a finger down the two facing pages and flipped to the next one.

"But you seemed so calm about it."

"I suppose I was calm because I could *see* her doing it. Ghosts come up to me pretty much all the time, but they normally can't affect the physical world. That only seems to happen in rare cases . . . or when I'm with *you*."

"So I'm a ghost battery pack?"

She shrugged. "It has something to do with your aura, I guess. I can't see auras, but they can, which is how they find me. Harriet seemed surprised you couldn't see her, so maybe there's something about your aura that—" she lowered her voice as a guy passed by our table, looking at his phone, and continued, "—helps them somehow. So no, my mom has never seen anything even vaguely like this."

I was in the *A* section of the *Encyclopedia of Signs and Symbols* I'd grabbed. Each entry had a listing with an illustration and an explanation of what it meant. Some of them were familiar words, others weren't. I scanned two pages: *Adoni, Air, Airplane, Alchemy, Alcohol, Ankh*, and more but nothing looked like the symbol I'd seen. I skimmed forward. "So . . . she thinks you're making it all up?" I asked.

Zoe looked up from the pages she was perusing. "At first, she thought I just had imaginary friends, like a lot of kids do. But then the pictures I drew of them got kind of gruesome—blood, gunshots, stabbings, cars crashing—and then little Zoe had to go see the nice doctor and talk about her feelings.

"Then there was medication, which made me sleepy and slow and uninterested in anything. I didn't see any ghosts for a couple of years. And then they took me off the meds and the ghosts came back. My mom said I was just trying to get attention and sent me back to the psychiatrist. So I learned that I couldn't talk about it with her."

"That must have been hard. Did you ever think you were crazy? Because no one else saw what you did? Because no one believed you?"

"It had been going on so long . . . I mean, it was just part of my life at that point. One thing that helped me, actually, was when I was in first grade, I read a book about dogs."

I looked up from the *B* section, where I was skimming *Bass Clef, Bat, Beard, Beehive, Beorc,* and so on.

"Dogs?" I asked. "How did that help?"

"Because it explained about how dogs can smell and hear things that people can't. And some dogs can hear and smell things that *other* dogs can't. It wasn't magic. It was science. Since I could see and hear things that other people couldn't, I figured I was like them. Just a different kind of dog." She smiled wistfully.

C: Caduceus, Calcinations, Cancer, Cannabis, Capricorn . . .

I shook my head in amazement. "You must have felt really alone, when you couldn't talk to anyone about it." Sometimes I felt that way myself.

"Couldn't talk about it with anyone, until I met my Gram." She said "Gram" warmly and tilted her head with a sad smile and turned a page.

"Your mom's mom?"

She scanned the page she'd turned to and turned to the next one. "My dad's. My parents got divorced when I was about . . . three, I think? He cheated. It was ugly. My mom refused to let him contact me. Then when I was thirteen, my dad convinced my mom to let me talk to him. He'd gotten remarried and I had a little half-sister and half-brother he wanted me to meet. So I flew to Florida for a summer and met them and that was when I met my Gram again. She's the one I got it from. She called it 'The Sight.'"

The *C* section was long. There was an entire page with symbols for *Christ*. Then *Chrysler, Cinnabar, Circle, Citroën, Clay* . . .

Zoe continued. "My mom and I were fighting a lot by then, and over the next year things got worse. She threatened to have me committed, and I threatened to run away . . . and then Gram invited me to live with her. Which I did until I was twenty, when she passed."

"I'm so sorry," I said.

Zoe nodded. "Thank you. So yeah, after that, I could always talk to my Gram about it, but not my mom, and not even my dad, because he always thought his mom was superstitious and crazy. 'Voodoo?' he'd say. 'How about VooDon't?' "

"She practiced voodoo?" *Comet, Copyright, Cow* . . .

"Yeah. She was born in Haiti. Learned it from her mother."

"Wow. So you're, what, a quarter Haitian?"

"A quarter Haitian, a quarter African American, a quarter Irish American and another quarter Italian American, and probably some other stuff I don't even know about. I'm a total mutt."

I turned to a full page devoted to different cross symbols. *Cross of Christ, Cross of Endlessness, Cross of Lazarus, Cross of Loraine, Cross of Palestine* . . .

"Are you having any luck?" she asked, gesturing at the book I was looking at with her chin.

"Not so far," I said, scanning yet another page.

"Ugh. I can't do this anymore," Zoe said, tossing the book she was looking at onto the table. Nearly an hour had passed.

"Me neither," I said, pinching the bridge of my nose. I felt like my eyes were beginning to cross.

Then one of the books that was lying open on the table began flipping pages on its own. The hair on my arms raised again. I tried looking out of the corner of my eye and could almost see something, but as soon as I looked, it disappeared again.

"Zoe?" I asked.

The book stopped flipping and fell open on a section labeled *Alchemy*. The book then rotated about ninety degrees.

"Wait, what's that?" I asked. There in the center of the page was a symbol that on its side looked just like part of the eye symbol I'd seen on Hank's forehead.

"That looks like it!" Zoe said excitedly. "Thanks, Harriet!"

"But what is it?" I grabbed the book and read the caption: *The alchemical symbol for lead.* I flipped back to the beginning of the chapter, then skimmed. The chapter discussed alchemy and various symbols used by its practitioners.

I asked, "Alchemy? Yeah, I saw a symbol for alchemy in that encyclopedia. That's like, chemistry, right? Except in the old timey days, they were trying to transform lead into gold?"

"Oh!" Zoe said, picking up a book she'd left open on the table. "Yeah, over here. This book mentions this thing called the philosopher's stone that could do that. Turn lead to gold."

"Right. But what does this have to do with zombies?" I asked.

"Wait, wait, wait," Zoe said, pushing books aside until she found the one she wanted. She turned to the back of the book. "This guy. Right here. He says that lead and gold are metaphors for death and life. Lead is dark, gold is light. Lead is . . . Saturn? I don't really get that, but 'gold is the sun' . . . that I can kind of see. Look, even the symbol for the sun and gold are the same." She turned the book toward me and pointed.

"Well," Zoe said, turning pages. "It says here that one of the other things that alchemists were trying to do was create a potion that would cure all diseases and let people live much longer, if not indefinitely. So this guy thinks that when alchemists talked about transforming lead to gold, what they were really trying to do was turn death to life. To bring people back from the dead so they could live forever. Which is essentially necromancy."

"Necromancy?"

"Death magic. A necromancer can control the dead."

I felt my eyebrows raise. Zoe shrugged helplessly.

"So look here," Zoe said, placing the other book next to the symbol I'd drawn and the book I'd been looking at. "This symbol. That's the alchemist's symbol for lead, right? But here it says it's also the astronomical sign for Saturn. And here, this says that necromancers study alchemy and astronomy. So . . . yeah. I think we're looking for a necromancer."

"Wait, are we looking for the necromancer or his creation?" I asked. "I mean, Hank—or the zombie, whatever he is—is haunting his wife. If a necromancer made him and controls him, which makes some sense, then what *doesn't* make sense is why he would bother. What would a necromancer have to gain by harassing a widow? So is Hank out of control of the necromancer who created him?"

"That's a good question."

"And why would he attack me? And why not you? No offense."

"No offense taken! Um . . . well . . . I haven't seen him. You have. You chased him. Maybe he sees you as a threat."

"Maybe. But then either the necromancer that's controlling him has plans for Hannah, or Hank has gone rogue. Either way . . . how do we stop him?"

"An even better question."

I checked the time. "I need to go to work soon. Let me see that?" I said, taking the book from her and beginning a sketch of the other symbols in my notebook.

"What are you doing? Oh, right. You poor confused cavegirl. Hang on, allow me," Zoe said, pulling her phone out of her pocket.

"You're going to call someone?"

"No, silly. Here in the future, technology has many uses," she said, holding the phone steadily over the book. I heard a click and realized she was taking a photo. Duh. "And now," she said, taking a small device from her bulky purse and attaching it to her phone, "I'm going to print it." Mere moments later, she handed me a small two-inch by three-inch photograph of the symbol for lead.

"I can take pictures with my phone too, you know," I said.

"That thing? You'd be better off snapping pics with a potato."

As we stood and gathered our things, Zoe said, "I won't."

I looked up and saw her looking to her left at nothing. "Harriet?"

"Yeah. Telling her I won't forget to tell her son where to find the jewelry."

"I don't know how you can stay so calm about all of that."

"It just is. Oh, look, it's Hipster Santa again," she observed.

"What?"

She elbowed me. It was Roland, the helpful, oddly athletic senior librarian. He was pushing a cart of books, dressed in the same suit and bowtie he'd been wearing the last time we saw him. "Hello, goodbye," he said. "Have we met?"

"Yeah, you helped us with the zombie books the other day."

"Of course, of course. And what about today? Find everything alright?"

We said that we had and he wished us a good afternoon.

"Wow, how sad. Santa's gone senile," Zoe commented as we walked down the stairs.

Once we'd gotten to her car, Zoe said, "I do know a guy who knows about this stuff . . ."

"But?" I asked.

"But what if he knows who is doing this and hasn't done anything about it? I don't know where his allegiances lie."

"Or what if he's the one who did it?" I asked.

She frowned. "I hadn't even thought of that."

"So maybe you shouldn't be alone with this guy. Wait, is this the guy who did the magical symbols in your apartment?" Zoe's apartment, which I'd visited in the spring, was completely covered with mystical symbols as protection from ghosts. Clearly very necessary, given what I'd just witnessed. Otherwise, they'd bother her at all hours.

"That's him," Zoe said.

"So he knows where you live. Maybe don't contact him yet," I said. "I still have one more place I can go for research."

"Where?" she asked.

"Thirteen Books," I said.

"Oh no," she said. "Do you want me to come with you?"

CHAPTER THIRTEEN

WALKING UP THE SIDEWALK TOWARD THIRTEEN Books after work, I felt nervous. The last guy I'd dated, Derek, was the manager there. It was a hole-in-the-wall place that covered any variety of bizarre subjects, from alien abductions to angels to witchcraft. I'd first visited the little store in the spring while trying to figure out what to do about the ghost in my apartment. Even though Derek worked there, he wasn't a believer.

Ultimately, that was why I'd stopped seeing him, when he wouldn't believe me about my paranormal experiences. When you know what you've seen, like Hannah knew that she'd seen Hank, or Zoe knew she'd seen ghosts, people telling you that they don't believe you, or that they believe that *you* believe . . . well, those aren't the kind of people you want to be around.

As I approached Thirteen Books, I noticed—among the books, crystals, tarot cards, and other occult accoutrements in the front window—there was a large fluffy black and white cat idly licking its paw.

That was new. There hadn't been a store cat when I was last there.

I opened the door and the bell jingled. I looked to my left, expecting to see Derek perched upon the stool behind the counter like I had every other visit, but the stool was empty. I took a few tentative steps, and said, "Hello?"

"Be right there," said a voice that was definitely not Derek's. It was a male voice. A cultured one. In fact it sounded sort of like—

"Hello!" said Hipster Santa. He was wearing a different suit and bowtie than he'd been wearing earlier at the library.

"Um, hi," I said, looking around the store to see if Derek was hiding somewhere. He wasn't. "Do you work here too?"

This was weird. In a city of eight million residents with another eleven million daily commuters, not to mention tourists, this was an extraordinary coincidence. What were the odds?

"I am and have always been the proprietor of this emporium of the esoteric, so while technically, you *might* say that I work here, I play more than I work," he explained.

"*You're* Derek's uncle?" I asked. When I'd asked Derek why he worked in an occult bookstore when he didn't believe, he'd mentioned that his uncle owned the store. Had he told me his uncle's name? I couldn't remember.

"You know Derek," he said, nodding. "Yes, I see that now."

"He told you about me?" I asked, feeling anxious about what he might have said.

"You are Madison, are you not?" he asked.

"Yep, that's me," I said.

"I'm Roland. And yes, I'm Derek's uncle. Derek, I'm sorry to say, has moved to Boston. So tell me how I can help you, Madison. Is this for your essay?"

I tried to remember my cover story. It was getting harder and harder to keep them straight. "Uh huh," I ventured.

"Tell me again what you're looking for," he said.

I pulled the sketch I'd made of the symbol and handed it to him.

"Curious. Very curious," he said.

"It looks like an Eye of Horus," I said.

"Except for here," he said, pointing at the swooping swish beneath the eye, "And the pupil on the Eye of Horus is usually filled in, isn't it? I've never seen an eye like this before."

"Unless you turn it on its side," I said, demonstrating. "Then it's—"

"It's lead!" he said with some excitement.

"You just know the alchemical symbol for lead off the top of your head?" I asked.

"I *did* say that I'm the proprietor," he reminded me. "Occult lore is my specialty."

Of course it was.

"Can you tell me anything else about this symbol?" I asked.

He studied it a moment, turning it back and forth.

"Well, in this context . . . while it's reminiscent, it's *not* an Eye of Horus or of Ra, for that matter— but why change the iris and pupil?" His finger traced the outside circle and then the dot in its center. "Ah! That's also the alchemical symbol for gold. Lead and gold combined. Very interesting." He handed the sketch back to me. "And the eyebrow . . . hmmm." He turned the sketch to its side again. "Looks almost like a sickle. Where did you happen to come across it?" he asked.

"In a book?" I half-lied.

His brow furrowed a moment. "Must have been some book. And what is it you want to know?"

"Well, um . . . if this symbol could be used to control a zombie, is there like, an antidote for it?"

Roland regarded me for a long moment. "Hypothetically, you mean?" he asked.

"Yes. Hypothetically," I said.

He regarded me a few seconds more before speaking again. "Hypothetically, as far I know, there is not."

"So, what if . . . if a . . . if there's a . . ." I kept stumbling over my words, trying to figure out a way to ask about stopping Hank before he killed me or Zoe or anyone else. Then I realized where I was standing and who I was talking to. If anybody was going to believe me, it was Hipster Santa.

"Okay, I lied. It's not hypothetical. It's not for an essay." I pulled my turtleneck sweater down a few inches. "I was attacked. Strangled. By a dead guy. There's an obituary and a disturbed grave and everything. And he's been haunting his widow. And he's real! He leaves footprints, and he's really strong and scary and I need to know how to stop him."

Roland regarded me with what seemed like a look of distrust, then concern and alarm. "Perhaps we'd better sit down and you can tell me more about this . . . thing," he said. "All about it. Starting from the beginning."

Perhaps ten minutes later I had poured out the whole story of everything I knew about Hank, as well as describing my two encounters with him, leaving out the parts about my flaming hands. We'd been sitting in a back room in two old stuffed upholstered chairs. The smaller room was lit by a hanging Moroccan lamp, with room for a desk and a smallish bookcase.

"I see. Yes. That is . . . troubling," Roland said. His fingers were steepled together and he tapped his bottom lip with his index fingers. "Hmm," he said.

"Hmm?" I asked.

"Thinking," he said. "Can you amuse yourself while I do so?"

"Uh, I guess," I said.

He reached forward and pulled a book from the lower shelf and opened it about halfway through. From where I was sitting, it appeared to be handwriting on the page, though I couldn't see what it said. He flipped several pages, then drew his index finger down and across the page. This went on for a minute or two.

"Ah," he suddenly announced.

Looking toward the front of the store, Roland called out, "Sterling, come keep our guest company." Then he exited the room before I could ask him who Sterling was.

I didn't have long to wait, however. Seconds later, the black and white cat from the window strolled through the doorway and sauntered up to the chair I was sitting on, rubbing his cheek against the upholstery.

I reached down and rubbed my fingers together. Sterling sniffed my fingers, then rubbed his furry cheek against my hand. Deciding I wasn't likely to eat him, he leapt into my lap, affectionately bumping his ear against my forearm and purring. He had to weigh fifteen pounds at least. It was like petting an insistent fluffy watermelon.

While we'd been talking, I'd mostly been looking at Roland. Now I looked around the room as Sterling settled into my lap, kneading my jeans with his fluffy paws.

There were tan curtains on the one window. The curtains were open and I could see iron bars over the glass and a brick wall somewhere beyond it. The desk held a blotter, with scattered papers and letters or bills, and an antique black telephone, a landline. The small bookcase held several fabric- and leather-bound books. Not a single one was labeled. Maybe they were private journals?

I checked my lap. Sterling appeared to have gone to sleep.

The chair I was sitting on was cream and brown plaid and the fabric had a rough, slightly bumpy texture to it. Roland's chair was a deep burgundy color and looked much softer. His had a higher back and a more rounded shape, while mine was more square.

Feeling antsy, I took out my phone to check the time and saw a text from Kip's new number.

Still on for 9pm?

Yes. Location TBA.

We'd made plans to meet when we were both done with work. I slipped my phone back into my pocket as Roland reentered the room.

"Made a friend?" he asked. I nodded and then wondered if he'd been speaking to me or the cat. "I think I have some ideas. This way," he said, leading me back towards the front of the store.

"Isn't it kind of late?" Kip asked. We were standing on the flagstone steps of the First Romanian Reformed Church of New York, and I was shaking the excess water droplets off my umbrella from my walk from the subway. A storm had rolled in while I was at Thirteen Books.

"It's supposed to be open," I said, trying the door. It was unlocked, just as Roland had said it would be. Inside the door was a vestibule with an umbrella stand. I put mine in with the others and Kip did the same with his.

We passed through the vestibule into a wide room with high arches, wooden rafters, and a center aisle that split row upon row of wooden pews. At the close end of the aisle was a font, presumably with holy water inside. At the other end of the aisle, three steps up, was an altar covered in white cloth and lit candles. Above it hung the crucifix, adorned with a life-size likeness of Jesus.

I had a sudden urge to touch my forehead, stomach, and then my left shoulder followed by my right and found my right hand doing so unbidden. I noticed Kip did the same just after I did.

"I didn't know you were Catholic," Kip said.

"I'm not. Shh," I whispered, gesturing at the few worshippers sitting in the pews, heads bowed.

Beautiful stained-glass windows dominated each of the side walls. Though I could see the shapes of saints and their vivid reds, yellows, blues, and greens, I imagined they would look even more spectacular with daylight shining through them.

I made my way quietly down the center aisle, not wanting to disturb anyone's prayers. When I reached the altar, I did a curious thing. I curtsied. *Genuflected*, some part of my brain corrected. Kip looked at me askance and I tried to play it off. But it had been like a sneeze: completely involuntary and somehow necessary. I wondered if Christina had been Catholic. The word *Christ* was part of the name, wasn't it?

I turned left and walked toward the wooden door marked SACRISTY and knocked softly. It was opened by a man dressed in black slacks and a black shirt with a white tab at the collar. He looked at us inquisitively.

"Father Altescu?" I asked. "Roland Benzies said—"

He nodded. "Come in, come in," he said, gesturing us into the little room. Father Altescu was in his forties. His black hair was curly and close to his scalp. His brown eyes were both kind and weary, as well as slightly bloodshot.

The room contained a dressing rack with several white robes and various vestments hanging on it, as well as a full-length mirror. Another door on the right wall presumably led to the altar. On one wall hung a white wooden shield bearing a red cross, an odd one, its arms of equal lengths with flanges at each end. It looked like this: ✠. Four smaller crosses of the same kind filled the spaces in the corners of the larger center cross. It looked like one of the crosses I'd seen in the encyclopedia at the library, but I couldn't remember which one.

The priest moved to a table beneath this shield where he picked up three glass vials and a metal flask.

"The ampule glass is fragile," he warned, "so keep it somewhere safe until you need it. The flask is full. I'm sorry I can't give you more."

Kip made a skeptical noise and I stepped on his foot. "Thank you, Father," I said. "We really appreciate it."

"*Annuit cœptis,* my child," Father Altescu said. "And good luck."

"And *what* in the bloody fuck was *that* about? Is that *holy* water?" Kip sputtered as the church door closed behind us.

It was still drizzling and I was futzing with my two-dollar umbrella which was now broken. I gave him a look. And then I said what the look was supposed to say, just in case my facial expression wasn't clear.

"What the hell is your problem?"

He ran a hand through his hair and sighed heavily. "Sorry, sorry. Just who is Roland Benzies and why in God's name do ye need holy water? That *is* holy water, isn't it?" His accent was coming out more again and it affected his "oo" and "er" sounds.

I descended the stairs and Kip followed. When we reached the bottom, I said, "Roland is an old man who knows occult lore. The holy water is for Hank. You know, the dead guy who tried to kill me last night?"

Kip shook his head and sighed heavily again. "It doesn't make any sense."

That hurt.

I walked quickly ahead of him toward the wrought-iron gate, trying to keep my emotions under control.

"Madison. Madison! Wait up," he said, hurrying after me.

I'd gotten to the gate and it took a lot of self-control not to swing it closed in his face. Well, that and the fact that it probably weighed five hundred pounds.

"I thought you said you believed me," I said, letting the hurt show in my eyes but biting my lower lip to keep it from trembling. God, my lips were melodramatic.

"I do. I did, and I do," he said, putting his hand to the back of my neck. "I do believe you. Sincerely." He looked me right in eyes when he said it. It was too dark to see how green his eyes were, but his lips were very soft looking.

He kissed me tentatively. I tentatively kissed back. The one hand continued to hold the back of my neck while the other stole its way to my jawline and held my face while we kissed. And kissed. And kissed.

I noticed then that I was very wet and that Kip had both of his hands on my face and I had mine on his. The drizzle had increased to a sprinkling at some point and was showing signs of becoming a downpour. The droplets were heavier and so was my wool peacoat.

"We need to get out of this rain," I said, resting my cheek against his.

"Yeah, come on," Kip said, taking my hand. "I know where we can go. It's not too far from here."

The building Kip took me to had a brass revolving door that led into a small lobby with two brass framed elevators. Large gray industrial rugs had been rolled out to soak up the rain. To our immediate right was a desk. Behind it was the doorman. He wore a dark suit with a brass name tag that read MAHFOUZ.

From beneath fuzzy eyebrows, Mahfouz regarded the two of us as we came in dripping. Kip had realized he'd left his umbrella at the church just as it began to pour.

"Going up to 6C," Kip said.

"Name?" Mahfouz asked.

"Jack Donovan," said Kip, squeezing my hand.

Mahfouz consulted a clipboard and grunted. "Go on up," he said.

All Kip had said was that we were going to an apartment that belonged to a friend of his who was out of town. Apparently it was one of the friends who knew Kip as Jack.

As the elevator doors closed, I saw Mahfouz's attention had gone back to whatever he'd been looking at on his phone before we interrupted.

I shivered, so Kip moved behind me. He put his arms around me and pulled me against his body. *Ding* went the elevator, to indicate we'd arrived at the first floor. I spun so that I was facing him and buried my head against his shoulder. I slipped my arms behind him and *ding*, went the second floor. He kissed my cheek, high on my cheekbone, and then again diagonally lower, again lower, until he reached my mouth.

Ding I heard faintly as the world around us faded away. It was just the two of us locked in embrace, my blood roaring in my ears while our mouths connected more than just our mouths. The elevator jolted to a halt and we broke off our kiss.

"This is our floor," Kip said.

"Distracted, were you?" I teased.

We stepped out before the doors closed on us and Kip led us to the second door on the right. He looked each way down the hall before reaching above the door jamb and bringing down a small tin box. Inside was a key, with which he opened the door.

The entry was a dark hallway that led into a foyer of sorts, where Kip clicked on a standing lamp. Though a doorway ahead was a tiny kitchen. To my left, there was a hall and a bathroom with the door open. On my right, two steps down, was a small sunken living room divided by a huge bookcase, and behind it, a bedroom.

Hanging on the back of a desk chair in the bedroom was an inside-out I ♥ NY t-shirt. "Is that—?" That's all I got out before we were kissing again. My coat hit the floor as I impatiently yanked it off and helped push Kip's off his shoulders. Next were my sodden sneakers and socks and his boots and socks too. I began pulling his shirt off and he let me. Then I removed my turtleneck sweater.

"Towel?" I asked. My hair was still dripping wet. Kip's had fared better beneath his hood.

He disappeared into the bathroom and returned with a folded towel, which he unfolded and draped around my shoulders, using it to pull me toward him into a kiss. Then he pulled back and gently towel-dried my hair until I couldn't take it anymore and gently bit his chin, then his jaw, and lower lip.

"But, your neck—" Kip said.

"Shh," I said.

The warmth of our skin touching one another's contrasted the chill from the rain and made our touching more addictive as we sought warm ourselves by the other's body heat. The towel slid to the floor as his hands came up to cup my face and our kissing intensified.

"This way," he said and began leading me toward the bed.

"But your friend's bed—" I said.

"He left clean sheets," Kip said somewhere between kissing my neck and ear and jaw and mouth. My hands were wrestling with his belt buckle while he undid my button-fly jeans, murmuring, "Oh, I like these."

He was walking backwards to the bed and his hands were caressing the lines where the top edge of my blue lace bra met skin. I finally got his belt unbuckled and slid it free of his beltloops and dropped it on the floor. His fingers were inside the bra's lacy edge and I undid the button on his black pants as the back of his legs hit the bed.

I gave him a little shove and he fell back onto the comforter. I tried to shimmy out of my jeans gracefully but they got stuck around my calves where they were wet from the rain. Kip got up to help me and I sat on the bed. He knelt in front of me and rolled the denim legs down and pulled each one off carefully.

Now I was just wearing my bra and underwear and he still had on his black pants. "Your turn," I said, watching him. His muscular torso was fair-skinned and his chest and shoulders and arms were well-defined. A line of dark hair curled from beneath his navel and traveled further south.

He stood and peeled the black pants off his hips, revealing a pair of gray boxer shorts with a small button on the fly. He let the pants drop to the floor and leaned down to kiss me. I met his kiss and lost time for a bit as we rearranged ourselves on the bed. He lay on one side, pressed against me, one hand supporting his weight while the other teased the waistband of my purple cotton bikini briefs. One of his fingers stole inside the waistband and teased the skin beneath it, then stole back to my bra, first the outside, then the inside.

I hadn't been sure what to do with my hands while he touched me, but now I knew what to do with them: I unclipped the bra's front closure.

Kip deftly teased a slow reveal of my breast, first one, then the other. He draped the straps down my shoulders and I rose so that we removed my bra together. He took a breath and gazed down at me. "God, but you're beautiful," he said.

"So're you," I said. I caught the waistband of his boxers and wiggled one finger inside, tracing his skin along his hip and he inhaled loudly.

Then his mouth was on my nipple, kissing, licking, nibbling, sucking, while his fingers explored the edges of my underwear, first the front, then the sides, catching the entire side panel so that he could have pulled them off my hips had he wanted to. Then his fingers returned, dipping beneath the cotton fabric's edges down the front of my thigh then across to the other side.

My fingers had been busy all this time as well and I had been teasing the solid shape of him through his soft cotton boxers.

His mouth switched to my other nipple and I squirmed and arched my back and sighed. At some point his fingers began to stroke over my underwear and then slid inside them, hovering without touching while his tongue and teeth continued to tantalize my nipple. Then his mouth returned to mine and kissed me deeply.

The hovering fingers pulled my underwear away from my most sensitive skin and I moaned at the proximity. My breathing was erratic and fast and I felt a building pressure, a need to be touched, and soon.

I squeezed him beneath his boxers and he moaned and I pulled at his waistband and said one word: "Off." The boxers were pulled down and discarded and he was all skin in my hand.

Then he was touching me outside my underwear and inside my underwear and inside me and our bodies slid over one another. I made incoherent sounds of ecstasy while his fingers circled and massaged and slipped inside me again and our mouths fed at each other. I could feel him pressed against my thighs and longed to have him between them.

I shifted my weight so that the front of him was pressed against the front of me and he moaned again. His fingers were driving me crazy and my hips were rocking with his movements of their own accord.

I slid one hip of my underwear down and he slid the other and soon we had them off.

He leaned over the side of the bed and from the pocket of his pants retrieved a small package that I recognized as a wrapped condom. He looked at me and seemed to blush as he opened it and rolled it on, then lowered himself down to me again and asked, "Now where were we?"

I kissed him and used my hands to draw his over my breasts, hips, and to the spot that had made me want my underwear off in the first place. "Here," I said, wondering how my voice got to be so breathy.

"Oh, yes, I remember now," he said, expertly stroking me and sending delicious shivers throughout my body.

"Kiss me," I demanded and then his mouth was on mine again. His arm and fingers stayed between us and between my legs while we kissed but the rest of him was hard against my inner thigh. I bucked my hips and squirmed toward him and then he was inside me for a moment but then pulled back. I made a sound of distress and he plunged forward again, slowly, so slowly, then back and forward, slowly once more, then again and again and again, slow, then faster, then slow again.

It felt like my body and the room and the world were melting away and the only existence I was capable of acknowledging was the absolute bliss of what his body was doing to mine. There was a sense of rising, building, climbing, until the crushing pleasure crashed over me again and again as the combination of our kissing and his driving push-and-pull left me crying out in climax.

He followed just a few seconds later, uttering a guttural groan and collapsing on top of me.

We lay there catching our breath and he shifted, pulling back, sending delicious aftershocks throughout my body. He took care of the condom, removing it and tying it off before placing it in a nearby receptacle.

"Be right back," he said. When he returned, he had a couple of washcloths with him and handed me one. I used it to tidy myself up down below.

"Well," I said.

"Well," he said back, lowering himself to the bed and kissing me again.

"That was fun," I said.

"Mm," Kip agreed, kissing me. And kissing me, and kissing me.

Some time and another condom later, we fell asleep, Kip holding me close, my head on his chest.

CHAPTER FOURTEEN

"WHAT'S THAT YOU'RE READING?" ERICA ASKED. She was on register and I was on bag check.

It was a book I'd been loaned by Roland. I showed her the cover, then put the book down as a woman approached my station. "More like failing to read," I said, unclipping the two of spades from the woman's shopping bag and handing it back to her.

"*Legends of the Golem?*" she read aloud. "That creature the rabbi made in Prague?"

I felt myself grin in incredulous surprise. "Yeah. How do you know about it?"

It was an all-hands-on-deck day, as new comics day this week also coincided with our monthly restock of other items. Trendon and Jackson were unloading the comics, Nidhi was putting them on the shelves, and Mac and our newest employee, Rae, were down in the basement, reorganizing and collapsing boxes to make room for new ones.

"*Nick Fury's Howling Commandos!*" Erica said. "There's a golem who kicks ass."

"See, I'm confused though, because I thought Golem was that creepy thing in Lord of the Rings that says, 'my precious' all the time," I said.

"No, that's Goll*um*, not Gol*em*."

"Isn't that needlessly confusing?" I complained.

"Blame Tolkien," she said. "That golem legend has been around way longer than his stuff. Though for a guy who invented two forms of the Elven language—" She broke off as a customer approached with a graphic novel and a few new comics. "Did you find everything alright?" she asked, ringing up his purchase.

"Did you know that Quenya was based on Finnish?" replied the customer. The two of them began nerding at each other hardcore while my mind wandered.

A golem. That was one of the ideas that Roland had had, saying there was a link between alchemy and kabbalah and that perhaps Hank's personal religious background tied into that.

At some point in the sixteenth century, a rabbi in Prague created a creature from clay, or so the legend went. It protected the Jewish people from their enemies, and when it was no longer needed, they put it to rest. I didn't know what that had to do with Hank, since he wasn't clay, but then I thought about the whole "ashes to ashes and dust to dust" thing and thought that a human body probably wasn't all that different than clay after all. What had gotten Roland thinking about it was the symbol on Hank's forehead. Roland had suggested that the combined symbols of gold and lead might represent some combination of life and death. Someone brought back from the dead.

In some legends of the golem, it had *emet*, the word for "truth" on its forehead. In one version, the creature ran amok and so its creator wiped away part of *emet* to make it just *met*, the word for "death," and it crumbled into pieces. Another version claimed there was a holy scroll or parchment in its mouth, and it took removing that to put the creature to rest.

Another story claimed that the golem was at rest in the attic of a synagogue in Prague, while others claimed it had been buried in a cemetery there. Both agreed that the creature awaited being called to service once more. That was as far as I had gotten in the book Roland had given me.

When I had woken at Kip's friend Dave's place, it was to the sound of the front door slamming as Kip returned from picking up breakfast. He'd already found clean t-shirts and sweatpants for us both to wear and had taken our damp clothes from the night before to the laundry room in the basement of the building. Our coats were flung over the apartment's two radiators and were still slightly damp, but no longer soaked.

We were sprawled on Dave's sofa eating bagels and drinking tea when we had begun discussing our visit to the church the night before. Kip had been raised Catholic as it turned out, and he suspected that I had been as well.

"Wait, do you understand Latin?" I asked. "Because I have no idea what Father Altescu said as we were leaving."

"Of course. I was an altar boy. Let's see . . . '*Annuit cœptis.*'" Kip recalled. "I never heard a priest say that before. *Annuit* that's 'approve' and *cœptis*—is that a form of *coeptum*? That would have to be . . . 'undertakings,' I think."

"Approve undertakings? That doesn't really make any sense."

"Yeah, well, the Latin. It's kind of understood, like *he* approves or *they* approve."

"He who? God?" I asked.

Kip shrugged. "Maybe."

We had had enough time to finish eating, take quick showers, change back into our clothes, and kiss goodbye a little too long. Then he headed to his job and I headed to mine.

I shuddered briefly, pleasantly, as I recalled the events of the night before. Tiny jolts of pleasure pulsed through me at the memory.

"Have a good night?" Erica asked, eyeing me with a smile.

I felt my cheeks flush with embarrassment, which was even more embarrassing. "Is it that obvious?" I asked.

"Well, when a girl wears a turtleneck, it's probably because its cold out, or because she has a hickey. When she wears what appears to be the same turtleneck two days in a row? Hickeys. Hickeys and maybe didn't make it home last night. How'd I do?" she asked.

"I'm impressed," I said, choosing to let her think she was right about hickeys so I wouldn't have to explain about being strangled by a golem.

"Batman's got nothing on me. World's greatest detective, my ass," she said, while bagging up a teen boy's purchases. "Did you find everything okay?"

When I took my break for dinner, I texted Kip to see if he wanted to meet when I got off work. There was no immediate reply, which wasn't so strange since he was working. When an hour passed, I figured he was just busy. When two passed, I got a sick feeling in the pit of my stomach. I waved it away. Tourists, I told myself firmly.

But I couldn't help checking my phone over and over again, thinking I might have missed the vibration and feeling disappointed every time there wasn't a **New Msg** notification. Then, after 9PM, when I knew he would've had enough time to drop off his carriage and stable Rosie and take the subway downtown, the disappointment came every time I heard the door open. It was never Kip.

At closing it was down to just me, Nidhi, and Jackson. I had already confided in Nidhi that Kip and I had slept together. She went from excitement to worry as the evening went on and I didn't hear back from him. She was all sympathy and full of additional excuses for him.

"Maybe his phone was stolen," she said as we exited the store.

"But no one would want his phone," I said. Sure, he'd gotten a newer phone, but it still didn't have the internet.

"Well, he lost his phone before, right? Maybe he lost it again."

"Maybe," I said. The metallic screech of the security gate coming down prevented me from adding anything to that.

"All men are dogs," Jackson volunteered in his lilting accent, placing the padlock on the gate and securing it.

"Oh, great, that's exactly what she wants to hear, *Jackson*." Nidhi said his name like an accusation. The three of us continued talking as we walked toward the West 4th Street station together.

"I'm just telling it like I'm seeing it. Disgusting animals, all of them," he said.

"Including yourself?" I asked.

"Ah, I was raised by a single mother. I respect everything about women. Everything."

"What does that have to do with anything?" I asked.

"My mother raised me right. My father left her when she was pregnant. She learned quick that she had to do it all on her own and expected no help from anyone. She got a job, her own apartment, put herself through college, now she's putting me through college. *She* is a survivor. *You* are too, Madison. Don't let this *Kip* get you down." He managed to make "Kip" sound like a swear word.

"Yeah," Nidhi joined in. "It's probably nothing, but if it is, it's his loss, you know?"

I nodded. "Yeah. His loss," I echoed, feeling hollow inside.

I sat alone in my room. All was quiet. After midnight on the 12th meant it was now the 13th of

October. One year since I'd awakened on Madison Avenue. *And a happy sort-of birthday to me.* I felt a melodramatic little tear forming in the corner of my eye and tightening my throat.

I had thought I'd be telling Kip about the anniversary of my awakening that evening, but instead I had spent the however many hours being upset over his lack of contact and trying not to check my phone a thousand times. I went from worry to anger to doubt and self-doubt and self-pity, and flipped the record and did it over again in reverse, as if I were playing all the sad slow love songs on Side B, ending with the "Was it something I did?" blues before it was time to replay Side A for angry rock ballads and power anthems.

I was miserable and syrup-heavy in bittersweet sad sugar cubes. A pity tea party, table for one.

I'd been listening to a lot of Journey on records that I bought in Times Square at an old vintage place. Vinyl felt right. CDs just seemed odd to me. Like shiny space age plastic coasters. Records. That was what I preferred.

Records. Of course. I should look at the flyer.

I pulled out the record album that had shown up in my apartment months ago. The bright circular label in the center of the record read: *"The Kiss" by Michael Adderly with Les Elliott and His Orchestra, Romeo Records, 1939.*

The record had arrived in the spring with Christina Marie Taylor's Missing Person's flyer and part of a newspaper. Each was yellowed with age and in folds that had been refolded many times, both with dates from October 1987. Christina

Marie went missing on October 13, 1987, and had been eighteen then. If I *was* Christina—and a year had passed since the day that I appeared on Madison Avenue—then that would mean I'd turned nineteen at some point. *If.* But a lot more than a year had passed since 1987.

So how could that be? How could I look so young thirty years later? I wasn't a vampire, so what was I? And how was I connected to Michael Adderly? He had seemed to think that I was working for another vampire, but that clearly wasn't true. It was my feelings for him that confused me.

I'd been flooding my senses so hard with Kip that I hadn't had any room left to think about Michael. But wasn't that for the best? What kind of future could I have with a vampire? For that matter, what kind of past did I have with a vampire?

I still held the paper sleeve with the record in it. I had only listened to the song twice before, the day I first heard it in Sleepy Hollow, at the old Adderly mansion, and the night I received it. The song had a bouncy, dreamy feeling to it, and Michael Adderly sang "like an angel." That's what the magazines in the 1940s had said about him, and they weren't wrong.

I flipped the record over to its B Side and found an instrumental version of "The Kiss." I hadn't bothered turning it over the last time. But what was the point of listening to the instrumental version when it was Michael's voice that had made me feel more alive that spring day than I had in all the months since I'd awakened?

Why didn't I have any memory of him, or of my life at all?

What had he meant when he said I reminded him of someone from before? Before what? And how was I different? What had Christina been like?

I put the record back in its sleeve and began to put it into the album, then changed my mind and took it out again and placed it on the turntable. The record began to spin and I gently placed the needle at the outside edge. First the familiar scratching sounds of recorded "silence" and then the orchestra kicked in song.

After a short prelude that would have allowed happy couples to find their way to the dance floor, Michael's voice—a clear tenor that dipped into baritone for effect—pierced like a dagger straight through the center of my chest. I closed my eyes and I could feel . . . *love*. I could feel *in* love and *being* loved and the *loss* of that love and there was no other way to explain it. There was no memory attached to this feeling whatsoever, yet I longed for, ached, burned, yearned for some unknown anonymous Him. Was it Michael? I could recognize these feelings better now, because I had begun to feel them for Kip.

The song finished too quickly and not quickly enough at the same time. I picked up the needle and put it back at the beginning again and reached for the tissues.

The next morning, I jogged down the stairs in front of my building and paused to button up my coat before walking up the block. The sun was shining, the air crisp and cool but not too cold. The dogwood tree in front of our building was blooming again, which seemed a little odd for the season. I hustled down the block toward the subway station, thinking about my plans for the day.

Since it was my day off, I had had more than half a mind to take the subway to Central Park and tell Kip off in front of every one of his whistling friends. Or to go to the stables and leave him a note with Rosie. Maybe I'd give her an apple and ask her to kick him for me.

A text came in while I was planning this portion of my sad little revenge scene. I braced myself for the inevitable disappointment and was glad when I saw that it was from Zoe, asking if I'd meet her to talk over our research.

I hadn't found anything else in the book I'd borrowed from Roland, but maybe that was because I'd been working—not to mention sitting around feeling sorry for myself when I wasn't.

I walked down the concrete hall that descended into the depths of York Street station, then walked all the way to the far end of the platform so that when I stepped off of the F train in Manhattan, I'd be getting out close to the exit.

A Brooklyn-bound train *whooshed* into the station, preceded by a bracing wind. The wind sent a McDonald's bag behind me skittering along and then a hand—a large male hand—clamped itself over my mouth.

It happened incredibly fast. One second, I was on the platform, and then next I was being carried down the access stairs onto the tracks.

CHAPTER FIFTEEN

Subway tracks are not a clean place. They are not a nice place to be, in any way. They are dark, strewn with garbage, crawling with rats and roaches, and they smell like urine. No one in her right mind would be down on those tracks in the smelly dark unless she was being forced to—as I was.

My kidnapper's hands held me in an iron grip, carrying me through the darkened tunnel. I was thrashing and wondering why my hands weren't lighting on fire this time. Maybe my life needed to be in immediate jeopardy for that to happen.

I could smell that my assailant was Hank. Cedar, mildew, spices . . . that was him alright.

At least he wasn't strangling me, which when I thought of it at the time, struck me as a little weird. Not that I was unhappy about not being strangled. I was so not unhappy about it, I started to laugh.

We were now down a side tunnel with some dim light coming from a series of bulbs on the wall. The smells combined from the tunnel and Hank made me think of an old hamster cage.

I knew exactly where I should look in my backpack for the holy water and was ready to grab it as soon as he changed positions. I didn't know what he planned to do with me and I wasn't about to find out.

He set me down on my feet and took two steps back to give me space. I grabbed the holy water ampule from the side pocket of my backpack and threw it at him.

Bullseye! The vial hit him in the chin, shattering. Water ran down his chest . . . and nothing happened. No screaming, no tearing at his flesh, no bubbling, nothing. So much for holy water. Maybe it didn't work because he was a golem, not a zombie?

His hands were palms out, held in front of him as if to say, "Easy, now. Nothing in my hands, see?"

But he said nothing.

I glanced around trying to figure out how to get back to the train platform and he gestured "Stop, wait" with his hands.

"Don't you talk?" I asked.

He shook his head.

"But you understand what I'm saying?"

He nodded.

The lighting was dim and it was hard to make out his features. He stood silhouetted in the tunnel with his hands at his sides, waiting. What should I ask him?

"Were you waiting here for me?"

He nodded again.

"But not to attack me?"

He put his two hands together in prayer shape and bowed toward me.

"To pray to me?" I asked, hoping I was wrong.

He shook his head vigorously and I sighed in relief.

Somewhere nearby something was dripping droplet by droplet into a puddle. *Bloop*. I ask a question. *Bloop*. The air currents in the tunnels began to stir and became a rushing gust as I felt and heard the F rain rumble into the nearby station. I could make out the direction, but wasn't sure which tunnel I needed to take. I needed an EXIT sign.

A sign. *Hmm.*

"Can you write?" I asked.

He shrugged.

I rummaged through my backpack until I found a small pad and a pen and handed them to him. His fingers were clumsy with the pen but he wrote SORRY in large shaky letters.

"You're sorry? For attacking me?"

He nodded.

"Why did you attack me?" I asked.

He shrugged sadly and wrote BLACKOUT on the next piece.

"So you don't remember attacking me, but you're apologizing for it?"

REMEMBER AFTER NOT BEFORE

"Do you remember who you are?"

NO

"Do you know who Hannah is?"

NO

"Pretty nurse, lives in Staten Island . . ."

WIFE?

Now it was my turn to nod. "She . . . was."

He hung his head then raised it and shouted something long and incoherent to the ceiling. It was a sound of anguish, a howl of grief that descended into hopelessness.

"Do you know what happened to you?" I asked when he had control of himself again.

DEAD

"Yes. Do you know what happened after?"

NO. WAKE COLD. PULLED TO CITY

"What do you mean pulled?"

LIKE MAGNET

"You were pulled like a magnet? Towards me?"

SOMETIMES. DON'T KNOW. NO.

"So . . . what do you want from me?"

HELP

Somewhere in the nearby dark, something scuttled by. A rat, probably. The thought gave me the creeps.

"Do you think we could maybe have this conversation somewhere else?" I asked, stepping from one foot to the other.

"He knows he's dead," I told Zoe.

I'd gotten Hank out of the subway tracks and onto a train car, where the fluorescent lights did his complexion no favors. We'd gotten kind of lucky in that no one else wanted to be on this particular subway car because a foul-smelling man was passed out on the other end, surrounded by several trash bags.

Another oddity occurred when I tried using my phone to take a picture of the symbol on Hank's forehead: it didn't show up on the screen. Hank's discolored forehead was there, along with his eyebrows, but not the symbol, even though I could see it as plain as I could see my own hand when I looked at it with my bare eyes. Speaking of eyes, Hank's were also different than the last time I'd seen him. Instead of fogged-over with gray-white, they were jaundiced and brown.

I explained all of this to Zoe. "He doesn't know what happened to him. He felt drawn to Hannah and didn't know why until he saw the pictures on the walls in the house. He didn't even know her name!"

Zoe and I were sitting in a Starbucks. Someone had left a newspaper behind on the table. Its lurid headline about a grisly hate crime read: REST IN PIECES. So classy. I folded the newspaper so I didn't have to look at it.

"So what Hank wants is our help," I said, taking a sip from my too-hot hot chocolate.

"With what?" Zoe asked.

"He wants to see Hannah."

"There's no way."

"I know."

"It would be so traumatic for her," she said, poking her straw around dregs of whipped cream at the bottom of her cup.

"I know," I said. "But I promised him I would try. I mean, Zoe, the guy is built like the Hulk and he almost killed me the other night. He hangs out on the subway tracks for fun. I wasn't going to tell him no. And maybe this sounds ridiculous, but I feel sorry for him. He's drawn to her 'like a magnet' and he's confused and he doesn't remember anything. He has vague feelings of being pulled places but then it stops and he just wanders, feeling emotions with no memories to attach them to. I mean, I can relate, you know?"

"I'm sorry," she said in a small voice.

"It's not your fault, Zoe. You thought you were dealing with a ghost."

"I know, I know. I just feel like a horrible person for putting you in this situation."

"Well, don't. It's a good distraction for me anyway," I said.

"You still haven't heard from that jerk?" she asked, putting her hand on my forearm.

I exhaled. "No. I'm not even sure I want to now."

"His loss," Zoe said.

"You know, everyone keeps saying that, but I mean . . . here's a normal guy, a very attractive guy, and we have great chemistry and then, I sleep with him, and as if my life were some horrible high school novel, he ghosts me after we sleep together."

"You know, I wish that was what ghosts really did, just disappeared, instead of turning up like fish oil burps."

"Fish oil burps?"

"Don't ask," she said.

Later that night, at home, I tried to engage Sylvie in yet another conversation about why I hadn't heard from Kip. Sylvie had only two words to say: "Good riddance." When pressed for more information, all she'd say was, "Didn't like him."

"But why?"

"Just didn't."

I supposed she'd go and talk to her plants about it later. Julie was more sympathetic, her own relationship being in a bit of trouble at present as well. Apparently, Tad hadn't appreciated Julie's night out or her drunken accusations and was mad at her.

She'd been terribly hungover the next day when I told her that her car had been "broken into" in Hoboken. She was extraordinarily grateful that I'd come to get her and brought her home. She had had no memory of the night whatsoever and was just glad she'd woken in her own bed.

The two of us were sitting in the living room, watching TV with the sound off because we'd found out in the past several months that I couldn't pay attention to a show and have a conversation at the same time. We hadn't had much time to talk about Kip, but when she asked, I spilled all the pertinent details.

"Twice? So he definitely didn't have a bad time," she said.

"It seemed like not? But I don't know."

"Tell me you used protection," Julie said.

"What? Oh, yes, he had condoms."

"Are you on the pill or anything?"

"No . . ."

"Did *you* have condoms?"

"No."

"Eesh. Hang on." She went into her room and returned with a box. "Here. Just in case."

I took the box from her. Inside were four foil packets not unlike the one Kip had used. "Um, thanks?"

"You gotta take responsibility for your own stuff, you know? Not every guy's a Boy Scout. Can't just expect the dude to be prepared. I *like* that he was. But what I *don't* like," she said, "is that he took you somewhere that wasn't his place—I know, I know," she said as I tried to interrupt, "It was raining and you were soaked. But then you said you thought you saw the t-shirt that he'd been wearing there, so then it seemed like his place? But then what was the other place he took you the other time? And that one had no decorations or anything. It's just weird. He disappears and then shows up again and then disappears again and takes you to weird apartments. It's deeply suspicious man-slut behavior, like a guy cheating on his live-in girlfriend. And then he ghosts you? *Again?* You know you're probably better off without someone like that, right? And it's—"

"His loss. I know," I said.

"Good riddance," Sylvie said, passing through the living room on her way to her room, carrying a large yellow mug.

"Sylvie, I meant to thank you for that tea you made me in the thermos. It helped my throat so much. What was in it?"

"Just herbs," she said. "And some sticks, flowers, a little tree bark. Most people ignore the healing plants that Mother Nature has to offer, but her remedies are all around us."

Julie rolled her eyes at the latter but only I could see it. "Where do you get all of that stuff, anyway?" Julie asked.

"A few herb shops in Chinatown," Sylvie said. "Goodnight." The door closed quietly after her.

"God, she's so weird," Julie whispered.

"You thought I was weird at first—you told Kip you didn't like me when you met me!"

She giggled. "Well, in *vino veritas*, right? And you're still weird. But I like you fine—now."

"In vino what?"

"It means, 'in wine there's truth,' or something like that. Like how people who have been drinking wine aren't shy with their real opinions. Oh, wow, have you ever heard this story?" Her attention diverted to the TV for the moment and she reached for the remote control to turn it up.

I glanced at the screen and saw a picture of an infant and the words 30 YEARS AGO and BABY JESSICA on screen. "Yeah, sure. The little girl who fell in the well, right? Took 'em a few days to get her out, etcetera."

"—the story of Baby Jessica shocked the nation as—"

"How have you heard about this but not, like, *American Idol?*" Julie demanded, muting the sound again.

"Huh? Oh, uh, I must have seen it in a magazine. Look, there's a *People Magazine* cover right there," I said, gesturing at the screen. I really needed to be more careful about my references. "I think I'm going to head to bed," I said, getting up from the couch. "Night."

"Goodnight," Julie said, turning up the volume once more.

A male voice continued, "—that's right, Susan. As of tomorrow, it will be thirty years to the day that Baby Jessica began her incredible ordeal. We're going live now to our correspondent in Midland, Texas, where eighteen-month-old Jessica McClure fell into a well on her family's property on October 14, 1987."

That couldn't be right, could it?

I stopped short outside my room. "What did he say?"

She muted the TV again. "She fell in the well October 14th 1987. Why?"

"Uh, no reason. Sorry to interrupt."

"—it would be almost *sixty* hours before firemen and other emergency workers were able to free her—"

Sixty hours? I closed the door to my room and sat down at my desk.

October 14, 1987. Plus sixty hours. Nearly four days past October 13, 1987. But I knew. I knew this story of the baby girl who fell down the well and who was rescued the same way that I knew the lyrics to "Billie Jean," the same way that I knew Murdock on the A-Team wanted trash bags, the same way I knew Ferris Bueller was a righteous dude. But those things had entered pop culture before October 13, 1987, the date that Christina went missing.

What did it mean?

A quick internet search confirmed the dates. The reporters had it right.

I started getting a queasy feeling and closed my laptop. There were no answers there.

I needed sleep, not to obsess over the past and weird things I couldn't explain.

The past was in the past. Let it stay there.

The weekend arrived and I worked both days as usual, taking a double on Saturday to make up for the previous weekend. I hadn't seen a sign of Hank since our encounter in the subway, which was fine by me. Zoe had left a message for Hannah to call her, but as far as I knew, she hadn't heard back.

Coming home from work Sunday night, I exited the subway and walked down the block toward home. Since my encounters with Hank and Michael Adderly, I'd become even more vigilant than before about being aware of my surroundings, looking up and down the block before turning a corner and making sure there was no one sneaking up behind me or hiding just out of sight. But even though my guard was up, I was still absolutely shocked to see Kip sitting on my stoop.

Chapter Sixteen

HE LOOKED TERRIBLE, WHICH WAS GRATIFYING. His clothes wrinkled, hair a bigger mess than usual, he certainly didn't seem his usually cocky self. For all of the things I had thought I'd say when I saw him again, here he finally was and I was speechless. For a second, I wanted to turn around and walk back to the subway, but I was tired and it had been a long day. So I walked up to the stoop and stared at him instead.

Now I noticed the circles under his eyes, the sharpness of his cheekbones that was exaggerated by the hollows beneath them. Had he lost weight? He had a couple of scratches on his cheek and forehead too—not like fingernail scratches but something else. Thinner, sharper. A razor, maybe.

I tried not to be worried about him and it made me angry. If Julie was right, maybe his girlfriend had thrown him out on the street and sliced him up for good measure.

"Please hear me out," he said, his accent thick. "I know how it looks. I know, yeah? But please, I'm begging you, please listen."

I shook my head. "You really had me fooled," I said. "But you and me? We're done. Broken up, if we were ever even together. It's been—" I counted inside my head, "five days. Five days!"

I went to walk around him to climb the stairs and he stood up and blocked my path.

"Please . . . wait."

"Look, Kip. I'm tired and I'm not going to stand here and listen to lies about how you lost your phone or whatever. That won't work anymore. It's over, okay?"

"I didn't lose my phone. I had to throw it away. For five days, I've been on the run because I couldn't get back to you. Just, please, let me come inside and talk to you, yeah? Please? And maybe I could use your bathroom?"

I would not fall for his accent or pretty green eyes or be concerned about him in anyway, I told myself firmly. And what the hell was he talking about? On the run? What the crap is that?

"Just tell me the truth for once," I said.

"I'll tell you inside, I promise. And then if you want me to go, I'll go, I promise. But I hope you'll listen."

When Kip came out of the bathroom, he looked a bit more like his old self. He'd neatened his hair and washed his face and used Julie's mouthwash, from the minty smell of him.

Sylvie took one look at him, frowned, and went to her room. Julie was out for the night, trying to make up with Tad.

"Well, thanks for stopping by," I said too sweetly. I walked toward the front of the apartment to show him out.

"I deserve that. I know I do," he said. "And you asked me for the truth and you're right, I should have told you the truth a while ago, but once we'd gotten started it was so hard and you were so pretty and I just couldn't tell you."

I experienced so many emotions—from anger to hope to fear to anger again—in such a short period I felt like my ears were ringing. "You have a girlfriend," I said.

"A girlfriend? God, no," he said.

"A boyfriend?" I asked.

"No, not a boyfriend either."

"So what's the truth then? You're secretly a priest? You were abducted by aliens?"

Kip looked towards the door of Sylvie's room and back at me. "I'm not—it's hard for me to talk about it, yeah? Can we sit, in your room, maybe? A little privacy?"

The self-righteous part of me wanted him thrown out while the hopeful, sad part of me thought we might hear something that would make sense and that meant he cared about me, and another part wanted to put hands over its ears and yell "No! No! No!" until he went away.

"Come on," I said, disgusted that the hopeful part had won. I was also curious, wanting to hear this supposed truth.

Once we'd gotten settled with him in the desk chair and me on my bed with the pillows fluffed up behind me, I crossed my arms and gave him an expectant look.

"You know, I meant to tell you that I liked your room the last time we were here," he said. "The green and purple. It suits you."

"I didn't pick the colors. Don't stall, Kip. It's unbecoming to us both."

He nodded. "You're right. You're right. It's—I—" he stopped and gave a short laugh. "Where do I begin?"

"I hear it's traditional to begin at the beginning, but you feel free to start *in medias res* if you prefer."

"I deserve that. That and more. Alright, then. Here goes. You know how you went through all of your trouble with the haunting, back in the spring, yeah? And so you believe in ghosts because you've seen them, you've seen things that no one else would believe if they didn't see it too. And so have I—no, no, wait—"

"You are *not* going to tell me you are being chased by a ghost!"

"No, by your bloody zombie, Hank, or whatever his name is!"

"What?! But why would he be chasing you?"

"Because," Kip paused and took a deep breath. "I . . . am . . . fey."

"Fay?" I asked.

"Fey," he corrected, pronouncing it like "fee-y".

"I don't know what that is."

"The fey . . . well, they're faeries, basically."

We stared at one another for a beat and then I couldn't hold it back any longer and the laugh escaped through my nose in a snoring, snorting sound.

"I'm not having you on," he said. "I swear."

I gave him a look. "Faeries. Swear on . . . swear on Rosie," I said.

"I swear by Rosie's soft ears and her long mane and tail, by the sound and soundness of her hooves, and by her love of apples, I am not having you on."

It was a pretty weird way to swear, but I was mostly convinced by it, possibly because it was weird. "You're a faerie," I said, trying it out.

"I am," he confirmed.

"You asshole!" He seemed surprised at this exclamation from me. "You let me tell you all of this stuff about ghosts and zombies and whatever and you go on letting me believe that you're a normal guy who's taking a risk and believing me all the while knowing yourself that there's a secret supernatural world—with faeries? Asshole."

"You're not wrong," he said.

"Do I have a sign on my back that attracts weirdos? Why? Why go out with me and—and—everything—and pretend this is all new to you?"

He seemed to stare at the ceiling before continuing. "I've come a bit clean so I might as well finish the whole thing, yeah?"

"There's more?" I said. "Are you a secret agent too?"

"So. When we met, it couldn't have been better timing for me. Not so much for you, but for me it was great. You asked if you have a sign on your back. No. Not a sign. But you do have . . . well, an aura, you might call it. Your aura—it's all light. It's big. Big enough to shelter in if you don't want to be found."

The aura thing again. Just like Zoe had said. "Continue."

"So when we met, I didn't want to be found—but I had been. That *thing*. I think it was him. It followed me onto a train. I didn't know what it was at the time—I didn't get a good look—I just knew I was being followed. I had to start a track fire to get away. And that was when I saw you, when I was getting out of the station, looking for a bolt hole. You were like Christmas. Like a beacon. My puny light would disappear next to yours. I was safe with you. Safe enough that he couldn't find me."

"So you were just . . . using me," I said.

He took a breath as if to deny it and then said, "At first, yeah. Yeah. I was. But then . . . then you were different! You were like me. A person out of time, out of place. You were funny, smart, beautiful, unpredictable, and Jesus, you know how to kiss. I liked you for your own self, then. Then it was just— I felt lucky. And then—then that fucker attacked you. And I should have left but I couldn't leave you—not with him out there somewhere."

"So then you slept with me and disappeared? Do you have any idea what that did to me? How it made me feel?"

"Jonas is dead," Kip said.

"What? Who?" I asked.

"Jonas, the bartender, Wonderland?"

"The guy with the rabbit ears? He's dead?"

"Yeah. I got the call that he had disappeared right after we went to dinner at the Thai place that night. I got the call and had to leave you, ditch my phone because you don't know how they're tracking you and if a person has your number and that person disappears then you have to disappear too."

"Was he a faerie too?"

"Yeah. Half the people at that club were. And at first, I thought you knew about yourself and weren't telling me but then you didn't notice any of the others. Then when you told me about your amnesia, I thought that must be why. But I still wasn't sure if you knew about yourself or not."

"Knew what about myself? I'm not a faerie too, am I?"

"No, no. I think you must be a witch, or a sorcerer or magi or whatever they're called."

"You think I'm . . . you know what, just table that. Finish your story. What happened to Jonas?"

His expression became grief stricken. "They found his body . . . five? Yeah, five days ago. He'd been tortured. Cut to ribbons. Starved and burned and blinded. They cut off his ears."

I had seen the headline on the newspaper at Starbucks. The police had thought it was a hate crime.

"I'm sorry about your friend," I said. "But there's still a lot of this I don't understand." A yawn interjected itself into my speech. "Plus, I'm tired, I'm hungry, and honestly, I'm still mad at you."

"I don't blame ye a bit," he said. "But I wanted you to know. I'm being honest here. The reason I left you the first time was to save my own skin, but when ye didn't hear from me—well, after—that was because I wanted to save yours. I had to get magical protection. Otherwise, as long as I was by your side, that thing would come for you. I do care about ye, Madison."

I rubbed my temples, feeling a hunger headache coming on. "Come to the kitchen while I have some ramen. You want some? It's boring but it puts something in your stomach. You look like you could use it."

Early the next morning, I sat bundled in a scarf and gloves and earmuffs on a bench at Brooklyn Bridge Park. I hadn't come to enjoy the spectacular views of Manhattan, the Brooklyn Bridge, or the boats traversing the East River.

I'd agreed to meet Hank there to let him know when or if Hannah would be willing to see him. It was a short walk from my apartment building, and very public, which I hoped would keep him from attacking me or carrying me away.

Sitting there in the cold, looking across the way at Jane's Carousel—the antique carousel encased in glass in the park—made me wish that I'd chosen somewhere else for us to meet because the carousel of course made me think of Kip.

He'd told me some incredibly strange things the night before and I'd asked him to leave at the end of it. He seemed surprised by this. It was like he thought that explaining would make everything better, that now that I knew I just had to forgive him. But Kipling Jack Donovan wasn't as quite as charming as he thought.

Beyond that, I needed time to think about all of the ramifications of this supernatural world and how I did or didn't want to interact with it. Had Hank been responsible for the death of Kip's friend Jonas? Or was that someone—or something—else? Was Hank still dangerous? Had he gotten control of himself again? Or was it Kip's proximity that caused him to go into attack mode?

A woman with a toddler in a stroller walked up. She sat down on a nearby bench, handed her child a baggie of multicolored Os, and began fiddling with her phone. I questioned my reasoning of asking Hank to meet in a public place. A mortal man would refrain from violence in public, but Hank was no mortal man. Was I endangering this woman and her child?

The arranged meeting time came and went, and I wondered if the problem was that Hank didn't have a watch. The woman left with her toddler, which was a relief, and I found myself watching a couple of pigeons pecking at one another over fallen Os.

I was getting up to leave when I recognized Hank's lumbering walk, coming from beneath the Brooklyn Bridge.

He surprised me by having a piece of paper with marker writing on it:

WHAT DID SHE SAY

"We haven't been able to get in touch with her," I said. Zoe had called and sent text messages, but there had been no response. "She mentioned something about her parents wanting to take her on a cruise to get her mind off things, so we think maybe that happened and she didn't tell us?"

A boat passed by, traveling down the East River and passing under the bridge.

He frowned and sat down on the next bench over.

"I'm sorry. But you know, I wonder if it's for the best? Have you thought about how hard it will be for her to see you like this?"

He set his jaw and grimaced. I could tell he wanted to say something.

I had more questions for him anyway, especially about Kip, so I pulled the pad of paper out of my bag. "Do you want some—?" I began to say but then the words died in my mouth.

An odd, thick fog was pouring upwards from the river and over the embankment and coalescing around Hank's feet and the bottom of his bench. It climbed up the back of the bench and hung in the air, where a small diamond-shaped patch of darkness seemed to open. Like a playing card in size, it seemed to be made completely of inky black shadow but without an object to cast it. It hovered over and behind Hank. The darkness then stretched, impossibly growing larger and larger, eating all of the light in its area.

I pointed and made a sound but before Hank had finished turning around a huge clawed hand with elongated fingers reached out of the darkness toward him. The two pigeons fluttered away with startled coos. At the same time, a low voice spoke in elongated vowels. The words were in a language I didn't understand, but the voice then repeated them in English, in the exact same sneering tone: "Faithless hound. Obey!" Then the clawed hand snatched him up and pulled him into the darkness, which instantaneously shrank to nothing, disappearing with an audible *pop*.

The fog rolled back out again to the river.

I was alone in Brooklyn Bridge Park, glad that I hadn't peed myself.

"What happened to you?" Sylvie asked as I entered our apartment, I was apparently looking somewhat shaken.

"Oh, I, uh, saw a dead rat outside. Really gross."

"Is that so?" Sylvie asked, her head cocked at an odd tilt.

"Huh?"

"A dead rat. You can do better than that." Sylvie said. "You're a terrible liar."

Caught in my stupid lie, I felt my expression freeze. "Why would I lie about a dead rat?" I asked, hoping that the heat in my cheeks wasn't apparent.

"I don't know. Why would you?" she asked, her hands on her hips.

"I don't know. Maybe I'm tired of you judging me," I said, suddenly feeling defensive.

"I am just trying to look out for you. You are young and inexperienced and you bring home that . . . that Kip—"

"That's none of your business, Sylvie! We're just roommates. You're nice, you make me tea, but you don't get to tell me who I should or shouldn't be with. Geez, you're worse than—" I clapped my hand over my mouth.

"Worse than?" Sylvie asked.

Billy. She was worse than Billy. Billy who had suddenly developed an interest in my personal life, Billy who was *just watching out for me*, Billy who had been missing for months . . . Billy who had been hypnotized by Michael Adderly to spy on me. Was Sylvie Michael's new spy? Was that what he had been doing in my neighborhood? Getting info on me from my roommate? That was a different kind of stalking altogether, and it scared me to death.

"Never mind," I said, picking up my backpack and heading right back out the door.

It was trash and recycling day in our neighborhood. Piles of garbage bags and bundled cardboard boxes crowded the curb and sidewalk.

"What the fuck? What the fuck!" I said aloud, walking toward the subway. Was every part of my life infested with supernatural flimflam?

Where could I go to get away from it? Couldn't go to work: It was my day off. My apartment possibly housed a vampire's spy. A vampire which my old self maybe was in love with. My now-ex-maybe-boyfriend was a faerie. The zombie—or golem—I had been trying to help was just stolen from reality by something with claws. Oh yeah, and maybe I was a witch or something.

"What the fuck!" I yelled, kicking a blue bag of beer cans. It sailed through the air a couple of feet, then hit the sidewalk with a satisfying *clankity-clank*.

"Yeah, girl, you give that trash hell!" yelled a guy across the street.

"Fuck," I said dejectedly.

I needed someone I could talk to about all of this. Someone who would believe me. Of course. The library. I'd talk to Roland and see what he thought.

"What do you mean he's on hiatus?" I asked the woman at the information desk.

"He had a lotta vacation days left and he needs to use 'em," she said. "Policy."

"Vacation days," I muttered on my way out.

CLOSED UNTIL FURTHER NOTICE
SORRY FOR ANY INCONVENIENCE

This was the sign on the door at Thirteen Books.

"Fuck," I said.

Then resigned, I picked up my phone.

He answered on the second ring.

"I need to see you," I said.

"I was hoping you'd say that," Kip said suggestively.

"Not like that."

"I was surprised to hear from you," Kip said, sliding into the booth at the diner I'd chosen. "After you made me promise not to call or text. But I'm glad you did. You look . . . what is that look?"

My eyes flicked toward the window at our table, looking for my reflection so I could see what look he was talking about. But the reflection was blurred by the lights behind the counter on the opposite wall.

"So tell me this. If *you* were talking to a zombie on a park bench and then a diamond of darkness opened up and grabbed him, what would you do? And what would you think that was?"

"I would think, *Jesus, Mary, and Joseph, they've come!* But—wait, that happened to you?"

He was a little slow, but he got there.

"Yes. Yesterday morning."

"Coffee?" the waitress asked, holding a carafe. She'd brought me tea just minutes before.

"No thanks, maybe some more hot water?"

"Not you, him," she said, smiling at Kip.

"Oh, uh, tea please," he said.

"Mint, Orange, Earl Grey, Darjeeling, Chamomile—"

"Chamomile, thanks."

"Lemon, honey, sugar, milk? I bet you like it sweet, huh?"

Was she flirting with him? She was flirting with him.

"Milk and honey," he said.

"Right away," she said, leaving.

"Was it me or were her hips swaying just a little more when she walked away from the table?"

"Jealous?" Kip asked.

"I don't know yet. Back to the weird stuff. What does it mean? Is it important?"

"It confirms that he was sent by the High Fey, which shouldn't be possible. It's just not done. Fey magic is charm, and divination, the elements, animals, nature. We don't deal with the dead. At all. That's why I didn't think that your zombie and the tracker that was after me were the same. But that diamond of darkness, that? That I've seen. And it's never good."

"Tell me again why you think the High Fey are after you. And why would they would use undead, even if it isn't *done*—like that's just a thing you do or don't do: Do you wear white after Labor Day? Do you wash darks and colors together? Do you wear black shoes with blue pants? Do you use undead? Oh, no thanks, cheers! It's just not done!"

"They're after me because I'm an insult to their honor, to their pride, to the favor they think they've done me—taking me from the mortal world and bringing me there."

"Here's your hot water," the waitress said to me, "and here's your tea, with milk and honey." She turned to Kip and flashed a saucy wink. "I'll be back to take *your* order in a min, sugar."

"I think she is swaying more," Kip observed.

I rolled my eyes at him. "Yes, you're very pretty. Finish your story. Do you mean you weren't born Fey?"

"No, when I was a boy, growing up in County Roscommon, in Ireland. I was taken. One of the High Fey had taken a liking to me and took me. She raised me as one of her own.

"Five years passed, five long years, before I found my way out again. And fifty had passed here."

"Fifty?"

He nodded.

"How could fifty years pass in one place and only five in the other?"

"Time flows differently in the Ever Realms. You ever hear the story of Rip Van Winkle? It's like that. The Ever Realms are like a dream. Time moves slow there. And the world out here moves on without you."

"What did you do?"

"I was stupid. I didn't know how long it had been. I went home. I went home and I saw a woman, standing in the back of the house, hanging laundry on the line. At first, I thought it was my gran, but she was singing, like my mam always did, which my gran didn't. It was my mother. Grown old, she had. I was happy, but sad too. Confused, yeah? But happy. 'Mam,' I called. 'It's me.'

"I thought she'd be happy to see me. But she? She called me monster. Began throwing things at me, calling for her menfolk to come and drive me away. My own little brothers, grown men now, came running. No one recognized me, or if they did, that was worse, for they thought I was—well, what I am . . . now. Fey.

"Five years there, five years of eating and drinking their food, their wine. It changed me. And my family grew old while I was gone. I'd grown older, but just from a boy of ten to young man of fifteen. My own mother didn't know me. So, I fled. Made my way here, where I have been hiding from the High Fey since. Going on six years now."

"But why do you need to hide from them?"

"Because I'm their property. Their pet. And what kind of master lets a pet run away without looking for it?"

"After all this time?"

"It's not long. Not to them. To them, it's like I've been gone weeks. It's still fresh."

"So you're saying this is revenge?"

"It's more than that. It's duty. It's honor. It's the law. It's the way it has to be. There can be no dispute."

"But why don't they just come here and get you themselves?"

"Well, that's just it. They can't be here. Steel, iron, metal, plastics—everything the city is made of is toxic to them. It's why so many of us who've rebelled are here. That diamond of darkness? That's faerie magic. I've been avoiding it, hiding with magic of my own. So they send out their hounds to track their property and either we run back to them for protection or . . . we die."

"Jesus, Mary, and Joseph," I said.

Kip was finishing his slice of pie while I explained about Sylvie and how I thought she might be a spy for Michael.

"So you didn't just make up a vampire ex-boyfriend to scare me away. You're a monster magnet, woman. It's got to be your aura."

"So every supernatural creature can see auras? Vampires too?"

"How I would I know? I've never even met a vampire. But," he said, "I do know a charm that can reveal a person's hidden motives, makes them reveal the truth. You could use it on Sylvie. Interested?"

"I guess? But I think I'm more interested in helping Hank. He doesn't want to be whatever he is. Somebody made him this way. He may not even be undead. The holy water had no effect on him. He has no memories, but all of these feelings that are unexplained. Don't you see, Kip? He needs my help. You don't. Clearly."

He fingered the silver and moonstone amulet he'd been wearing since he'd found out that Jonas had been murdered. "Do I have to need your help in order to want it?" he asked. The look on his face was both sad and hopeful.

I almost weakened for a second, but his eyes flicked over my shoulder as the waitress swayed past again and I found my resolve once more.

"I don't see how I can trust you, Kip."

"One problem at a time." Kip said. "I have an idea about somewhere I can get information about your zombie—or whatever he is. But first, you need to be able to go home without worrying that it's been infiltrated by vampires. So let's go see about your roommate, eh?"

Sylvie sometimes took weekdays off since she worked some weekends and was on call others. (The New York Parks Service takes the care of their trees seriously, I suppose.) So I knew there was an equal chance that she might be home or that she might be out. I snuck into the apartment with Kip behind me, the two of us tiptoeing into my room and closing the door behind us very, very quietly.

Kip opened up the paper bag that included a bundle of dried sage, a book of matches, a white candlestick, a small brass brazier, and a jar of finely ground pink salt.

"Here is the sequence: you light the candle first and then—"

"*I* light the candle? I thought you were going to do this?"

"I can't. You're the one that the intentions are being hidden from, so you have to do it."

"Great. Okay, so I light the candle and then what?"

"You pass it through the air like this," he said, "making a five-pointed star."

I took the candle from him, lit it and mimicked his movement.

"Then you light the sage. Put it in the brazier, waiting, like this . . ."

I carried out each of the steps as instructed, except the last, which was to toss the salt on Sylvie while making a declaration of what I wanted to know.

Once smoldering, the dried sage leaves had a pleasantly pungent, smoky odor. It hung in the air of my room.

"I can't believe I'm doing this," I whispered. We'd been sitting with my door cracked and the lights off.

"We can do something else if you'd like," Kip said nonchalantly.

"Have you forgotten that I'm still mad at you?" I said back between gritted teeth.

The front door opened and Sylvie let herself in, carrying a potted plant with one arm and a small grocery sack in the other.

"No time like the present," I whispered.

Kip nodded. "Go."

The door swung silently on its hinges and I came out of my room, a handful of pink salt clenched in my fist. I'd thought carefully about what my declarative statement should be. I'd planned to say, "So Sylvie, why are you really here?" Kip had thought it might be too wishy-washy.

"You also need to be careful about *how* you say it," he'd said. "Don't use the name 'Sylvie' because you don't know if that's really her name, yeah? There are always loopholes in magic. Why do you think I always say 'High Fey' instead of using a name? Names have power. Words have power, and if you aren't precise, that power can be used as a means of evasion or a weapon against you."

I padded down the hall, thinking she was in the kitchen. Then the door to her room opened and we collided into each other. I reached out to catch myself and the entire handful of salt poured out and down Sylvie's front, sparkling in the afternoon sunlight. I'd planned to say, "Are you keeping any secrets from me?" Then I would toss the salt on her feet and say, "Tell me the truth."

But when I bumped into her and dropped all of the salt on her at the same time, I wasn't prepared and the statement fled from my mind. I panicked, so I grasped for the first thing I could think of.

"Reveal your secrets!" I shouted, which made me feel rather silly.

I was ready for Sylvie to look at me like I was crazy and tell me to get out of her face, but that wasn't what happened. Instead, it seemed like everything stopped.

The pink grains fell through the air and down Sylvie's front. But instead of hitting the floor, they formed swirls of pink dust that curled upward and back down upon themselves, like a murmuration—a flock of birds moving through the sky seemingly as one entity. The grains climbed higher and higher until they had rained on Sylvie from head to toe.

She cried out and grasped the doorway with each hand, crushing the wooden frame in her fists. Her skin went pale as cracks erupted in her skin, not fine cracks like you see in a ceiling but like gouges, going from the red of blood to black. Her skin turned from pale to gray, dark gray. Her eyes went dark, completely black—and then leaves sprouted from her hair.

"What have you done?" she cried, putting her hands to her head.

Chapter Seventeen

WHEN HER TRANSFORMATION WAS COMPLETE, the woman I knew as Sylvie was no longer standing before me. Her skin was like bark, her eyes completely blacked out with no iris, no whites. They were all pupil. The leaves in her hair, shaped like bulbous feathers, were numerous. In fact, they *were* her hair. Her fingers were spiky and knobby and her ears ended in points. There were dark tears on her face and then she collapsed to the floor, moaning.

What. the. fuck.

The door to my room opened and Kip exclaimed, "Sweet Jaysus, she's a dryad!"

"A what?"

"A dryad! One of the Low Fey, not as low as goblinkind but not—"

"What's wrong with her?" I cried as she lay twitching on the wood parquet floor.

He furrowed his brow. "Dryads . . . What do I know about dryads? Right! They need their trees. They *live* in trees! How she's survived away from her tree for so long—"

Sylvie let out another moan and shuddered again. The leaves in her hair, which had sprouted green, were turning yellow around the edges.

"What's happening to her?" I cried.

"I'm dying," Sylvie rasped. No longer did she appear to be in her thirties. More like her sixties or possibly older. It was kind of hard to tell with all the bark.

"What? No . . . What did I do? How do I stop it?"

She had another spasm of pain. Then her hand shot out and grabbed Kip's arm. "The market," she said. "Go to . . . the market." Then she fell back again.

"Spare us your pleas. We'll do you no service," said Kip. "Why should we help you when you were spying on Madison for a vampire?"

Sylvie coughed, and spoke haltingly. "What . . . vampire? Madison, I am not— There is a magus. His name . . . is Rowan. He was the one who asked me . . . to watch over you. To . . . help keep you . . . safe."

"A magus?" I asked. "Like a wizard?" Sylvie nodded. "So you aren't working for Michael Adderly?"

She shook her head, and her eyes fluttered closed and she moaned loudly as one leaf from her head fell and wafted to the floor.

"We have to do something." I said. "This is our fault."

"We need to get her outside," Kip said. "She needs fresh air and bare earth. He picked her up off the floor and walked toward the front door. She seemed to weigh no more than a bundle of dried sticks.

"Kip! Stop! You can't take her out there like that! Even jaded New Yorkers will notice she's not human," I said. "Let me get a blanket or something."

"It's fine," he said, touching something to her forehead.

She shimmered a moment and then looked like her previous self, though a sick, sleeping version.

More faerie magic. That's just what we needed.

I opened the door.

"Careful, careful," I said.

We'd gotten her outside to the front of the building. Kip set her gently down at the foot of the dogwood tree and placed her hands in the dirt beneath it. Her moaning seemed to quiet some.

"Will that help her?" I asked Kip. "Will she get better?"

"No, child," Sylvie said, her voice cracked with pain.

"What can we do?" I asked again.

"Nothing," she said, "Unless you can get to the market."

The market? "Is something you need from the grocery store, Sylvie?" I asked. "It's probably closed but there's a bodega around the corner."

"She didn't mean the supermarket, Madison."

"Changeling. Take her to the market," she wheezed. Her voice seemed a little stronger from her contact with the soil, but not much. "If you can find it."

"The wunderkinde know a lot more than yours do about the Dark Market," he said, like it was a competition. "And don't call me changeling."

"I'll call you worse!" she hissed.

"Stop it, you two!" I said. "What's she talking about? What's the Dark Market?"

Sylvie chuckled, and then the chuckle turned to a cough. More of the leaves in her hair were yellow now, though some green remained.

"The only way I can live is if you find me a new tree," she croaked.

"What about this one?" I asked, indicating the dogwood. I looked up at the blossoms I'd been wondering about. They were also dying now. Was that why it had been in bloom? Was it reacting to Sylvie's presence?

"No . . . it must be . . . an oak," she said.

"Um . . . how do we bring you an oak tree?" I tried to imagine carrying a tree in a planter on the subway and how much trouble it would cause people trying to get on and off of the train.

"The acorn. Bring me . . . the acorn . . ." she said as her voice fell away. She began to snore softly as a petal slowly wafted through the air, falling from the dogwood.

"Sylvie. Sylvie, wake up. What do we do then?"

She stirred. "Botan . . . ical Gard . . . en. I can . . . get there. Friend. Need . . . phone."

"We need to hurry," I said, rushing up the stairs to my building to find Sylvie's phone. "Where is this market?"

"I'll go. You stay here with her."

"And let you disappear for another six days? I don't think so."

"You can't go, Madison."

"What do you mean I can't go?"

"It's the Dark Market. Only lower fey are welcome. Unless . . ." he trailed off.

"What?" I asked.

"Do ye have a mask or anything to hide your face?" he asked.

While most people have heard of the Brooklyn Bridge, there aren't a lot of people outside of New York City residents who know the Manhattan Bridge. It just isn't as famous or picturesque. My neighborhood was between the two bridges on the Brooklyn side, in the wedge of land beneath the two of them. It's called DUMBO: Down Under Manhattan Bridge Overpass.

Beneath the Manhattan Bridge, there is an arch. A huge arch that's nearly fifty feet tall, just as wide across, and over a hundred feet deep—the entire width of the bridge. It's more like a tunnel, made of big blocks of stone, covering enough area for a good-sized flea market bazaar, which is hosted there several times a year.

I'd briefly thought Sylvie meant that flea market (which wouldn't open again for months) and was confused when Kip brought me to the arch.

"Now we wait," Kip said.

"For what? I don't think Sylvie has much time, Kip!"

"We're waiting for the entrance to the Dark Market, also known as the Goblin Market or the Tekram Nilb Og. There's a door here. It doesn't open until sundown, which should be—" He shaded his eyes with his hand and looked toward the sun, "—in less than half an hour. She can hang on that long, I think."

"What the hell happened back there? I don't understand. I thought you said it was a truth spell." I spoke in hushed tones.

"It is! I've never seen that spell do what you just did. Never."

"So it's me, then? I made the spell go plooey?"

"No, no. Do you know what a glamour is?"

"No," I said.

"It's a charm, a minor illusion. All fey can change our hair color with a glamour, or the color of our eyes, the color of our skin, or clothes. We can make ourselves appear just a bit taller or thinner or shorter or fatter. More powerful fey can change the look of objects as well, you know, make a wooden coin appear to be made of gold, that kind of thing. Usually a glamour is used to deceive mortals. Like when I made Sylvie look human again, yeah? That is a glamour."

"So she was glamoured and that's what the spell uncovered?"

"Ah, no. That was something else, that was. That was no glamour. A glamour is just a mirage. Just on the surface, nothing more. That? That was different, powerful magic. Your dryad didn't just *look* human. She *was* human. No fey could—or would—do that."

"Why's she gotta be *my* dryad?" I asked. "So is she fey or isn't she?"

"Oh, she's fey, alright."

"How do you know?"

He laughed a rueful laugh. "She called me *changeling*. That's what those of us taken from the mortal world are called among the fey. But we call ourselves wunderkinde."

"Why 'changeling'?"

"You've never heard the myth? The faeries come and steal a child away, leaving one of their own behind, a fey child that is sickly and frets and dies, usually. Then the fey raise the human child as their own and he grows in the Ever Realms and changes. Some from curses, some gain magic or talents, some change form altogether. Changeling children always change, in some way, making them part of the fey forever."

"But that's terrible," I whispered. "Why do the fey send their own children off to die?"

"They would die anyway. They have been for centuries. The children of the High Fey, that is. That's why they steal human children. Because their own don't survive. No one knows why. Or if they do, they're not saying."

"But it's cruel to make the human parents go through that, don't you think?"

"Cruelty is just another card in a deck of emotions the High Fey use in their immortal quest for whatever it is that drives them. If it wins them what they want, they wear it like a mask until it no longer serves a purpose."

"You're kind of mixing your metaphors there," I said.

"Anyway, yeah, I'm sure she's fey. Just as sure as I am now that you, you've got magic of some kind. That spell would have made a glamour slip—but if she'd been glamoured, I would have seen through it, just as she saw through mine."

"Wait—"

"What you did," Kip continued, "was transform her back to her own true self. And that is *powerful* magic."

"Uh huh. Skip back to the part where you just mentioned your own glamour. Just what, exactly, do you have glamoured about yourself?"

"Take off your jacket," Kip said.

"What?"

"Take off your jacket."

"Why?"

"Why must you be so difficult, woman? Just take it off!"

"But it's cold out here."

"You'll put it right back on in a moment. Now hand it to me. Thank you." He folded it over his arm for a moment and then turned each sleeve inside out and held the inside-out jacket in the air for me the way he had at Wonderland when he helped me with my coat.

"Inside-out," I said. "Like my plaid?" I recalled the way he'd stopped me from putting my plaid shirt on inside-out that night.

"Come on," he said, and shook the inside-out coat at me.

"Fine," I said, and slipped my arms into it.

I faced him and gasped involuntarily.

I hadn't been sure what to expect. I'd sort of pictured green skin and webbed feet, but Kip with no glamour was even more beautiful than Kip with. His eyes seemed slightly larger—or was it just that his lashes were longer and darker? His cheekbones had more definition, his lips slightly darker and his skin fairer. The only other physical difference was his ears, which were pointed.

"Jesus, Mary, and Joseph," I said.

I could still see the glamour version of Kip, sort of superimposed over the other version I was seeing now. But the glamour was translucent, almost a shimmery outline.

"Look there," he said, raising his chin in the direction of the wall. The sunlight was petering out and had condensed to a single ray illuminating one group of stones that formed a dark, arched door.

"Can anyone see that?"

"Not unless they can see through a glamour."

"So the only way to see through it is by wearing your coat inside out? That's awkward."

"There are magical ointments, I've heard, or if you can find a four-leaf clover, but those are rare. You also can touch them with an iron nail. Mothers used to sew them into the hems of their children's clothing to keep them from being taken—unfortunately, mine didn't." He shrugged. We were quiet a moment.

The beam of sunlight on the far brick wall was slowly waning.

"Come on," Kip said. "The market awaits."

Chapter Eighteen

When Kip was sure we wouldn't be noticed, he took my hand and walked toward the brick wall. One second it was a wall, but as he stepped forward, it became an archway that led into a cave-like tunnel that was dimly lit by phosphorescent lichen. The temperature was cooler, and root tendrils trailed down the walls and hung from the ceiling.

"We're not under the bridge anymore, are we?" I asked.

"We're not anywhere," Kip said and grinned.

We continued through the twilight dark for several feet before Kip stopped walking.

"Put this on," he said, unclasping the silver and moonstone amulet from around his neck. "It will mask your aura."

"If this is what kept you hidden," I said, "you shouldn't be taking it off, should you?"

"I told you, the Dark Market is neutral ground. No High Fey, no hounds, no undead. They can't get in. I'll be safe there."

"What do you mean, 'They can't get in'? Why not?"

"The Dark Market . . . how can I explain? It's magic. The nature of the market itself bars High Fey and undead from entry. There are magical boundaries to prevent them, their hounds, things like that."

"But what's to keep one of the High Fey from putting on one of these things?" I asked, clasping the silver chain of the protective amulet around my neck. The moonstone pendant was heavier than it looked and prettier up close, with swirls of iridescent azure and shimmering purple running through the gem, as if it were faintly glowing. "Or putting one on the undead?"

"The protection works both ways. Putting one of these onto a hound or undead would make no sense. It would lose its ability to track its prey. And the High Fey . . . the only time they can get into the market is on *So-whin*."

"So-*what*?" I asked.

"Maybe you've heard it called *Samhain*?" he asked.

"Sounds a little familiar?"

"Yeah, you probably know it better as All Hallow's Eve, or Hallow E'en."

"Oh. Sure. Um . . . should I change now?"

"Now's a fine a time as any," he said.

"This is weird. I should have just changed in the apartment," I said.

"Yes, but then you'd have run the risk of calling attention to us."

"But what if someone comes?"

"They can't. We're Inbetween, just you and me here."

I wanted to ask what he meant by "Inbetween," but it was more magical merry faerie mumbo jumbo and Sylvie didn't have time for that. "Fine. Turn around," I said.

"It's nothing I haven't already—"

"Turn. Around. Now. Or have you forgotten that—"

"You're mad at me. Fine," he said, and turned his back.

I turned away too and peeled off my jacket and shirt and pulled the dress over my head. "Tell me more about this Dark Market," I asked.

"Right. Like I said, the market is neutral ground, and the High Fey can't go there except on Samhain. That's when it belongs to the Wild Hunt—and the Wild Hunt, made up of the Mad High Fey and their hounds, answer to no master or authority."

"The Wild Hunt? What do they hunt?" I turned to make sure he wasn't watching and pulled off my boots and jeans beneath the dress. Kip appeared to be studying the brickwork on the wall.

"Whatever they want. Anyone and anything they come across. Only the most vile and wicked of creatures venture forth to the Dark Market on Samhain, in hopes of getting caught up in the Hunt and its malevolence. Hunt or be hunted. Become predator or you'll be prey."

"Yikes. So why are we going there again?" After pulling my boots back on, I stuffed my jeans and shirt and jacket into my backpack.

"That's only one night of the year. The rest of the time, it's the Dark Market. It's a kind of supernatural black market for faerie kind, used by us wunderkinde and lesser fey, nymphs, satyrs, goblins, knockers, pixies, brownies, all sorts of other magical creatures as well. It's never in the same place twice, except on Samhain."

"So how do we get there?" I tightened the laces on the bodice of the dress.

"It's magic. I can't really explain it."

I finished pulling on the red cloak and picked up the basket. "Okay, I'm done. Are you sure this is necessary?"

The Little Red Riding Hood costume I'd borrowed without Julie's knowledge was a little tight, but not uncomfortable. Kip had said that my modern clothes were a problem and the old-fashioned look of the dress with its dark skirt and bodice with white sleeves would better obscure my humanity. He promised I wouldn't feel out of place once we were in the market.

He turned around and gave me an appraising look from my toes to the top of my head. "It's perfect. But you still need the mask."

"Why?"

He pulled a black mask out of his jacket and slipped it over his eyes. "It's tradition in the market. Maybe it was started by wunderkinde, I'm not sure. It's just like on Samhain; you wear a mask so the monsters mistake you for one of their own."

Kip's mask was simple: unadorned and black, made of leather. It fit the top half of his face perfectly, leaving the bottom half uncovered. I stared at his mouth for longer than I meant to and had to remind myself that his luscious lips were off limits.

I sighed and pulled the red mask on. It limited my vision, which I didn't like. I did like wearing red and black, though. It made me feel a little dangerous.

"C'mon, this way," Kip said.

We emerged from the tunnel onto a hillside overlooking a small bazaar of cloth and wooden stalls of many shapes, sizes, and colors. Brown canvas, magenta silk, sky-blue linen, decorative scarves, a rainbow of fabrics. Some of the stalls had been built with boards and some had thatched roofs. One had been built from barrels, another from logs. Some were just poles and cloth. Controlled wisps of smoke came from some areas, scenting the air with wood smoke, sandalwood incense, and roasting hazelnuts.

The vendors and shoppers themselves came in a multi-colored, oddly shaped variety as well. Here was a bat-faced creature of small stature, dressed in a three-piece suit, standing on a wooden stool bickering over prices with a loincloth-clad, yellow-skinned frog-man twice his height. Both were wearing masks over their eyes. There was a slender woman whose hair was downy white feathers that contrasted with her fine black filigree mask and full black eyes. She caressed a carved hand mirror at the stall of a tiny man with a full beard wearing a conical red hat.

"Wait, is that a garden gnome?" I whispered to Kip. "Garden gnomes are real?"

"Try to be serious," he said.

I caught whiffs of cinnamon, the sea, and fresh baked bread while we walked. Several languages were being spoken. I heard Russian and Spanish and possibly Chinese in addition to English, as well as other languages I didn't recognize.

Everywhere I looked, I saw masks and strange faces. A lilac-skinned child in a golden mask went running to a goat-footed man selling balloons. He had small horns on his head, long hair, and a goatee. The child gave the man something and he handed her a balloon. She took it, sat down on the stone wall next to him, put the balloon stem in her mouth, and inhaled. When she exhaled, trickles of blue smoke ran from her mouth and nostrils and she had a horrific, blue-fanged smile. Seconds later, blue wings erupted from her shoulders and she flew away.

"Well, I can see you were right about me not feeling out of place," I said. "I might even be underdressed."

Movement, hustling and bustling. Voices raised in bargaining, describing, complaining.

Standing head and shoulders above the throng of vendors and shoppers stood a minotaur—a man with a bull's head, complete with huge horns. He must have been eight-plus feet tall, wearing a studded leather jerkin and holding a spear and shield. The head of a huge double axe blade was visible just over his shoulder.

"Security," Kip said when I nudged him. "And speaking of security, Christ, I didn't give you the warning. Listen to me now. Carefully. You must remember these rules: One, ye must stay on the path. Two, accept ye no gifts of any kind, *especially* not food nor drink, and three, do *not* lie. Can ye remember that?"

"Sure. Now how do we find an acorn?" I asked.

"We ask the right questions of the right people."

"Okaaaay, well, where do we find them?"

"Good question. Maybe let me do the talking, yeah?"

I shrugged.

To our right, a rotund blue man with golden eyes sat smoking a pipe in a booth that featured small brass teapots—or lamps, I suppose, but . . . no. It couldn't be. "Are those magic lamps?" I whispered to Kip. "With genies?"

"Lesser djinn, maybe some imps or other minor daemons," he said, keeping his voice low.

"And they grant wishes?"

"They serve their masters."

"Wait, so they're . . . slaves?"

"Not exactly. More like indentured prisoners," he whispered back.

"Prisoners? Did they commit crimes?" I said, louder than I meant to.

"Shh," Kip chastised. "Stop asking so many questions. You're supposed to blend in, remember? Try to act like you've been here before, yeah?"

"Oh," I said. "Right."

At the next stand, a woman wearing a translucent red gown with a translucent red veil waved her hand toward a display of small, apple-shaped stoneware jars, each plugged with a wide cork. They seemed to come in every imaginable color. "Dreams, my darkling dears?" she murmured in a melodic voice to Kip and me.

"Not today, thank you, milady," Kip said.

The veiled woman inclined her head graciously as we continued past. I wanted to ask Kip about how she sold dreams, and where she got them, but it would have to wait.

"Ah, here we go," Kip said, picking up his pace. We passed several more stalls, coming to the booth of an elderly man with leathery brown skin, unkempt grayish brown hair, and a scraggly mustache and beard beneath a tiny snub nose. Though his posture was stooped, he appeared no taller than a five-year-old child. Shirtless, he wore a raggedy brown loincloth.

"Greetings, Meurig," said Kip, bowing his head. I did a small curtsey behind him, not really knowing what else to do.

"Changeling," Meurig said with a nod.

"I come with a gift and a question," said Kip.

"Give your gift and if it should please me, your question I will answer," Meurig said, with a formal air.

"A moment?" Kip asked, inclining his head.

Meurig waved him away, seemingly bored of their interaction already.

Kip turned to me. "I need the basket," he said quietly. I was carrying it over my arm.

Kip had raided our kitchen before we left and placed several items into the basket and my backpack, which I wore beneath my red cloak.

I handed the basket to him, and after hunting through it, he spent a few moments slathering a corn muffin with honey before he spun and bowed to Meurig again, the muffin held out as an offering.

This time Meurig perked up, a sparkle in his eye and a half-grin tugging at the corner of his mouth. He took the offered muffin and devoured it in two bites. "You bargain gifts of gold, of summer sun, and autumn harvest," he said, sucking up muffin crumbs and licking honey from his fingers. "It is good. You remember the old ways. Ask your question."

"Where can I find a dryad's acorn?"

Meurig paused in his finger licking, surprise evident on his face. "An acorn for an Oakmaid . . . I've not seen one in . . . scores of years. Perhaps in the deepest, most remote woods—or you could find the Owlwife and see what she may bring. It is said she can fetch most anything . . . for a price."

Kip nodded. "I count this bargain paid," he said, and began to move away from Meurig's booth. I was going to start asking him questions again, thought better of it, and just followed.

We had now reached the center of the market and were only ten feet away from the minotaur. Up close, he was even more impressive.

The bull head on his shoulders was a deep brown with a golden ring through the nose. Several gold hoops also adorned the base of his ears. His head slowly swiveled on his neck and he inhaled mightily and blew air out in a rushing snort.

Eight feet tall, with shoulders nearly four feet wide, I could see why he was in charge. I wouldn't want to mess around with him.

His weapons and shield all reflected torchlight as if they'd been carefully sharpened and polished. His boots were clean and well-cared for. His Roman-style armor was intricate and impressive, the studded leather burnished and the buckles gleaming.

This was no monster in the center of the market. This was a soldier, a disciplined warrior who took his duties seriously.

His large brown eyes regarded me for a moment and he snorted again, dismissing me.

A golden-haired Barbie-sized pixie in a diaphanous dress landed on Kip's shoulder. Her butterfly wings stopped fluttering almost immediately. Her green eyes were large in her small face, though her head was proportionally larger than her neck should have been able to support.

"Now look what the cats have dragged in," she said, running a tiny hand along the cuff of his ear. "Where've you been, handsome?" Her voice was high and musical.

"Ah, Eurwen," he said. "Allow me to present my . . . companion, Madison."

"Pleased, I'm sure," she said and curtsied at me, wispy blonde hair falling into her face.

I curtsied back.

"Whatcha lookin' for today?" she asked, continuing to pet Kip's ear.

"Do you know the Owlwife?"

"Whatdya wanna see her for?" The pixie's wings fluttered with agitation.

"An acorn. For a dryad," I said.

"Ooh, don't see too many of them around these days," Eurwen said.

"Eurwen knows the layout of most of the market, as well as the vendors. Who's the market master today?"

"You mean he's not the master?" I asked, eyeing the minotaur.

Eurwen tittered and launched herself from Kip's shoulder, flying within a foot of me. "Oh, you *are* new, aren't you?" she asked, giggling.

"Come on Eurwen, don't be petty. It's . . . unbecoming," he said.

I figured that swatting her wasn't a great idea, though it was very unsettling to have her hovering there like an oversized fly.

"Aw, you're no fun," she said.

"True. I guess I'll just have to give this honey to someone else," Kip said, turning away as if to walk off.

"HONEY?" She darted back to Kip, hovering in front of his face. "What kind?"

"Organic, wild flower," he said.

"O, sweet, orgiastic nectar!" she said, and held out her tiny hands. "Gimme!"

"Make your bargain first, little one," Kip said.

A sound like a bee went whizzing past my right ear and a small dark figure with wings buzzed into view and collided with Eurwen.

"Did somebody say honey?" a high, squeaky voice asked.

"You can't have it, Apis! It's mine!" Eurwen replied, crossing her arms.

The small figure had antennae and yellow stripes on its body, looking like a cross between a person and a bee, though smaller, maybe half the size of Eurwen. It buzzed around her in a few circles, then hovered. "I'll bargain my services times two," Apis squeaked.

"Thrice," Eurwen said to Kip, "but only if it's real."

Kip paused a beat, waiting to see if the little bee-man wanted to counteroffer. The dark figure shrugged and flew away.

"Thrice it is," Kip said. I took the very small jar of honey from the basket over my arm and handed it to Kip, who showed it to Eurwen. "A smell?" he asked, unscrewing the lid.

Eurwen breathed deeply and her pupils dilated. She exhaled happily. "Oh, yes. I strike this bargain," she said, and once again the words had a formal air to them.

"One taste per service, and when the remainder of your services are complete or dismissed, the contents of the jar are yours," Kip said.

"Fairly bought. This way," she said, flying away from us toward a path between the stalls. Kip inclined his head and we followed her.

We passed stall after stall. Here a hooded vendor selling swords and daggers, there a snake-headed man charming snakes in a basket. Another stall with sparkling jewelry in glass cases, then a stall filled with baskets of odd fruits of various sizes and colors—none that I'd ever seen before.

The goblin selling them was terrier-like and spoke with a gruff voice. "Goblinfruits, goblinfruits for sale," he said. "Come taste them, come taste! A sample for my lady?" He proffered a platter of beautifully cut pieces of fruit, slices the color of pomegranates, juicy and shining. I could smell the fragrance of them, like flowers and cherries, tart and sweet and fragrant. My mouth watered.

Kip grabbed my hand. I blinked a few times, feeling as if I'd just almost fallen asleep. I had been about to reach forward and take one. "Sorry!" Kip exclaimed to the goblin, "We're a bit rushed for time. Looks good, though. Maybe next time!"

Eurwen tittered again as he hustled me away.

Kip held the honey jar aloft and unscrewed the lid. "Keep us away from the fruit merchants or I'll pour half out on the ground," he said to her.

" 'Twas a joke! Just a joke. I meant no harm to the lady!" Eurwen protested.

"That is entirely too close to a lie. Speak—and act—with care, Eurwen," Kip said. "And you," he gave my hand a squeeze before letting it go, "No eating, no drinking, remember?"

Several wondrous sights later we reached the outskirts of the market, to a large tent that appeared to be made of burlap bordering on the edge of woods. "Another smell?" Eurwen asked sweetly, hovering near Kip.

He obliged by opening the jar and letting her breathe in the honey. She inhaled deeply and sighed happily again. "My taste?" she said.

"Once I have seen the Owlwife," Kip said.

Eurwen's eyes narrowed, but she flew upward over the tent's entrance and hovered above it. "Enter and see if what you seek is within," she said.

Kip entered the tent and I followed him.

The tent was larger on the inside, or at least seemed so. It was dim and hard to see and the ground beneath my feet felt sturdier than the earth and grass we'd been walking on. There was a strong scent of earth and leaves, a mossy smell. Huge leaves two or three times the size of my hands hung from . . . was that an enormous branch hanging from the ceiling? Wait, where was the ceiling? Everything above us was huge branches and leaves and darkness. As if it were suddenly night inside the tent.

Ahead of us was a darkened opening, like a cave. No, not like a cave. The edges of the opening weren't stone, but gnarled wood. Wait. The leaves, the cave, the firm ground. There was a dizzying sensation as I realized I was standing on a branch of a gargantuan tree. The cave was a hollow in that tree, and from within it came an awful sound of tearing and crunching.

I made a face at Kip and he shook his head at me.

"Don't just stand there," came the deep and commanding voice of an elderly woman from the opening. "Enter."

The tearing and crunching had stopped, but my eyes had adjusted to the dark enough that I was able to see the huge owl raise her head to slurp down a mouse's tail that was much larger than any mouse I'd ever seen.

Kip spoke. "We're in search of an acorn for a dryad's oak," he said.

The owl stared at him with orange eyes the size of dinner plates. "Why?"

"Will you bargain an object for an answer?" Kip asked.

The owl laughed an unpleasant laugh. "You're canny for a changeling," she said. "No, I'll not bargain object for answer, but answer will answer like."

"We don't have time for this," I muttered to Kip.

The owl tilted her head. "What's that, girl?" she snapped, then swiveled her head back at Kip. "What have you brought me, changeling? Is she to be my snack?"

"She is friend to a dryad. The dryad is dying. She has no tree. So we seek an acorn for her."

"No tree? But still alive? How can this be?" Her feathers were ruffled and she flapped her wings and settled down.

"Powerful magicks, my lady," said Kip.

"Magicks, pah!" she spat. "What color are her leaves?" Her head swiveled toward me as she asked.

"Gone yellow, mostly, my lady," I answered, mindful of the title Kip had used.

"There's still time then," she said. "A day, no more."

Her head turned back to Kip. "You answered me true and so I must answer you: To find this object that you seek, place your hand within my beak."

"No, Kip," I said.

"Silence, girl! What say you, Changeling? Is it important enough to you?"

"You should take my hand," I said, surprised to hear the words tumble from my lips. I knew that Sylvie wasn't important to Kip. It might have been his fault because he'd given me the spell, but he wouldn't risk a limb for her. It was because of me that she was dying now, so it was my responsibility.

Plus, I was hoping that maybe the hand thing was a metaphor.

Or maybe the acorn was in her mouth?

"Come then, girl," the owl said.

I glanced at Kip.

"We can still leave," he said. "There's no bargain struck."

"So you'll let the dryad die after all? Tsk. Shame shame," the owl said, blinking her great orange eyes at us.

"A hand for an acorn doesn't really seem all that fair to me," I said, hoping the owl would explain she didn't want to eat my hand.

No such luck.

"Make your offer then," said the owl.

"My service, for one hour."

"I am not interested in your service."

"Then we are at an impasse," Kip said.

"The necklace," the owl said. "It has value."

I reached for it, but Kip shook his head at me. "It's not hers to give," he said.

"What is yours to give, my girl?"

"Careful," Kip said under his breath.

I thought about all of the things inside my backpack under my cloak. I thought about the objects that Kip had put in the basket that he said we might need. I couldn't think of one that might appeal to an owl.

"I don't suppose you like kimchi?" I asked.

"Tempting, but no. It must be a fair-bought trade. For an item as rare as this, girl? Something of value must be given."

"I have no name, nor memory, either. My body is mine, but I have no desire to lose any part of it. Service is all I can offer, my lady."

The owl leaned close and the large orange eyes regarded me a moment. "Oh, you are an interesting one, aren't you? Well, why didn't you say so?"

The air around us was stirring, the tree branches shifting, the leaves withdrawing as the air around us shimmered and changed and we found ourselves standing in a small room of what appeared to be a small cabin. The room was warm and bathed in golden light from a fire in the fireplace. A rocking chair sat near the fire, a bed against the nearby wall, a small table with a single chair at it across the room.

The owl had shimmered and changed too and was now a wizened crone with a beak-like nose and orange eyes standing before the two of us, dressed in smocking cloth layers and scarves. The room rumbled beneath our feet and I had a sense of sea sickness as the floor tilted slightly, becoming a regular, rolling sensation.

"Are we on a boat?" I asked.

The crone cackled and flung her arm toward a window. "Have a look."

I looked at Kip and he had a very odd look on his face. He seemed a bit pale as well.

"Go on, go on," she urged.

I looked out the window as instructed to find daylight. The surroundings were not the sea as I'd thought, but rather a deep forest with tall trees. Then how was the cabin moving, I wondered, and how were we so far off the ground? Then I saw it, a huge bird foot, just peeking from beneath before disappearing again as another moved forward. The little house was walking. On giant bird feet.

I had an urge to pinch myself to see if I was dreaming, but what was the use? I pinched anyway and made my arm hurt.

"Fun, isn't it?" she asked.

I nodded. "Oh, yes," I said politely.

"Messy though," she said, gesturing toward her fireplace and nearby shelves, where cannisters had fallen onto their sides and spilled their contents among the ashes on the hearth: rice, beans, grains, kernels. "Separate these for me by the time I return, and I will give you what you seek."

"When will you return?" I asked.

"When I do. And no helping, little rabbit," she said, wagging a finger at Kip. The wooden chair came scooting across the floor behind Kip. He went paler and sat down on it, sitting on his hands. She cackled once more and then climbed onto an old broom that had been leaning against the wall and flew out the window.

"I'm going to strangle that pixie if I ever see her again," Kip said. "Do you have any idea where we are?"

"We're in the Owlwife's house, aren't we?" I asked, kneeling among the spilled grains and things.

"She's *not* the Owlwife. We're in the hut of the Baba Yaga," Kip said.

"Is that supposed to mean something to me?" I stood the four jars that had spilled their contents back on their bottoms.

"She's legendary. Maybe a witch. Maybe a goddess. Maybe one of the low fey who stole power. No one knows."

"Okay, so she's powerful," I said. There had to be tens of thousands of grains here.

"She eats people, Madison," he said, looking sick.

"Tell me you're kidding," I said. Kip shook his head sadly. "Well, don't just sit there, help me!"

"I can't. I can't get up. She bespelled me."

"Well, shit. What are we supposed to do now?"

"I don't suppose you happen to have an army of enchanted mice or ants or birds you can call to do the arranging for you?" I gaped at him. "Yeah, didn't think so."

I pushed a few beans to one side and then rice to another and grains, then kernels, creating four gathering points. "I can do this," I said.

"Not in the time she's given you. It's never enough time. If you can get magical help though, then you will complete the task and she will help you. If you don't? We're owl pellets."

"Magical help. Where am I going to get magical help?"

"Your own self, of course. You did it earlier, with the salt. Now do it with the grains."

"That was different. That was . . . crazy. This is crazy. Have I gone completely insane or what?" I felt dizzy suddenly and thought I might start screaming.

"No. No, ye haven't. Calm yourself. Breathe, Madison. Come on now. Breathe."

I inhaled and exhaled.

"Slower. Slower. That's right. Like smelling roses and blowing out candles."

The wave of panic and vertigo passed. "Okay, okay," I said. "Tell me what to do."

"I can't do this," I said.

"You can. We've seen that you can."

We'd been trying for at least thirty minutes, maybe an hour.

"Just close your eyes and concentrate," Kip said.

"But—"

"Close your eyes. Concentrate."

I glared at him.

"This is stupid. All of this stuff is dirty anyway! Why would she want to eat it?"

He stared at me a moment. "Do you think a creature who eats raw children cares about a little dirt?"

"Ew."

"You'd be surprised what sounds good to eat when you're really hungry," he said.

There was something about the way he said it. Something wistful and sad.

"I'll never take my cereal and ramen noodles for granted again."

"You have to try, Madison. She'll be back soon."

"You're asking me to do magic. Which until recently I was very happy thinking didn't exist."

"I'm sorry to hear that. Now close your eyes and concentrate or: We. Will. Get. Eaten!"

Time passed while I practiced. My eyes were closed but I could hear a high, almost tinkling, whooshing sound. I opened them and grains and beans fell to the floor.

"UGGGG," I said. "It's no use! I can't! I can't do it." I was near tears: hungry, thirsty, and my head ached. How long had we been doing this? How many hours?

"Damnit, Madison! Pull yourself together!"

"Fuck you, Kipling Jack Donovan! I'm trying my best here!" I yelled, gesturing at the seeds and grains on the floor. And just like that, just like *that*, I could feel them. Every grain, every kernel, bean, and pebble. The dust, the ashes, every little bit of it, like I was a puppet master and each one was a link in a disconnected chain.

When the Baba Yaga returned, flying through the window on her broom, it was to a neat and orderly home. The grains had been separated and put away. The fireplace and floor had been swept, the table cleaned, the shelves and all the items on them dusted.

"Ah, I knew you could do it, my dear," she said. "And extra points for the rest. For that, I'll let your changeling leave with you . . . eventually. As for your acorn, here, catch!"

She pulled a golden object from her smock-cloth pocket and tossed it toward me. It went high so I took a step back to get under it and tripped. I fell backward out of the burlap tent and landed on the ground outside with a fist-sized acorn cradled to my chest.

It was still twilight outside the tent at the edge of the woods, as it had been when we went into it. But now I was alone.

Sounds from the market reached me, voices in argument, hawking their wares, striking bargains, making deals. Pounding, grinding, jingling. All the sounds of commerce.

And then I heard a low growl that raised the hair on my arms and the back of my neck. I glanced behind me and caught a flash of glowing green eyes and black fur.

I ran for my life.

Chapter Nineteen

I gasped in pain as the dog's teeth locked around my booted left calf. I stumbled and at the same time heard a yelp of pain from the creature. I looked over my shoulder and saw the beast shaking its head from side to side.

It was the biggest dog I'd ever seen. Its head resembled that of a German Shepherd, but with huge ears at least twice the size. Its spindly legs were unnaturally long, as if it were on stilts. Bigger than a wolf, at least another foot taller than a Great Dane, its fur was so dark green it looked black. The cold green light from its glowing eyes created disturbing highlights across its face.

I braced myself for another attack, but the great green dog halted. It growled, pacing back and forth almost as if faced by some unseen barrier. It appeared unable to move any closer. But why?

Then I realized. Of course. The path, the boundary Kip had told me about, the one that kept unwanted creatures out. The path ended before the Baba Yaga's canvas tent, and I'd been thrown out and off it. So was that why I needed to stay on the path? To keep goblin dogs from trying to eat me? What the hell was wrong with this place?

I took a look at my leg. There were teethmarks on my leather boot. As I dusted myself off, I made a mental note to wear tall boots more often in the future.

I wanted to stay near the tent to wait for Kip, but I also wanted to get away from the dog. I looked around to see if I could find Eurwen anywhere, and then remembered the little bee-man she'd called Apis. Maybe he could help. But he worked for honey and I had neither basket nor backpack.

I passed a vendor stall that had a stone wall as its counter, with a large, winged gargoyle seemingly for sale with several smaller ones behind it, but no vendor. I paused, confused, and stood on tiptoe to see if there was someone very short hiding behind the stone wall. "Excuse me," said a voice near my ear, nearly giving me a heart attack.

But there was no one there. Except the same winged statue, now with its tongue sticking out and its stone eyes crossed.

"Oh!" I said. "I beg your pardon. Are you a gargoyle?"

"That depends. Gargoyles on buildings spout water. Grotesques stick their tongues out . . . and breathe fire. Drago! Iskra! *Zhar!*"

Two of the smaller gargoyles belched out jets of flame and chirped before resuming their former frozen positions. I refrained from clapping because I was supposed to have been here before.

"Which are you?" I asked. "If you don't mind me asking, I mean."

"I can be both . . . or neither. Which do you seek?" it asked, crossing its stone arms with a sound like one cinderblock being dragged across another.

"Oh, I apologize for my rudeness. I'm afraid I'm not shopping for your kind today."

"Accepted." The grotesque's lip curled and it stuck its tongue out once again.

I stood there awkwardly a moment, wanting to ask so many questions. Could it fly with those wings or were they merely ornamental? Would the little ones would grow in size over time? Were they its children? But I also felt I'd been dismissed.

As I tried to decide whether to ask or walk away, I heard a male voice say, "Memories for sale. A full set of human memories."

I passed a topless blue-haired mermaid who lay recumbent in a bathtub of water, her iridescent tail dangling over the edge. At a canvas a few feet away, a spider-woman with four hands—each holding a paintbrush—fast-painted her portrait.

In the next stall over was a crocodile-headed man with an open-mouthed grin of jagged teeth. He wore a burgundy bathrobe—or was it a smoking jacket?—over a white-collared shirt and black ascot with a diamond-studded pin in it.

"Memories for sale," he said. "Interested?" His mouth didn't move at all. Was he talking in my head?

"Whose memories?" I asked.

"I have many memories available from all sorts of creatures. Memories of their best and worst: a mermaid's wedding, for instance," he said, with a head tilt towards the next stall. "Didn't last long."

His mouth still hadn't moved during this speech, remaining completely open the entire time. It was a mask, I realized. There was black mesh at the back of the mouth that let the wearer see and breathe.

"Perhaps you'd be interested in a werewolf's first transformation? Maybe you'd like to experience flight, hmm? Or the sadness of losing a child? Are you one of those dreary types who wants a perfect day? I have five." He gestured at a wall of fluffy ostrich feathers, their quills carved with intricate symbols.

While all of the feathers had a base of black or white, almost all of them had been dipped in colors: a black feather dipped in red, a white feather dipped in blue, another feather of yellow and green, and so on. A single fully white feather stood out amongst the others.

"What's that one?" I asked.

"Ah, those are very rare, very rare indeed. That feather contains the complete memories of a married human policeman, very much in love with his new wife, up to the moment of his most inauspicious death."

What? A policeman with a new wife? My god. He was talking about Hank. Or at least, it sure seemed like he was talking about Hank. What were the odds? It had to be more than a coincidence.

"Where do you get all of these memories from?" I asked, hoping I sounded casual.

"Oh, here and there. In trade, mostly. Would you like to examine the policeman's memories?"

"Sure," I said. "What do I do?"

He pulled the feather down from the wall. I noticed he was wearing black leather gloves. As he handed me the feather, I could see that the tiny symbols that ran up and down the quill were not only hieroglyphics, but they were moving, flowing around the shaft.

Feathers. Hieroglyphics. It reminded me of something, but I couldn't quite remember what.

"The sample memory—it's at the tip here. Place the feather over your forehead and trace an eye just here," he said, poking me in the mask between my eyebrows.

"How much does something like this cost?"

"Depends on the buyer. What do you have?"

"Oh! Um, not much, actually, at present. My friend is carrying my things and he's elsewhere in the market." I fervently hoped that Kip was a) alright and b) would at least remember to grab my backpack.

"No, no. I meant what *memories* have you to trade?"

"Oh! Um, well, not too many, actually."

He was silent a moment and his head tilted as he regarded me. He then stepped closer to the edge of his counter. "Do you have a name?" he asked.

I wanted to step back from the toothy grin of the latex crocodile head, but forced myself to remain in place. "I'm called Madison," I said. Kip had warned me not to lie while in the market, and since my name wasn't legally Madison, I figured it was better to play it safe.

Some kind of ruckus was happening somewhere else in the market. Voices were raised and I heard a crash.

"Called Madison. *Called.* How interesting. You know, you seem familiar to me, Madison," he said. I didn't like the way he said it.

AAHOOOOOOHHOOOOOHHHH came the unearthly howl from nearby. It sounded like the goblin dog had found its prey. More ruckus was happening and it was getting closer.

Pop. Pop. POP.

Stalls began folding up and in on themselves and disappearing.

"Maybe I could take a look in your head for you, hmm?" the memory vendor said. He was suddenly too close, putting both of his gloved hands over mine.

The gloves were very soft.

They were made of black leather, with very fine stitching.

Was he hitting on me? So gross. From the sound of his voice, he was probably old enough to be my grandfather.

"So how does this work?" I asked, pulling my hand away. I held the feather between us as the hieroglyphs marched and spiraled around its shaft. "The sample memory, I mean." Getting his mind back on business and less on me seemed like a good plan.

"Place the feather's tip here between your eyebrows—you will have to remove your mask of course—and then use it trace the outline of an eye on your skin." He said I'd have to take my mask off like it wasn't a big deal, but there was something about the way he said it that gave me the creeps.

"And I'll just see it?"

"It will, briefly, appear in your mind's eye," he murmured, tilting his head toward the commotion. Perhaps he'd finally heard the din of the disturbance through his full-head mask.

"But that's just for the sample memory?"

"Correct."

The ruckus was much closer now.

Kip came skidding around the corner, running at full speed, grabbed by me the hand and yanked me away, still holding the white feather.

"STOP THIEF!" yelled the memory seller.

I could hear the growling and slavering of the goblin dog behind us as we fled through the market, stalls collapsing in on themselves like stop motion videos of flowers blooming in reverse. *POP. SLAM. THWAP. POP. SHOOP.*

The panicked throng of shoppers were running this way and that, disappearing through doorways that appeared at the end of the row of the market as they approached.

We reached a central area where several of the stalls had already disappeared.

The minotaur was striding toward us, rushing to the call of "Stop thief!"

I looked frantically around and yanked Kip to the left as the minotaur came bounding toward us, pulling the enormous double axe off his back and swinging it through the air.

CHAPTER TWENTY

THE AXE WAS COMING STRAIGHT AT US. I BOWLED into Kip, knocking us both backward onto the ground.

The goblin dog nipping at our heels chose that moment to leap. Instead it sailed over us.

The massive axe connected with and beheaded the goblin dog in one slice. Its head spun through the air and landed in my lap, heavy as a cantaloupe.

It had a horrible look on its green face.

I should have been up and moving. I should have jumped up to run. Instead I was staring into the dead eyes of the goblin dog, its dark green tongue hanging out of the side of its mouth in a morbid semblance of a dog smile.

"Come on!" Kip said, tugging on my arm. I let him pull me up as I saw the minotaur retrieve his axe from the wooden post where it had lodged itself.

We had gotten past one stall when the crocodile-headed memory seller emerged from one of the rows some fifty feet ahead. He seemed to be straightening the cuffs of his burgundy jacket as he walked, a gesture that would seem harmless under other circumstances but seemed filled with malice coming from him. We skidded to turn back but the minotaur was bearing down on us.

Then to our right I saw Hank.

Hank emerged into the intersection, lumbering toward us, hands extended in the pre-strangulation position. His eyes were fogged over—practically white once again. Whatever it was that had a hold on him had obviously regained control.

A guttural voice came from the minotaur. "Undead? *Here?*"

The large bovine head swiveled from Hank back to us. He dismissed us with a snort and pulled the spear off his back.

"Undead are *not* permitted in the market!" he bellowed, hurling the weapon at Hank.

Kip grabbed my hand again, pulling me away from Hank and the minotaur, away from the memory seller, who cried out, "Stop them!"

A horrible roar of pain and fury came from behind us.

I glanced over my shoulder to see the minotaur yanking his spear out of Hank.

Sawdust poured from the wound.

As I looked back, a pale figure in black joined the fray, leaping onto the minotaur's back.

Kip and I both ran as fast as we could toward the opening at the end of the row.

CHAPTER TWENTY-ONE

WE EMERGED FROM WHAT SEEMED TO BE A TINY round guardhouse into a concrete and cobblestone courtyard, near a four-lane city street and a four-way intersection beyond that.

I paused, trying to find my bearings. A Wendy's fast food restaurant was on one corner. On another, an art structure of three pillars with multi-colored bubble-shaped tree canopies read **Flatbush Ave.** That's when I knew where I was. Brooklyn's Prospect Park was behind us, and against all odds (but probably due to magic?) the Botanic Garden where Sylvie had said we should meet her was across the intersection.

A goblin rushed past us into the park, a masked yellow frog-man loping after him.

Kip had been about to pull me into the park, but I pulled back and said, "This way!"

Our timing couldn't have been better, as the little pedestrian figure in the **WALK/DON'T WALK** signal disappeared and a countdown from 15 began.

15

Step off the sidewalk

14

Feet continue moving

13

12

11

Cross the first lane

10

9

8

The second lane and yellow line

7

6

5

The third lane

4

3

A scream, coming from Prospect Park

2

The fourth lane complete

1

Step onto the sidewalk

0

Pandemonium.

We looked back, which you should never, ever do.

He stood at the edge of the park. It was the same figure I'd seen jump onto the minotaur's back, but now he was closer. A shirtless dead man in black leather pants.

I say dead, because he was paler than pale and scorched and missing skin from vital places on his torso. His eyes were a bloody ruin.

Something struck me as familiar about the figure—but I didn't know why. It seemed as though something was missing.

Kip gasped. His face was stricken as he stared at the walking cadaver.

That was when I noticed the bloody gouges on the sides of the figure's head where his ears were supposed to be. Where delicate bunny ears had once curved so beautifully. Both eyes and ears had been cut or torn away.

"Jonas," Kip choked out.

Jonas was headed right for us, seeming to know where we were despite his lack of eyes. He appeared to be foaming at the mouth. His posture was crouched, ready, his hands out to his sides, palms up.

"Jesus, Mary, mother of God," Kip said in a panicked voice, gripping my hand tightly. We should have already been running but Kip appeared to be rooted to the spot.

"Kip, c'mon!"

"Jack! I can feel you, Jack!" Jonas screamed.

People on the sidewalk were scrambling to get away, except for the one guy in baggy jeans who was filming with his phone.

Jonas charged into the street, causing a bus to swerve to miss him. The bus swerved into a car. *CRASH*. Another car ran into the back of that one. Glass breaking. A third car didn't slow down in time. *CRASH. SCREECH CRUNCH.*

SCREEEEECH THUD! Jonas was hit by a car traveling in the opposite direction. His body went flying through the air toward the park and landed twenty feet back. *SCREEEECH CRASH. Screech crunch. Crunch.* More cars piled up. More screeches followed as other drivers hit their brakes. Horns began to blare.

A white-haired woman got out of her damaged SUV and yelled "You sons of bitches!" at the mini-van behind her.

A wizened and warty green woman trundled over a Volkswagen bug and disappeared into a sewer grate, followed by several cat-sized rats.

A taxi driver in a turban checked his yellow cab's shattered headlight, shaking his head sadly. He completely missed the squad of masked satyrs running for cover not ten feet from him.

The body remained motionless in the road.

A man in a blue coverall rushed toward Jonas's body, and two young women in jeans and fur-lined parkas came from the other side of the street, all trying to get to him, to help.

I stood, clutching Kip's arm hard, willing it all to be over.

Then Jonas's hand shot upward, grabbing the man in the coverall's face.

The two women turned and ran, and so did we, through the side door of the arched entryway into the Brooklyn Botanic Garden, followed by the sound of screams.

It was twilight and the turnstile doors were miraculously open.

A young man in glasses and a green polo shirt tried to ask us something while offering us some kind of program book, but we kept running. "Hide!" I yelled to him. "Run!"

Trees were all around us, except on the concrete path. We ran past a swath of pink and purple wild flowers arranged in geometric shapes. I was having trouble catching my breath and felt like my lungs were going to give out. Kip had already removed his mask somewhere along the way. I yanked mine off as we reached a fork and paused, hands on my knees, just trying to breathe. The white ostrich feather was in my hand still and I shoved it up inside my sleeve, hoping that the elastic at the wrist of the costume dress would keep it safe.

We took the right-hand path. The sound of multiple sirens joined the distant honking but was quieting as we hustled further along the path.

Classical music. I could hear classical music from up ahead. Pachelbel's Canon in D being played by a string quartet. We came in view of a large building made of glass panels. Near it, several round tables and chairs hosted people in fancy dress who drank champagne passed by servers from silver platters.

The path went straight through them, so we did too.

"Jack!" came the guttural scream from somewhere behind us. "Don't you run away from me, Jack! This is your fault!"

Jonas ran straight into and through the string quartet, knocking the violinist over and kicking the bass. Men and women screamed and fled.

Champagne glasses shattered on the concrete.

"Sorry!" I yelled over my shoulder.

A server dropped his silver serving platter of hors d'oeuvres, which rang out musically as it hit the ground.

Kip let go of my hand. "Go!" he yelled at me.

And then Jonas was upon him.

The car accident hadn't done Jonas any favors in the looks department, as half of his face and torso were now razed with road rash. His fingers and mouth were pulped, his eyes bloody blasted pits. There was dirt mashed into the places where his bunny ears had been.

He was trying to push Kip to the ground and Kip was struggling for all he was worth. "Come now, Jack! Sweet Jack! Jack-o-the-lantern!" gibbered the beast that was once a bartender.

Jonas seemed to be trying to get Kip's mouth open. Whether to put something in or take something out, I wasn't sure.

I needed a weapon.

The dropped serving platter was feet away.

I grabbed it, pleased that it was heavier than it looked.

I closed on Jonas and hit him in the back of the head with it.

It vibrated in my hands, and I hit him with it again.

"What is this disturbance?" he bellowed.

Now Jonas was facing me. The next time I tried to hit him with the platter, he caught it, but I ripped it out of his hands and smacked him in the face.

"Use holy water!" Kip yelled.

"Backpack!" I yelled, thankful that I'd noticed it on Kip's back. First he came up with one of the small ampules, which fell out of his hand and the tiny glass container shattered on the concrete.

He smashed the second one into Jonas's chest, and it broke on impact. A sizzling sound followed by a stink of decayed flesh made me sick to my stomach.

Jonas made a horrific howl that sounded more like a monkey screaming than a human.

He then turned and grabbed Kip once more, but not before Kip tossed the backpack in my direction.

I grabbed it out of the air, then pulled the flask of holy water from the side pocket and let the backpack fall to the ground. The steel cap was cold beneath my fingers as I unscrewed it, and poured the contents onto the silver platter.

"Open up, Jack!" Jonas had gotten his bloody fingers into Kip's mouth and was trying to pry his jaws apart when I hit him in the side of the head with the flat of the consecrated platter. Another sound of sizzling and Jonas howled another unholy howl.

In the distance, I heard an answering one.

I could see glimpses of skull beneath the ruined side of Jonas's face. He fell to the ground, clawing at the blasted skin and making it worse, all the while producing a high-pitched keening whine that was horrible to hear.

The brain. Some forgotten piece of lore surfaced in my mind. To kill a zombie, I needed to hit the brain.

I turned the platter on its edge but it was hard to hold onto or put much force behind it until I raised it above my head and let gravity do most of the work.

Again and again I slammed the platter down until there was an awful *crunch* and splattering noise and Jonas stopped thrashing.

I dropped the platter to the ground, breathing hard, trying not to look at the mess of what had once been a person at my feet.

My hands were shaking. My shoulders too.

What had I just done? I had just *killed* someone.

I felt panicky. My mouth was dry. My eyes were wet. My teeth began to chatter of their own accord.

Kip stood with his hand balled in the collar of his shirt, wiping at his mouth.

I looked at my shaky hands and saw they'd caught a shower of dark droplets. Should I wipe them on my dress? I felt sick. My breath was still coming hard.

I had maybe thirty seconds of self-inflicted horror and recrimination.

Then Hank arrived, knocking aside a table-for-ten like it was a cardboard box. Glasses and plates clattered to the ground and shattered.

Two large puncture wounds in his chest had sawdust caked around them, but he seemed unharmed otherwise. I briefly wondered if the minotaur had survived.

"Hank. Hank?" I said, positioning myself between him and Kip, holding my hands up in a placating gesture, but he knocked me to the side. He was so fast. So strong.

"Run, Madison!" Kip said. He'd gotten a chair and was trying to fend Hank off with it, but Hank ripped it out of his hands and flung it away.

Hank's eyes were still clouded over as he put his huge hands around Kip's neck.

"Hank! Hank! Stop!" I yelled, to no avail. I picked up the silver platter again and hit him on the back of the head. The platter dented, but Hank didn't seem to notice.

Kip's face turned red, then purple.

"Don't do this!" I cried.

Kip's eyes were fluttering and I thought he might pass out soon.

The weird symbol on Hank's forehead was prominently exposed, and I wished that I'd figured out how to change it some way like in the story of the golem.

And then, like pieces of a puzzle all coming together at once, I understood.

The almost Egyptian eye.

The parts of the Egyptian soul, judged against a feather.

Hieroglyphics.

Place the feather over your forehead and trace an eye just here.

The feather!

I pulled it from my sleeve and smashed it against Hank's forehead.

A bright light flashed as the hieroglyphs on the feather's shaft glowed first red and then white, a glow answered and repeated in the symbol on Hank's forehead.

As the symbol disappeared, the feather turned black and crumbled into ashes in my hand.

Hank shook his head and staggered, moaning, his hands to his head. He fell to his knees and shuddered violently.

Kip fell to the ground, coughing.

As I watched, the fog lifted from Hank's eyes and they returned to their jaundiced brown. He sat for a moment, shaking his head and looking around in confusion and wonder. I could see a personality in his face for the first time. There was a person there, behind his eyes. Then his eyebrows drew together as he covered his eyes with his hands and let out a heartbreaking cry of pain that I felt reverberate in my chest.

My eyes teared up and my throat tightened.

Sitting on his haunches, Hank wept silently, his face in his hands. The shaking of his shoulders was unmistakable. What could I say or do in the face of such despair?

I left him to his grief.

Kip coughed, still catching his breath.

I surveyed the scene: the lawn strewn with broken plates and shattered glassware, the destroyed instruments, overturned tables and chairs, my backpack lying with its contents scattered on the ground, the bloody mess that had once been Jonas.

I killed Jonas, I thought, my throat going tight and my breath quickening.

No.

Jonas was already dead.

I'd killed the monster he'd been transformed into.

Once again, I looked at Kip. He was gagging but alive. He was okay.

We were both okay.

Against the odds, we'd won.

A sound, a choked sob, came from Hank, and Kip, looking alarmed, clambered to his feet.

"It's okay, Kip," I said. "He's got his memories now. It's going to be okay. We won."

But I spoke too soon.

Fog was stealing from between the nearby trees, pouring over the shrubbery, racing along the ground and coalescing around the three of us and rising.

The black diamond appeared. It stretched, leaking pure darkness into the twilight shadows of the gardens.

The low voice spoke in a strange language once more as the huge clawed hands emerged, grabbing not only Hank this time, but Kip too.

"No," I said quietly. Then, "NO!"

I had not just faced the Baba Yaga, gotten chased by a minotaur, survived the Goblin Market and a creepy memory seller to save Kip from two dead guys just to have him dragged away now.

For that matter, they couldn't have the living dead guy either.

A feeling of built-up heat expanded from my chest, down my arms and out to my fingers, pulsing like it was just waking—that pins and needles feeling of a body part that was "asleep."

That body part was wide awake now.

"STOP! Stop it now!" I shouted, and from my hand pure white light emanated in a ray that hit the hands and disappeared inside the diamond.

The huge talons abruptly dropped both Kip and Hank and were sucked back into the diamond, which immediately fragmented into tiny pieces of black smoke that blew away into the sky.

I now realized I'd been holding my breath. A wave of dizziness came over me and I staggered. For a moment I couldn't feel my hands at all, but then feeling came back to them. I leaned forward, clenching and unclenching them against my thighs while breathing slowly.

I had barely caught my breath when I heard the applause. The green hag and her rats stood beneath a tree, each of them softly clapping. Apis, the little bee-man, was there buzzing and clapping over a patch of white flowers. Two masked squirrels wearing musketeer outfits clapped from the seat of a nearby bench.

The hag hobbled over towards me as if she wanted to talk but paused next to my backpack and its spilled contents.

"Is that kimchi?" she asked, looking it over. The jar had broken and the juices, pickled cabbage, and other vegetables were splattered over the rest of my belongings, including my change of clothes. "Too bad. Very impressive spellwork though." She nodded sagely. "Now, let's see. Take care of that, will you, boys?" With a toss of her head, she indicated the backpack to her cat-sized rats, and they moved up and began picking up the pieces with their little hands.

"Looks like your coat was spared," the hag said. "Toadflax, bring her that."

One of the cat-rats bounded over to me on its back feet, pulling my coat along.

As I was trying to think of a response to this odd form of kindness, a lovely blonde woman emerged from behind some bushes. She wore khaki pants and a green polo shirt with the Botanical Gardens logo on it.

"Are you Madison?" she asked in a thick New York accent.

I was folding the coat I'd accepted from the rat into a compact shape. "Yeah." How did she know?

"That was incredible!" she said. "Did you get Sylvie's acorn?"

Ah. "You're Sylvie's friend?"

"Yeah. I'm Michelle. Sylvie's this way," she said, taking a step back where she'd come from and gesturing that I should follow her.

"But what about this mess?" I asked. "I mean, the body—the musicians and guests—the police will be here any minute!"

"Oh, that?" the hag said. Her eyes scanned the trees and she cawed twice. A large black crow glided down, landing on her arm. Cupping her other hand to her lips, she whispered to it and it took off, cawing. Suddenly the air was filled with other crows, forty or fifty of them, all flying away from the area in different directions, cawing loudly.

"As for the rest of this—it's mealtime, fellas!" the hag said.

One of the cat-rats opened its mouth and the mouth seemed to stretch and widen to four times its size as it shoved a silver platter in.

"You got it?" Michelle asked the assembled group of lower fey creatures.

The hag made a dismissive noise. "Piece of pie," she said.

Chapter Twenty-Two

"Where is she?" I asked as we emerged into a grove of trees. We'd been walking several minutes.

While there was no moon, the lights of the city reflected off the low cloud banks above, providing dim light. Enough to see where we were going, but not enough to illuminate the deep shadows.

"Here," came the croaking voice from beneath a towering oak. The leaves in her hair had turned brown and there were far fewer of them, revealing patches of her gray scalp.

I knelt next to her. "I got it, Sylvie. The acorn," I said, pulling it from my bra where I'd stuffed it for safekeeping.

"I can hardly believe it," Michelle said, her New York accent thick. "No one has seen one for years."

"Can you do it, Michelle?" Sylvie asked, her voice quiet. "I'm too weak."

"I'm on it," Michelle said. "You two need to be over here."

Kip and I walked to the area about a hundred feet away where Michelle indicated. A hole had been dug in the ground, and near it a huge watering can awaited.

"Alright. You guys wait here while I get Sylvie," she said.

"No need," said Hank in a deep baritone. He emerged from the trees, scooped Sylvie up as easily as I might pick up a kitten, and brought her to us. Our faerie-kin audience from earlier appeared from the woods behind him and joined our little group.

I wanted to comment on the fact that Hank could talk now or ask how the fey had cleaned everything up so quickly, but it seemed like the wrong time.

"Okay, big guy, you put her into the earth. Carefully," Michelle said. "Now, Madison, you give her the acorn."

The hole wasn't very deep, nor was it very shallow, perhaps three feet deep total. Sylvie opened her hands and cupped the golden acorn, holding it over the center of her chest. Then she laid back and closed her eyes.

"A handful of dirt," Sylvie whispered. "No more."

Michelle sprinkled the dirt into the hole.

"A sprinkle of water," Sylvie murmured. "And then, bury me. All of you."

"Alive?" I asked, horrified.

"Shh." Michelle put her hand on my arm. "She'll be okay."

The burying took several minutes to completely cover Sylvie and fill the hole, but as the dirt fell around her, her face—which had appeared drawn with pain and exhaustion—seemed to soften to a more peaceful expression.

When the dirt that had been dug from the hole was depleted and formed a small mound, Michelle indicated that it was enough. She watered the mound with the large watering can, then took a step back.

"What now?" I asked.

"Now we grow her," Michelle said.

The clouds had become more sparse overhead and a few rare stars were visible high in the night sky. The motions that Michelle asked us to do in tandem seemed silly, at first, but as I carried them out, I felt a jolt of energy connect from below my feet. From the acorn? Or possibly from Sylvie herself? I felt it travel from my feet as I crouched down, then upwards through my legs as I stood up, then through my torso and up my arms and hands into the sky.

The hag giggled as if she'd been tickled and her kitty-rats stood on their back feet, performing the same movements as the rest of us.

Again and again, we crouched and pushed next to Michelle as she guided us, the squirrels nattering at one another, Apis flying into the sky at the end of his push. Kip grinned at my side with Hank on the other, a look of wonder on his face.

A leaf popped out of the dirt, and then another, and then a small plant began growing upward, climbing, growing more leaves, forming bark, shooting up, up, branches sprouting green leaves and spreading above our heads until the tree was perhaps fifteen feet tall.

We all stood there, marveling at our creation, the tall slender tree silhouetted against the night sky. A feeling of well-being permeated from my feet to the crown of my head, and the others all grinned at one another, even Hank.

Then a fine tremor, a vibration of some kind became evident as the leaves whispered against each other. There was no wind.

A cracking sound followed, and then another, and then a sound of thrashing among the foliage.

A small girl with brown skin and green leaves for hair dropped out of the branches. She landed on her feet and, giggling, disappeared into the trunk.

Magic.

Chapter Twenty-Three

In the days after the events at the Botanical Garden, I saw newspapers in the stands with headlines like PCP PERP TRAFFIC TERROR and GARDEN PARTY GAS LEAK that completely covered up the supernatural aspects of it all.

Zoe and I sat on a bench at Brooklyn Bridge Park, waiting to meet with Hank. We'd just driven back from a local Verizon store where Zoe had facilitated the purchasing of my first smartphone, connecting it to her account. We'd left the phone at my apartment, charging.

Before that, we'd been in Staten Island, where we'd seen Hannah for the last time. Zoe had explained that spirits sometimes get confused because they don't remember their lives. She told Hannah, "After we helped Hank remember who he was, he was able to move on." It wasn't a lie, technically.

Grateful for the peace of mind we'd brought her, Hannah had paid us extravagantly for our services, which we then split 70/30, with me getting the larger amount, since Zoe said I'd done more to solve the case. Those funds had allowed my smartphone purchase.

It was a sunny day. Multiple joggers, strollers, and dog walkers passed by. Boats and ferries floated down the river and cars traversed the Brooklyn Bridge to one side of us, while more traffic and subway trains went over the Manhattan Bridge in the distance. The city's skyline loomed on the far side of the river.

"Is that him?" Zoe asked, seeing a large man walking in our direction.

Hank had been sort of "healed" by the magic involved in the dryad growing ceremony. The jaundiced and livid color of his eyes and lips, his pallor, as well as the holes in his torso, were gone. Now he just looked human.

"Yeah, that's him."

He'd changed from the track pants and hoody he'd worn before to khakis and a polo shirt. "Hello, Madison," came his deep voice.

"Hi, Hank," I said. "This is Zoe."

Zoe was staring at Hank with an expression I hadn't seen before, something between fascination and confusion.

"Wow," she said. "It's almost like you're haunting yourself!"

"Nice to meet you too," he said.

"I'm sorry! How about my bad manners? It's good to meet you too, finally."

They exchanged handshakes, and Zoe shook her head as though mystified. "What do you mean 'haunting myself?'" Hank asked.

"I can see your spirit," she said. "I can't see spirits in other people, unless they're possessed. But you, I can see you in there. And you look alive."

"But I'm not alive," he said. "There's no blood in my veins, no heart that beats."

"Yeah, but to look at you . . . no one would be able to tell." It was true. He just looked like a regular guy now. To me, at least.

"You've seen Hannah?" he asked.

"Yes, this morning," Zoe said.

"How is she?" His tone was wistful, and hopeful too.

"She's going to be okay. We told her—this is what you wanted, right?—that you had moved on?"

He nodded.

"There is no way that I could return to my previous life," he said. "I can't go home and have everything return to normal. More than anything, Hannah has always wanted to be a mother. That's something I can no longer give her. I have hope that someday she will be happy again. That's why I'll be staying away from her, for good."

Zoe and I acknowledged how hard that must be, though we agreed that keeping his distance from Hannah was probably for the best.

We were all quiet a moment, as if giving his past with Hannah its own moment of silence.

Then I remembered. "I brought you something," I said, offering Hank my old pay-as-you-go flip phone.

His surprise and gratitude were evident on his face, and that dimple that appeared so charming in the old wedding photographs—and seemed so wrong previously—reacquired its appeal.

"It has a new phone number," I said. "So you don't have to worry about people looking for me calling you."

"I am beyond grateful," he said, taking the phone and charger. He looked at the phone a moment, then flipped it open and closed. "To both of you. Not only for what you did for me—I'm still not really sure how you did it—but also for what you've done for my Hannah."

"I put my number in there—and put yours in my new one." It seemed like a good idea. You never know when a supernaturally fast and strong guy might come in handy.

"Do you know what you're going to do now?" Zoe asked.

"I'm going to travel west. See if I can thumb my way out there."

"How very *The Hitchhiker* of you," Zoe said.

We both blinked at her.

"You know, the old TV show with the guy moving from town to town?"

"Oh, wait. I think maybe . . . I don't think I ever saw it," I said. I wondered when it aired.

"On HBO?" Hank asked.

She nodded. "That's it! My mom has them all on DVD. I guess there's nothing wrong with your memory, huh, Hank?"

I felt my face go red.

"Oh, jeez, I'm sorry, Madison."

A boat filled with tourists sailed past and several of them, wearing Statue of Liberty hats, waved in our direction.

Zoe and I were walking back to my apartment.

"I meant to ask, how's your roommate taking the news?"

"Oh, she's not happy, but she's also got her mind on other things," I said.

I'd told Julie that Sylvie had to go back to Canada, but she hadn't even seemed to hear me. Tad had broken up with her and she'd been miserable the past couple of days.

"What about you?" Zoe asked.

"What about me?"

"Are you happy?"

Was I? I didn't think about it much.

"I'm okay," I said.

"I'm sorry about what I said to Hank about memories. I just stick my foot in my mouth sometimes. Leather, yum," she said, gesturing at her booted foot. "How is all of that going for you, anyway? Any leads?"

"Kind of?" I said. "I don't really know what to make of it." I hadn't shared the information I learned from the newsprint or flyer about Christina with Kara or Julie. I hadn't shared that with anyone. It was just too weird.

But here was Zoe who not only believed in and saw ghosts, but who now knew about faeries and golems too. She hadn't run away screaming.

"Maybe . . . would you come upstairs? I've been wanting to look into something further but I haven't been brave enough."

"Girl, you are probably the bravest person I've ever met. But sure, of course."

"Even if it's weird?"

"I'd be surprised if it wasn't."

"Wow. Just wow." Zoe had just finished looking over the flyer and the newspaper article. "You're right. It does explain why you would have so many gaps, but wow. She looks exactly like you. And the same clothes you were wearing too? Freaky."

"And then there's the Baby Jessica thing," I said, explaining the discrepancy in the two dates. "So even if no one knew where I was, I must have still been around. How else would I have learned about her falling down the well and being rescued?"

"But maybe you just read about it later?"

"No. I would remember if I'd read about it in the past year. This is different."

She frowned. "So where do you go from here?"

"I was thinking internet search."

"Good call."

I sat down at my desk and opened my laptop's internet browser. My fingers hovered over the keyboard and the same old queasy feeling began bubbling away in my stomach. I closed my eyes.

"What's wrong?" Zoe asked.

"I can't do it. Every time I've tried, I feel sick."

"You want me to give it a go?"

I nodded. Zoe sat down at the laptop and I stood behind her. She typed the name "Christina Taylor" inside quotation marks. Then she added *missing* and *1987*.

There were a lot of hits, but one news article grabbed our attention.

Zoe read the article aloud while I read over her shoulder.

> NEW YORK, NY – It was over a year ago that teenager Christina Taylor was reported missing in Soho. The date was October 13, 1987. Days later, several items that belonged to the teen were located in a condemned East Village loft along with the dead body of Dylan Murrow, a known heroin addict found dead of an overdose at the scene.
>
> Items belonging to Christina, including several rings, a purse and wallet, and a bloody leather jacket were recovered, though her remains were not. Cops also discovered bone fragments in an incinerator in the building, though they were too burned to identify.

"There was no body!" Zoe said.

"Keep going!"

A Bowie knife discovered at the scene with Murrow's fingerprints also had blood on it. Incredibly, while forensic scientists took a full year to complete their tests and investigation, the blood found at the scene has been matched to that of the missing girl in this landmark case.

"This is one of the first cases in New York State involving DNA evidence," said Dr. James Edward Todd, the interim Chief Medical Examiner for the state. "From all the physical evidence found at the scene, we know that Murrow killed her and we believe he disposed of her body in the building's incinerator. At some point after he killed her and burned her remains, Murrow overdosed. The case is closed."

"So I was *assumed* to be dead! And my stuff was found in a condemned building with a dead heroin addict? That's gross. But *I* didn't die, right? I mean, here I am. And I'm not a golem, am I?"

"No. You aren't a golem."

"I'm not a vampire or ghost or faerie, either," I said. "I guess, I suppose, I'm a magus—or at least a pre-magus?"

While Michelle had packed up Sylvie's plants and things, she had told me a bit more of what she knew about Rowan, the mysterious magus that

Sylvie had mentioned. He had been the one who had saved a dying dryad after her tree had been cut down by transforming her to human. Michelle didn't know Rowan, but she suspected I'd hear from him soon. I hoped she was right.

"A magus. Yeah, I guess so. It makes sense from everything you've told me and the way ghosts act around you. But listen to this."

She read aloud:

> The victim's father, John Taylor, said, "Well, of course it would be a relief if her body had been found. It would be over. It's likely I'll always live with some degree of uncertainty."

I inhaled sharply. Christina's father. *My* father?

"Do you think he's still alive?" I asked Zoe.

"Let's see."

She opened a tab and searched for "John Taylor 1987."

If you're an 80's new wave music fan, you'll already know what we found. Nearly 400,000 hits, most of them about the bassist from Duran Duran, and probably a few thousand about other John Taylors as well. It was just too generic a name. We'd need a lot more information to do a successful search.

"Let me see that?" I asked, gesturing at the screen.

She unplugged the laptop and handed it to me. I read quickly over the article again. "I knew something stuck out to me. John Taylor says 'I.' It should be 'we,' shouldn't it? There are no statements from Christina's mother. Nothing about the family. Just a father. Maybe they got divorced?"

"Let me try something," Zoe said, holding her hand out for the laptop. She went back to her original results, entered a few more search terms and found a few more archived articles about Christina's disappearance, which she skimmed quickly. "It seems like there was some kind of trouble at home. An older brother, Jeremiah, stopped talking to the family the year before."

"I have a brother? *I* was the one with the long-lost brother?"

"Because of the domestic problems, initially cops thought Christina ran away with a boyfriend— the guy she'd last been seen with—which delayed the investigation. Also, it says here that she had just turned eighteen, so she wasn't really a juvenile anymore. That added to the runaway theory."

"When?"

"When what?"

"When did she turn eighteen?"

"Hmm," Zoe said, tabbing through articles. "Oh! It was the day she disappeared!"

"Wait, so, October 13th is my birthday?"

She switched tabs and skimmed a different article. "Yeah. Hey, Happy Belated Birthday!"

"Dude, this is so weird."

"Oh, wow, here's a statement from a waitress at Raoul's restaurant. She served Christina and her date, a man she described as having 'brown hair, blue eyes, a slightly crooked nose, and lots of money.' Oh my God. It does sound an awful lot like—"

"Michael Adderly. Yeah, it does. Which would explain why he called me 'Chris.' "

"So you're a time traveler from 1987 . . . who was dating a vampire . . . presumed dead by her family and police . . . who showed up in 2016, with no memory of how or why you traveled? Man, I thought my life was weird."

"At least I wasn't a government assassin," I said.

"Huh?"

"Sorry, joke from work. Yeah, I don't know. It sounds totally insane when you put it that way."

"Helloooo? Maddy, are you here?" Julie's voice called as she entered the apartment.

"Yeah, in here," I called back.

"It's so weird with all the plants gone!" she exclaimed, closing the door. "I was just getting used to them!"

When Michelle had come by to clear out Sylvie's things, I asked if she was taking the plants. Michelle seemed shocked that I'd even ask, calling them Sylvie's "oldest friends" and packing them carefully with everything else.

Julie appeared in my doorway, wearing jeans and a burgundy leather jacket with big buttons on the front over a black shirt. She was rummaging through a shopping bag.

"Hey, I—oh! Sorry, I didn't realize you had someone over! You never have people over! Hi, I'm Julie."

Zoe introduced herself in return and they exchanged nice-to-meet-yous.

"So what's up?" I asked Julie.

"Well . . . Tad is coming by tonight—that's my boyfriend—" she said for Zoe's benefit, "well, ex-boyfriend, but maybe not ex for long . . . and I went shopping and what do you think, blue or green?" She pulled two dresses from the shopping bag.

"Oh, please. You know you need to try those on," I said.

"Well, I *would* have sent you the pictures I took in the dressing room but you don't have a smartphone so—"

I picked up my new smartphone and smiled brightly at her, framing it with my hands like a game show model.

"Oh my God, finally!"

"I couldn't have done it without Zoe," I said, and Zoe shrugged modestly. "So show me the pictures."

Julie swiped through her phone and handed it to me. "See, the blue one is a little tamer and the green one is more . . ."

"More va-va-voom," I said. "Well, what are you going for?"

"I don't know! I can't decide. Oh, were you in the middle of something?" Julie asked, taking in the newspaper article, flyer, and internet windows.

"Oh, just a research project I'm helping Zoe with. For . . . school."

"Cool," Julie said, her focus immediately going back to the all-important question of what she'd wear. "I think . . . I kind of want him to see what he'll be missing," she said.

"Good call," I said.

"I could always ask my Instagram followers," she said. "But then he might see it beforehand. Oh, and I'm up to 9500! 10k here I come!"

"Congratulations," I said.

"Wow," Zoe said. "What's your secret?"

Julie straightened her posture and stuck her chest out. "Boobs."

I laughed, and Zoe laughed too.

"Well, boobs and lingerie," Julie said and grinned, picking up her shopping bag again. "Okay, well, I'll let you get back to your project. I'm going to take a long shower. You need the bathroom before I do?"

I looked at Zoe and she shook her head and I did too. "Nope."

Julie withdrew and I heard her go into her room and close her door.

"She's nice," Zoe said.

"Yeah, she is. Mostly. I wonder if she'll get back together with Tad."

"How long have they been broken up?"

"A couple of days."

"A couple of days? And they're already seeing each other again? Yeeaah. You might not want to be around tonight."

"Good point," I said. "Now, where were we?"

"Don't you mean *when*?"

"Ugh, I guess."

She picked up the flyer and newspaper article again. "Alright, you disappeared on October 13, 1987, but you know about things that happened through . . . October 16th." A quick internet search gave her the date of Baby Jessica's rescue. "Your stuff was found at a death scene with a guy who overdosed . . . Maybe you were there for a few days before you time traveled?"

"Yeah, but what was I *doing* there?"

"Well, hmm. Tamara was killed by Irina Van Horn, right? Because of Michael Adderly? Maybe you were hiding from her?"

"And time traveled to the future to escape her?"

"Sure. But the time travel wiped your memory, and here you are."

"So . . . do I need to get back to 1987?"

My head swam with a panicky, dizzy feeling.

"No, I . . . Whoa, are you okay?" Zoe stopped looking at articles on the screen and was now staring at me in dismay.

"I just . . . I don't even know what to think!"

"Just breathe for now, think later. You are here. You are okay. You *are* okay, aren't you?"

I took a deep breath and let it out. "Yes. And no. It's just too weird. It's the proverbial can of worms. Pandora's Box. A cat out of a bag. A—"

"Yeah, I get it."

"I just don't know what to do next. You don't have a spare flux capacitor handy, do you?"

"Well, this magus Sylvie mentioned is supposed to find you, right?"

"Yeah, but that's just sitting around and waiting. I want to do something."

"I can only think of one thing besides doing more research," Zoe said.

"What?"

"Ask Michael Adderly."

Michael Adderly. If he was the last person to see Christina before she disappeared, then Zoe was right: I needed to speak to him.

Maybe he would tell me how he knew Christina and what happened to her. I could ask him about Billy, too, and why he hadn't returned my calls.

"I saw him, you know," I said.

"No! When?" Zoe exclaimed.

I explained how he'd shown up just after Hank attacked, and what happened. "So many secrets!" said Zoe. "Why didn't you tell me?"

"I don't know. It just seemed like we should concentrate on Hank and Hannah, I guess. Or maybe I didn't want to think about it."

"Maybe because you were tempted to kiss him?"

"Maybe. I guess that could be a danger. He said he wasn't using his vampire mojo on me, but he could have been lying. I mean, he's a vampire. Traditionally, they are not the good guys."

"True. I think you do need to contact him. Not, you know, date him or anything."

"No. Definitely not. Maybe I need a break from romance. Time to sort myself out."

"Is that what you decided about Kip?"

"I don't know yet."

Like Hank, Kip had also been healed by the dryad growing ceremony, suffering no major ill effects after being attacked by Jonas. I'd asked him not to contact me for a while. He said I could call him if I ever needed him. There was something implied in that "needed," a promise of sex and comfort that I hated to admit was very appealing.

I just wasn't sure I could trust him.

I had sewn a nail into my coat pocket to protect against future fey glamours, just in case.

In the hallway, Julie called, "Last chance on the bathroom!"

Zoe shook her head and I yelled back, "We're good!" The bathroom door closed, and moments later, the shower started.

"I don't suppose Kip has any single friends?" Zoe asked.

"Zoe!" I said, laughing. "Do you want to date a faerie?"

"Well, it's not like I can date normal guys. I talk to ghosts. What normal guy wants to deal with that?"

I knew what she meant. With all of the magical stuff happening around me, it seemed that I was stuck with the supernatural in one way or another. Although dangerous, it wasn't all bad. Sure sometimes it was horrible and full of death. But it was also about nature and reaffirming life. It could help people. *I* could help people. That seemed like something to be proud of.

No matter who I had been before, I could be proud of who and what I was becoming.

"You know what?" I said. "I'll ask him, but on one condition."

"What?"

"If you ever need help with another case . . ."

"Don't call you?"

"*Do* call me. I want to help."

Zoe squealed and hugged me, then apologized for hugging me.

After Zoe left, I called Billy's number and heard the usual message: "This is Billy. Say something," and this time, I did: "Hi. It's Madison. I hope you're okay. Listen, I need to talk to Michael Adderly. The last time I saw him, he said you were fine. Are you fine? Please text or call me. I miss you, and I hope you're okay."

Within minutes my new phone dinged with a text telling me where I could meet Michael that evening, with a side note.

I'll try to be there too.

A couple of hours later, having given Julie the thumbs up on her outfit, I locked the door to our apartment and walked down to the first floor feeling good about life, my life, for the first time in what felt like forever. The sun had just set, and the sky was golden with pink clouds. I could see the dogwood tree through the glass of my building's front door, bare of blossoms, bare of leaves, but still alive.

Coming up the stairs was a white-haired man, carefully moving a dolly that had a large footlocker on it. He wore a brown uniform and work gloves and had a kind face. I opened the door to hold it for him and his work gloves caught my eye.

They were made of black leather, with very fine stitching.

My eyes jerked up to his face in time to see him smile a reptilian smile.

"*Sleep*," he said, and then everything faded to black.

THE END

Madison will return

in

A MAGE IN SHADOW

Book 3 of the *Madison Roberts* Series

OCTOBER 2020

To keep up with Tracey Lander-Garrett's
new releases, visit her website and sign up for
her newsletter at **traceylandergarrett.com**

ACKNOWLEDGEMENTS

GOOD GRAVY. WHO'D HAVE GUESSED I'D BE writing another acknowledgements section for yet another book?

First, I will acknowledge gratitude to my editor, Marcel Leroux, who is amazing, very patient, and very funny. This time he ruthlessly slayed an alarming number of "and then" constructions while picking off more than a handful of nods and shrugs.

I want to believe I write so many of these movements not because I am a lazy writer, but because—at least when sugared and caffeined up—I am a Muppet. I naturally nod, shrug, growl, squeak, and speak with strange accents at odd moments. In short, I appear to behave as though I were an animated stuffed toy, not a human adult. Therefore, if my take on expressive movement in conversation is redundant, I say: Fair enough. *nods and then shrugs*

The first draft of this novel was written over NaNoWriMo 2017. I wrote over 50k words in 29 days and felt enormously proud of myself.

I thank Brian Williams, Amy Marcoux, Staci McGranaghan, Diana Ballard, Miriam Lover-Williams, Evette Alvarado, Tina Hudec, Lindsey

Wisneski, and Karsen LaRue for encouragement and insightful comments in the early versions of this novel. Thanks go to Sheri Sikes for letting me steal her cat Sterling for my occult bookstore and to Pete Altescu for letting me steal his last name. I'd also like to offer a retroactive shout-out to Heidi Charton for her suggestion of the name of the store Thirteen Books. And to Valery Chen, who swooped in and saved the day when my photo-editing skills were excessively challenged: thank you. Not all heroes wear capes.

I seriously thank Amy Goudy and Janelle Lannan Schittone for sticking to their guns with their opinions about thematic series titles and Jordan Rosenfeld for her authorly insight and cheerleading during the editing process.

I continue to be grateful to Anna Castle and the Austin Indie Author Society for all the things.

Of course, I must offer a bouquet of undying gratitude roses to my husband. He deserves them for appreciating the weird way station that is my brain, for sharing my enthusiasm for tabletop adventures, and for creating delicious dinners and beautiful brunches: he makes my whole world a better (and yummier) place.

Penultimately, I'd like to share some additional words about the person to whom this book is dedicated: Eric "Ric" Saterstrom. Ric was my stepdad, my mom's second husband. His influence ignited my interest in fantasy, comics, vampires, and horror. He inspired by example, showed me unconditional affection, and embodied kindness always. His last birthday gift to me, sent just before I moved to Texas, was the book *100 Things to Do in Austin Before You Die*. He passed just three months after sending it.

His inscription, in part, read: "What better thing than the stuff that dreams are made of sent with love." That was always his legacy for me: love and dreamstuff.

I love you, Ric, wherever you are. Thank you for showing me that otherworlds were worthy of my attention, imagination, and energy. I miss you so much.

Finally, because I am a nerd at heart, tributes of fandom and literary allusions are strewn throughout the novel; here are some: Those who are familiar with Kate Chopin's "The Story of an Hour" may recognize some traits of a comic book store patron with an unfortunate nickname. Lewis Carroll and Alice aficionados will easily identify quotations and the Tenniel art and other imagery described in the Wonderland scene.

The Dark or Goblin Market owes debts to Christina Rossetti's poem of the same name, E.E. Cumming's poem "[in Just-]," Ted Naifeh's *Courtney Crumrin* series, artwork by Charles Vess, and scenes from Guillermo del Toro's *Hellboy 2: The Golden Army*, while many bows of unworthiness are made in the direction of Neil Gaiman's *Sandman* series (the Owlwife and Baba Yaga scenes especially). Lastly, the dryad growing ceremony was inspired by a scene in Hayao Miyazaki's *My Neighbor Totoro*.

www.ingramcontent.com/pod-product-compliance
Lightning Source LLC
Chambersburg PA
CBHW032219050726
47591CB00001B/191